Readers love
KATE MCMURRAY

What's the Use of Wondering?

"This is a beautifully done, sweet, sexy, romantic, true love tale! Highly recommended to bring a smile to your face!"

—*Divine Magazine*

"…a sweet coming of age/transitioning to adulthood story."

—Jessie G Books

There Has to Be a Reason

"…a beautifully written story. Very realistic. Definitely a book I would recommend to others."

—Gay Book Reviews

"…I really enjoyed this. I had never read this author before but will definitely read more of her work."

—Night Owl Reviews

The Boy Next Door

"The story was unique and not something I've read over and over, which is refreshing!"

—Alpha Book Club

"I was completely captivated by this book."

—Inked Rainbow Reads

By KATE MCMURRAY

Blind Items
The Boy Next Door
Devin December
Four Corners
Kindling Fire with Snow
Out in the Field
The Stars that Tremble • The Silence of the Stars
A Walk in the Dark
What There Is
When the Planets Align

DREAMSPUN DESIRES
The Greek Tycoon's Green Card Groom

ELITE ATHLETES
Here Comes the Flood
Stick the Landing

THE RAINBOW LEAGUE
The Windup
Thrown a Curve
The Long Slide Home

WMU
There Has to Be a Reason
What's the Use of Wondering

Published by DREAMSPINNER PRESS
www.dreamspinnerpress.com

KATE MCMURRAY

STICK *the* LANDING

Published by
DREAMSPINNER PRESS

5032 Capital Circle SW, Suite 2, PMB# 279,
Tallahassee, FL 32305-7886 USA
www.dreamspinnerpress.com

This is a work of fiction. Names, characters, places, and incidents either
are the product of author imagination or are used fictitiously, and any
resemblance to actual persons, living or dead, business establishments,
events, or locales is entirely coincidental.

Stick the Landing
© 2020 Kate McMurray

Cover Art
© 2020 L.C. Chase
http://www.lcchase.com
Cover content is for illustrative purposes only and any person depicted
on the cover is a model.

Mass Market Paperback ISBN: 978-1-64108-221-1
Trade Paperback ISBN: 978-1-64405-346-1
Digital ISBN: 978-1-64405-345-4
Library of Congress Control Number: 2019957858
Mass Market Paperback published October 2020
v. 1.0

Printed in the United States of America
∞
This paper meets the requirements of
ANSI/NISO Z39.48-1992 (Permanence of Paper).

CHAPTER ONE

One year ago
International Federation of Gymnastics World Championships

JAKE HIT the mat so hard, he literally saw stars.

When he remembered where he was, he did a quick mental accounting and determined that nothing was broken, but he'd probably hit his head. What he should do now was get up, salute the judges, and pretend he hadn't just completely missed the landing on that vault.

But apparently he'd been lying there too long, because Alexei's face appeared in Jake's field of vision. "Are you dead?" Alexei asked.

"No." It came out sounding strangled.

"Good. Can you move?"

Jake tried experimentally to lift his arm. He managed to make it rise off the mat, but any further movement seemed like a lot of effort. "No."

Oh, this was bad. If Jake had managed to paralyze himself during the fucking Team Championships and thus prevented the beleaguered American men's gymnastics team from qualifying for the Olympics....

Alexei, Jake's coach, and Viktor, one of the other coaches, helped Jake to his feet. Jake wasn't hurt so much as stunned. "Do I vault again?" Jake asked, confused.

"No," said Alexei. "You get down and let Dr. Ruiz look at you."

"Am I supposed to vault again? Like, if I'd stuck that landing, would I?"

"No. It's the team competition. You only vault once."

"Okay."

Jake heard clapping, but it could have been a herd of bees buzzing, the way it sounded in his ears. All sound was tinny and distant.

He'd fucked up big-time.

"Score gets erased," said Alexei.

Well, yeah. Landing on his back was sure to earn Jake a zillion deductions. "What happened?"

"Over-rotated." Alexei guided Jake into a chair. "When you came out of tuck, you should have kicked your legs harder, but instead, you kept rotating."

"Ah," said Jake.

Dr. Ruiz, the team medic, swooped over and started asking questions. Did Jake hit his head (he didn't know, but probably), had he hurt anything else (his pride; otherwise, no), and did he know where they were (yes, Beijing). Really, he felt stunned more than anything else. This was like all the times he'd gotten the wind knocked out of him when he hit the mat too hard during practice; now he felt like he'd just got his breath back. Surprised, but okay. Not nauseous. No obvious pain.

"I'm fine," Jake insisted, though it started to sink in now how badly he'd fucked up. Sure, they'd toss out his score if it was indeed the lowest vault score for the American team. But fucking up in international competition—again—did not improve his chances of making the American Olympic team.

"You sure?" asked Alexei.

"Yeah. Just stunned. I thought I'd land that." Jake tried for a self-deprecating smile. Probably he looked crazy.

Alexei patted him on the back. Dr. Ruiz finished taking his vitals and ruled him okay to keep competing. Up on the scoreboard, his score flashed up: 13.333. Jake grimaced. Not embarrassing, but definitely not good, especially on a vault that he routinely scored better than 15 on.

"You didn't quite push off table hard enough," Alexei said, rewatching the vault on his phone. "You would have landed it if you got higher off table."

"Okay." Jake pretended to absorb that criticism, even though he was thinking, *Too fucking late now.*

"It's fine," said Viktor. "As long as you are okay?"

Jake nodded.

"We're in second place right now." Viktor pointed at the scoreboard. "One more event to go. We will podium."

"No thanks to me."

"Your high bar routine was very good," said Viktor.

"Good on parallel bars," said Alexei.

"Pommel horse not so much," said Jake, who'd biffed a skill there too.

Alexei shook his head. "When we get back to States, we change training. I've seen you do that vault a hundred times, no problem. Now, people watching, you land on your back. Why?"

"Oh, Alexei, if I could answer that question...." Jake shook his head. "Forget it. I'm all right. We'll qualify a full team to the Olympics, which is all that matters."

"You'll be on that team," said Alexei.

But Jake was not so sure.

On the other side of the world...

"YOU WANT me to do what?"

Topher stood in his kitchen with his cell phone wedged between his chin and his shoulder. It was very likely going to end up in the pot of boiling water below. The smart thing would be to fetch his headset from the other room and finish the call that way, but suddenly Angela, his agent, was saying strange words, and Topher felt dumbfounded.

"They want you to walk at Fashion Week. As a model. See, Jennifer Cole has a new collection—"

"She's a womenswear designer." Topher did not like where this was going.

"Yes, she is, but she collaborated on a menswear collection that is being put out under her label, and they want a couple of splashy stars to walk as models."

"It's insane, isn't it?" Topher stepped away from the boiling water. An onion sat half-chopped on his cutting board, next to the still-unopened package of pasta and a tomato that seemed to be shriveling up as it sat, whole and unblemished, mocking Topher. His dinner date would be here any minute, and he'd miss out on the pre-dinner flirtation if he didn't get this meal going. He sighed. "The collection, I mean. Hot pink feathers and, like, rainbows and whatever. I saw Cole's collection last year. She designs for teenage girls."

"I've seen some of the drawings," said Angela. "The collection certainly couldn't be called subdued, but I've seen crazier men's fashion. Hell, I've seen you *wear* crazier men's fashion. This could be a really good opportunity for you, Toph. You'd get the kind of positive press that would win over the TBC execs."

Topher harrumphed. TBC was the television network that had an exclusive contract to air the Olympics in the United States. Topher had been hired during the last World Championships as a figure skating correspondent—because who better than a two-time Olympic figure skater and world champion to comment on the sport—but because the old guard wasn't ready to retire, mostly he just interviewed the athletes off the ice. There had been rumors swirling that TBC liked Topher enough to have him replace one of their regular commentators, and Topher wanted that job more than he wanted his next meal. The ancient man who'd won his gold medal in 1960, when all one really had to do was spin around a couple of times, somehow still did the primetime commentary. Topher kept hearing that the old man could barely walk these days, let alone muster the energy to say anything informative about figure skating, so that spot was Topher's.

If he didn't blow it.

Or, not even blow it. More than one TBC employee had implied they wanted him to be less flamboyantly gay. Which, sorry, but no.

"I don't know if Fashion Week is the kind of thing the network executives really want me to do. Play football or hunt for wild game, sure, but prance around in frilly outfits? I mean, that sounds like a good time, don't get me wrong, and I'd sooner wear pink feathers than hold a gun, but I don't know if this is really what I need to solidify my position. Besides, the next Olympics are still three years away."

"What if I said you might have a job at the next *Summer* Olympics?"

Good thing Topher was nowhere near that pot of water now, because he moved his head so sharply, the phone slid down his chest. He caught it and held it back up to his ear. "What did you say?"

"TBC got a lot of flak at the last Olympics for having the same tired old commentators that they've had since the midseventies. And rightly so! I watched some of the coverage from the 1984 gymnastics finals—you know, Mary Lou Retton and all that—and it's the same damn people. Some market researcher finally suggested that the reason ratings are down could be that the broadcast has been basically the same for three decades. They want fresh blood. I think they want someone like you because they know you appeal to the youth market. As far as I know, they don't want you commentating on specific sports, but they'd like you to do puff pieces and some of the cultural stuff. They want you to build up your fan base and social media presence, though, which you can't do if you never leave your apartment. And if you do it well and they like you, this could pay off for you in the long run. Think of it as an audition of sorts."

Topher was having a hard time processing all this. "So, wait. What I hear you saying is that you want me to walk in Fashion Week so that I get some flashy, on-brand headlines and media attention, long enough, at least, for my name to stay in the news so that TBC will hire me, Christopher Caldwell, super gay figure skater, to do hokey human interest stories at the Summer

Olympics. And that if I do those hokey stories well enough, they may hire me to do a commentary for the sport I am an actual expert about."

"Yes. That is exactly what I am telling you."

"That doesn't make any sense."

"You want a job or don't you?"

Fuck yeah, Topher wanted the job. "I mean, I'm in, obviously. I'll go to the moon if it gets me a broadcasting job. But after what happened at my last Olympics and how much the network shit on me…."

"New management, buddy. There's a new head of TBC Sports and a new chair of the Olympics broadcast, and both are looking to shake up their coverage. It's all still in the early stages, but I think your odds are good. You're a household name, at least among the Olympic-watching demographics. I can't guarantee a lot of airtime, and this is all kind of experimental to see what pulls in ratings, but if it goes well, who knows? Maybe this is your ticket to that primetime commentary chair."

Topher took a deep breath. He'd retired from skating three years ago, after a post-Olympics World Championships in which he'd finished fifth. It was a last gasp more than a swan song, and a sign that it was time to hang up his skates. And this year he'd turned thirty, and was having the requisite crisis about it.

He'd once been a teenaged phenom, though he hadn't gone to the Olympics until after he'd turned twenty. Everyone expected him to win that first time. The pressure had gotten to him. He singled when he should have tripled one of his jumps in the short program, which had put him at enough of a point deficit that he couldn't make it up in the long program when everyone else skated flawlessly. He ended up in fourth place, which was basically the worst. The second time, he was still expected to win, but expectations seemed more tempered, and by then there were all these other rising stars and Topher was kind of the old man—at the ripe old age of twenty-five. Still, after a near-flawless short program that had landed him in first place going into the long program, something had happened and he'd choked. Actually, he'd fallen on his ass executing a jump he'd done without incident hundreds, if not thousands, of times.

Topher had won three World Championships, but something about the Olympics' stage was like a curse. He'd been hoping to try one more time, but fatigue and an old injury prevented him from doing so, and now he had bad knees that ached on rainy days and zero Olympic medals.

TBC generally hired retired athletes to comment on Olympic sports, but they got the guy who won a gold medal in Seoul or the woman who won a silver in Albertville. Not knowledgeable, albeit flamboyant, also-rans. Because Topher had been skating almost since the time he'd learned to walk, but he'd never won an Olympic medal. So what kind of expert could he be?

He shook off his shame spiral and said instead, "Hey, if Jennifer Cole wants me to dress like a unicorn and that's what I need to do to persuade TBC to send me to Madrid, then I'm already practicing my runway walk."

"Attaboy." Angela laughed. "I'll let the Cole people know."

CHAPTER TWO

One week before the Olympics
Transcript: Wake Up, America!

MORALES: As you know, we'll be starting our broadcast from Madrid on Friday morning, but in the meantime, we've got a bit of a preview for you.

HOLT: If you follow some of these sports, none of these people are strangers, but for the casual viewers, you'll be meeting a lot of these athletes for the first time once the Games start in Madrid.

MORALES: Each day this week, we'll be profiling one elite athlete who we think has got what it takes to win gold this year. Today, meet Chelsea Mirakovitch!

HOLT: Get used to hearing that name. Chelsea was too young to make the Olympic team four years ago, but she's been raking in the awards ever since. She's not only the reigning national champion, but she's a three-time World All-Around Champion as well. And she comes from quite a legacy.

MORALES: That's right, Joe. Her father, Valentin Mirakovitch, was a gold medal gymnast himself, winning the men's all-around in Seoul, representing the USSR. He's now her coach. Her mother was also a Russian gymnast and competed for the Unified Team in 1992 in Barcelona. Even her brother Jake is a gymnast. He'll be competing in Madrid as well.

HOLT: Wouldn't it be something if both Mirakovitch siblings won medals in Madrid?

MORALES: Oh, definitely. Jake has a shot at a medal. He's the reigning national champion, and he's the veteran of the team, having competed four years ago. But he faces stiff competition from athletes from Japan, China, Ukraine, and Great Britain, not to mention his own teammates. On the other hand, I'd say that gold medal is Chelsea's to lose. We haven't seen a gymnast this dominant since Simone Biles....

JAKE STARED at clouds out the window, surprised that this moment was already here. Just six weeks ago, he'd laid in bed at night imagining what this very plane ride would be like. Then he'd gotten sucked into training camp, and suddenly he was here. He let out a breath when a bit of turbulence bumped him. Yes, training camp. Even though the US men's gymnastics team was pretty spread out geographically, the new head coach, Viktor Chakin, had decided that the men's team should follow the women's model and spend some time bonding. Viktor, who had once been part of the Soviet gymnastics machine, did have a special gift for plucking boys out of fledgling programs and grooming them into world champions, but gymnastics was not a team sport.

Still, the American team had struggled the past few years. The dozen or so guys who had been on the national team in the past four years had a handful of medals between them, but mostly on individual events. The men's team hadn't won a team championship in… a while. Viktor Chakin, the champion-maker, had been hired to fix that problem.

Viktor Chakin had once been the teammate of Valentin Mirakovitch, the head coach of USA Gymnastics and lead women's coach. Jake's father.

So they were all one big happy family, apparently. After spending all of July at the men's team training camp outside Houston, everyone had been sent home for a week. Home for Jake was three miles from training camp. But no matter. Here he was now, on a plane with not only the entire men's gymnastics team—including the alternates, coaches, and staff—but the entire women's team as well. Which meant Chelsea sat three rows up, and dear old Dad was in first class, sitting next to Jake's mother, Lana. Lana didn't work for USA Gymnastics, but she was an honorary staff member, a team mother of sorts. And given that her entire immediate family was on this plane, it made sense for her to be here too.

Jake kind of wished he could escape them all, though.

His teammate Corey sat beside him. Corey had bought the Olympic preview issue of *Sports Illustrated* at the airport and currently had it open in his lap. "Too bad we won't get to see most of the swimming. You know that guy Isaac Flood?"

The name was familiar, but Jake couldn't place it. "Who?"

"The swimmer. Come on, Jake, he's a big deal. He won a bunch of medals at the last few Olympics and was on the Wheaties box and everything. Then he crashed hard. Got a couple of DUIs and went into rehab."

"Okay."

"He's back. Cleaned up at the Olympic trials. That's the kind of human interest story the morning show team at TBC eats for breakfast."

"Better him than me," said Jake.

"Well, look, there's you." Corey folded the magazine in half and displayed it for Jake.

Jake's official USA Gymnastics headshot was above a quarter-page box on a page headlined *Athletes to Watch*. He shared the page with three other athletes.

"Did my sister get a whole article?" Jake asked.

Corey smiled sheepishly. "Yeah."

Jake was genuinely happy for Chelsea. She was incredibly talented. She had a singular focus on gymnastics, she trained harder than anyone else in the sport, and she could do new skills with high difficulty levels that were pushing the sport forward. Unless she proved to be as doomed as Jake seemed to be, she could easily win five or six gold medals in Madrid, and she deserved them all.

He loved Chelsea to bits. She was his best friend in the world.

It was just… her shadow was sometimes a hard place to live in.

Corey frowned. "I mean, look, none of the rest of the men's team got any kind of write-up. You're our best hope, apparently."

"It's bullshit. This is the best men's team we've had in years. I hate to say it, but some of Viktor's crazier ideas seem to be paying off." What Jake thought, but did not say, was that while all that was true on paper, he didn't completely have faith that they wouldn't all choke on game day.

The men's team had a pattern. The previous Olympics and every subsequent World Championship bore it out. They killed it in the qualifying round, usually entering the team competition in first place, and nearly everyone made an event final. Then everyone choked.

Well, Jordan somehow managed to always stick his pommel horse routines, which was a goddamn miracle for a US gymnast, since the rest of them were particularly skilled at falling off when it mattered. Jake had always excelled at the bars—both high and parallel— but he was also famous for executing flawless routines and then landing terribly. Hayden was a beautiful vaulter, when he managed to stick the landings, Brad tumbled better than anyone in the world when he stayed in bounds, and Corey was freakishly strong and usually flawless on rings, except when he racked up deductions for not holding his poses long enough.

But the thing was, they were always perfect in qualifiers, so they *could* be excellent. In practice, Jake stuck his landings nine times out of ten. So did Hayden and Brad. Brad only stepped out of bounds in competition because his nerves wrecked his control; when he had control, he was unbeatable on floor. Viktor had been working with Corey on timing, and he had definitely improved. And, well, Jordan just needed to stick his pommel horse routines so that it didn't look like the US team as a whole sucked at the apparatus.

The new guy, Paul, was something of an unknown quantity. Jake liked him, though he was young. Paul had been a junior national champion and had won a bunch of college medals, but college gymnastics were a different beast. Jake had no doubt that Paul, just like his teammates, had the goods, but Paul had never been to an international competition before, so how he would react was anybody's guess.

"It's because you're the pretty one," Corey said, taking a closer look at the photo of Jake in the magazine. "They put your face on all the promo materials because you're the best-looking of all of us."

Jake scoffed. "That's not true."

"It is true. I mean, you'd have to compete with me for the honors if I hadn't broken my nose all those times." Corey rubbed the ridge where his nose hadn't quite healed correctly. "And let's face it, the TV network wants to spotlight guys with the kinds of looks that appeal to female viewers in middle America. Jordan is too Eastern European and Hayden is too black and Brad is too married. I don't say that to be racist. I'm just pointing out the network's Stone Age attitudes about these things. So you, my friend, as the most traditionally attractive, are our designated heartthrob."

"What about Paul?"

Corey scoffed. "Paul is a fetus."

"If Brad is too married, how am I not too gay?"

Corey grinned. "That's a memo even *Sports Illustrated* didn't get. See, it says here you're still single and ready to mingle."

"It doesn't say that." Jake reached for the magazine.

Corey pulled the magazine away and held it in the aisle. Jake gave up, so Corey read, "Male gymnasts tend to peak later than female gymnasts do, so this is a team not of teenagers, but of grown men. Some even have their own families of fledgling gymnasts. Mirakovitch's teammate Brad Porter is married and has a daughter who is three years old. She has yet to grace a balance beam, but it's only a matter of time." Corey rolled his eyes. "Blah, blah, yada yada. Oh, here's the part I wanted. 'But don't worry, ladies. Mirakovitch is still single.' See, it's right there at the end of the story."

"Why is *Sports Illustrated* talking about my romantic life? Why not the difficulty level of my high bar routine?"

"That's all here too. But see? You're a pretty boy. Teenage girls put pictures of you in their lockers and draw hearts over your face."

"Gross."

Corey laughed. "Seriously, though, are you seeing anyone? Is there a man tucked into your luggage and packed into the cargo hold I should know about?"

"No, of course not. When do I have time to date? I train all the time."

"Brad found the time."

"Yeah, well, Brad's father isn't a former Soviet gymnast."

"Fair point." Corey shook his head. "I like your father, but he can be a hardass."

"Not news."

"I'm thinking about asking out Jessica. She's twenty-two, so it's not completely inappropriate."

"Yeah, I could see that. I personally don't want to date another gymnast. I'd like to talk about other things sometimes."

"You have interests other than gymnastics?" Corey mock gasped.

"A few, as it happens." Jake rolled his eyes.

"Good luck finding someone who gets it. I dated a girl for a while who didn't understand why I had to train so much. She thought I was cheating on her because I spent so many hours at the gym." Corey shook his head. "I get why gymnasts marry each other. Who else would understand the hell we put ourselves through every day?"

It was a fair point. Jake hadn't dated much… well, ever, but certainly not in the past few years. Since before the last Olympics, really, and even then he'd gone on a handful of dates with a few cute guys who thought it was really cool Jake was an elite gymnast with the body to match… but not so cool that he literally lived at the gym. And once Jake started explaining about Valentin and the Soviet gymnastics machine, their eyes glazed over.

Well, whatever. He'd date after he retired.

Which hopefully wouldn't be for a while.

His thirtieth birthday loomed in the future. His injured body parts had begun to ache, especially first thing in the morning and late at night. He knew from a practical perspective that his days were numbered, that soon his body would give out on him. And Dr. Ruiz had already warned him that any more hits to the head could cause permanent damage.

But until that time, he was going to fight as hard as he could for that gold medal.

Because Jake Mirakovitch was the best gymnast in the world who had never won an Olympic gold medal. No, he was the best gymnast in the world, period. He just had to prove it.

TOPHER'S SEAT neighbor on the flight to Madrid was a retired gymnast named Natalie. TBC had hired her to comment over the gymnastics live feed, which would be airing online. The same crusty old commentators were doing the primetime coverage, as Natalie explained in exasperated tones.

"That's one step above where I was two years ago," Topher explained. "They had me writing cutesy articles for the network website. This is supposed to be my audition for a more regular gig. I'm hoping for primetime, but I'll probably just get relegated to doing videos for the website."

Natalie nodded. "Do you have a schedule here?"

"A rough one. My handler keeps telling me it's subject to change."

"I'm trying to get a ticket to the Opening Ceremony. It's not looking good."

"I clearly don't have a prayer, then."

The network had paid for a chartered flight, which Topher appreciated. TBC was paying for his hotel room too, though he was on his own for meals if he didn't eat at craft services. It wasn't a bad way to travel, and he'd never been to Madrid. Part of his job was to be a "cultural ambassador" for the network, so he'd be touring landmarks and filming short segments about them. They had him scheduled to show up at a few events to do stories that either profiled athletes or explained how the sport worked for laypeople, which was a little more in Topher's wheelhouse than talking about statues and art museums. His schedule was tucked carefully into his carry-on bag, so he'd worry about it when he landed.

There wasn't anything interesting to see out the plane windows, so he opened the September issue of *Vogue* and began to flip through it. He glanced at Natalie, who carefully paged through a dog-eared Madrid travel guide. Topher was somewhat at the whims of the network, so he figured they would tell him where to go and what to say, and he was content to wing it otherwise.

Natalie glanced over his shoulder—he was looking at an Anna Sui photo spread—and said, "Oh, that's gorgeous!" She pointed, getting a smudgy fingerprint on a bohemian-style gown that Topher thought was kind of a travesty of paisley and fussy design.

"She was better in the nineties. Anna Sui, I mean. I'm not really loving the boho trend. Everyone in this collection looks like they're going to Coachella," Topher said.

Natalie looked Topher up and down. "All right. So who are you wearing? Thom Browne?"

Topher was tickled she knew who Thom Browne was, so he said, "No. It's a newer menswear designer named Michael Bastian. I love the print on this shirt, don't you?" He fingered the sleeve of his shirt. It was a pale blue with little white daisies.

"It's pretty. I'd wear a dress with that print."

"I figured I'd go classy for the plane. The bright colors and sequins and things are reserved for next week." Topher grinned. "Joanna almost sent me home when she saw how much luggage I brought. But in my defense, I'll be in Madrid for three weeks."

Natalie laughed. "So if we crash into the Atlantic because the plane is too heavy, I know who to blame."

"I can't repeat an outfit on-air."

"No, I get it. I brought three suitcases myself."

Topher waved his hand. "Only three? Amateur hour. I have six. I had to give the cabbie an absurd tip to get it all in and out of the car."

"I'm glad your priorities are sorted out."

"Look, I'm a washed-up figure skater headed to the summer Olympics. I have to make a splash somehow. Why not with fabulous fashion?"

"Why not, indeed." Natalie winked. "I think this may be the beginning of a beautiful friendship, Christopher Caldwell."

Topher grabbed her hand and gave it a squeeze. "I agree. Call me Topher."

CHAPTER THREE

OVER BREAKFAST at the hotel where most of
the TBC talent and staff were staying, Topher asked,
"What is 'podium training'? Are these gymnasts really
so confident in their victory that they have to practice
accepting their medals?"

Natalie laughed. She looked cute today, in a black
matte jersey jumpsuit that made her compact figure actually look long and lean. "No. It's the official practice
session before the meet. The gymnasts get a chance to
run through their routines on the official apparatuses
before the actual competition begins. Like a dress rehearsal, kind of."

"Oh, okay. I'm supposed to cover it tomorrow, and
I thought it would be ridiculous if it was all, like, 'aw,
shucks' posing and Miss America waving." Topher cut
his egg-white omelet in half with his fork. The food at
the hotel was decent, if underseasoned. Topher made a
killer omelet when he cooked for himself at home, so

this was kind of a letdown. "You, my darling, are going to be my gymnastics translator."

"Not a problem. I did compete a couple of Olympics ago, you'll recall. I have a little bit of experience. So, you have to cover podium training?"

"Yeah. They're streaming it live on the TBC Sports website. This is, like, the first test."

"I'm covering it too."

"Excellent!" It was a relief, in a way. Topher had taken a gymnastics class as a kid, but he knew very little about the finer points of the sport. "They didn't tell me who else I'd be on the air with. I'm the token non-gymnast on the panel, I suppose. The audience surrogate. The dummy who asks all the questions." Topher frowned at his schedule. "This is like the cooking show I did. In one round, they asked us to cook with this wacky fruit I'd never seen before, and I felt like such an idiot for not knowing what it was. I still have this recurring nightmare where the judge hands me a mystery box full of things I don't know how to cook while millions of people watch on television."

"You'll be fine. I'll give you a primer before we get to the venue. I'm guessing there are a lot of parallels with figure skating." Natalie popped a piece of melon in her mouth. "Did you get an Opening Ceremony ticket?"

"Nope. There was a brief shining moment in which it looked like flight delays would keep Mary Ruggiero at home and they'd let me have her seat, but it looks like she'll arrive in Madrid in time after all." Topher sighed and looked back at his schedule. "I'm also supposed to do a short interview with a gymnast named Jake Mirakovitch. Do you know him?"

"Yeah. I've met him a few times." Natalie grimaced.

"What? Is he awful?"

"No, not at all. Super sweet guy, actually. Smoking hot."

Topher didn't even know what he looked like, so he nodded. "Okay, I hear you. Why the frown?"

"There are two important things to know about Jake." Natalie held up her index finger. "First, he comes from this gymnastics dynasty. His parents were Soviet gymnasts who won a bunch of gold medals in the eighties. And his sister is the world champion. I mean, literally the whole Mirakovitch clan lives and breathes gymnastics. And, well, they're all kind of intense about it."

"Okay."

"Second." Natalie held up another finger. "He's fucking amazing. He can do skills no one else in the world can do. He flies higher on the high bar than anyone in the competition."

"Huh. So why have I never heard of him?"

"He always chokes in international competition."

That surprised Topher, although he supposed it made some sense. There were plenty of talented athletes who just couldn't get it together on the world stage. Topher knew something about that. He nodded. "I guess the network is optimistic that he'll do well here."

"Sure," said Natalie, although Topher suspected she was actually thinking, *Or not, if they're sending you to talk to him.*

But whatever. Topher didn't want to waste the opportunity. "I think Joanna assumes skating and gymnastics have overlapping fan bases, so she thinks I'll have some affinity with the gymnasts." Joanna was Topher's handler. She had some official title that Topher could never remember, but her job mainly seemed to be telling the junior talent what to do. "Or, I don't know. I sometimes feel like the resident clown."

Natalie tilted her head. "They wouldn't have hired you if they didn't think you'd be good on-air. My guess is they think you'll bring in the Winter Olympics fans."

Topher suspected TBC thought he made good television, not necessarily that he was talented. But he nodded, not wanting to get into it.

Natalie seemed to sense that, and she asked, "So, who are you wearing today?"

Topher grinned and launched into an exegesis on that day's outfit. Figuring he'd ease into the fashion, today he had on a short-sleeve button-down tucked into dark skinny jeans, although the shirt was bright pink, and he'd put a little extra whimsy in his hair. He'd let it grow long on top so he could fashion a little pompadour. He'd gone light on the makeup too, just eyeliner and lip gloss, but he'd packed his whole kit. TBC had their own makeup people, but Topher hadn't decided if he trusted them yet.

Natalie gestured at her own shirt. "Not gonna lie, this was one of those big-name-designer collections for Target. This shirt was, like, twenty bucks. It's cute, though, right?" She picked at the shoulder. It was a blush pink lace top, and it *was* pretty cute.

"I like it, yeah. I won't tell anyone you bought it at Target."

Natalie took a bite of potato. "Serendipitous that we were seated together on the plane. We could be a good duo, you know."

Topher grinned. "I do know." He paused. "This Jake fellow. On a scale of, like, one to Matt Bomer, how hot is he?"

Natalie rolled her eyes. "You've got a phone, don't you?"

Topher pulled it out and Googled Jake Mirakovitch. And…. "Jesus."

"Photos don't even do him justice."

"How it is possible to have a face that pretty on a body that muscular?"

Natalie laughed. "Oh, sweetheart. Welcome to men's gymnastics. It takes a tremendous amount of strength, so they all have sculpted bodies like that, and most of them are short. You can't tumble as well if you're tall."

"I'm not exactly a giant." Topher gestured to his own five-eight frame.

"My point is that gymnasts are a rare breed."

"So are figure skaters."

"Fair."

"I'm just saying, you keep explaining things like 'living at the gym' as if I didn't spend most of my life living in an ice rink. Believe me, I get it."

Natalie gestured between their heads. "I think we get each other. Maybe we *will* be a good duo."

"Let's make the most of this podium training gig, then, eh?"

"I was feeling a little like I'd been relegated to the dark basement of the internet for this assignment, but you know what? I think you and I can have a good time together."

"We could be our own portmanteau. Natopher!"

"Topherlie!"

"Brilliant!"

Natalie laughed. She lifted her juice glass. "Here's to an excellent Olympic experience!"

"I'll drink to that." Topher clicked his glass against Natalie's.

THE HIGH bar in the practice gym was wonky.

Jake dismounted, stuck it, and made eye contact with Alexei. Then he turned around and walked back to the bar. "I think something's loose."

Alexei jogged over. "It's fine. I checked it myself."

"No. It felt uneven. A little wobbly."

"Do you plan to be this fussy all week?"

"No, I just—it didn't feel right."

"You need to catch your releases harder. These judges, they take deductions for everything. You grab the bar with your fingertips like you did on that last Tkatchev, you'll lose tenths."

"I know, but I think… you know, whatever, it's fine. I'll catch the bar next time." Jake didn't want to argue with Alexei. He could see plainly that one of the pins was not in all the way, so the bar had shaken a bit when Jake did the release moves, but another coach was already fiddling with it, so it was too late now. "I have to go do some bullshit interview for TBC."

Alexei slapped his ass. "Go. Do better next time."

"Next time is podium training, so…."

Alexei made a kind of strangled coughing sound. Jake knew Alexei hated that TBC aired parts of podium training, because it put more pressure on the athletes to do well, even though it didn't count. Jake was pretty good at forgetting about the cameras, though; he only fucked up when the judges were watching.

This was going to be a fun week.

Jake grabbed his stuff and went back to the locker room, where he changed into street clothes and fiddled with his hair. He put on a white button-down shirt—crisp enough to look good on camera, and it offset his summer tan nicely. Not that he'd had a lot of time for tanning, but Valentin thought it was a good idea to soak up some sun periodically, since his children otherwise spent so much time in a gym, they didn't get enough vitamin D exposure.

Jake walked to a press room deep in the bowels of the arena. When he poked his head through the open door, he saw that someone had strewn purple velvet curtains along all four walls of the room. Of all the choices…. Purple was one of the network's colors, so Jake figured this was some kind of branding, but still, it looked like a boudoir.

"Hello?" Jake called out.

The man who appeared looked vaguely familiar, but Jake couldn't place him. He was taller than Jake, and thin, but his clothes were tight enough to reveal an athlete's physique—sculpted muscles, a surgery scar near his wrist—and he carried himself with the sort of poise gymnasts and dancers had. Also, his shirt was blindingly pink and his blond hair was done up in some kind of crazy pompadour. He was… kind of a lot to look at, actually.

"Hi, can I help you?" asked the guy. He had a soft voice.

"Uh, I'm supposed to be doing an interview?"

The guy gave Jake an assessing look. "You're Jake, right?"

"Yeah, that's… uh, okay." Jake shook his head. He hadn't had to introduce himself to anyone working in gymnastics media in a while.

He looked around. A woman with a headset crushing her frizzy hair stood off to one side of the room, having an intense conversation with Natalie Pasquarella. There were a few other PAs and network employees buzzing around. The pompadour in the hot pink shirt stared at Jake expectantly.

"Oh, I'm sorry. I'm new at this," the pompadour said. "I'm Christopher Caldwell."

Jake's brain worked overtime to make the connection, but he drew a blank. "Okay."

"It's all right, darling. You probably don't recognize me because I'm not wearing feathers and completing a triple axel."

Figure skater. Flamboyant figure skater. Christopher Caldwell, yes. Jake had seen him skate on TV a couple of times. "Right, sorry. Of course. I just came from practice, so my head's in the clouds. Hi, Mr. Caldwell. It's nice to meet you."

"Likewise. So now you're probably wondering what I'm doing here."

"I… yeah, I guess." Jake felt confused more than anything else. What exactly was happening here?

Christopher Caldwell pointed to two purple director's chairs in the corner. Two cameras and a huge light were trained on the chairs, so clearly this was the interview set.

"They didn't tell me who I'd meet with," Jake said, trying not to seem like a complete idiot. "Just that I had to be here at the appointed time. Should I sit?"

"Yeah. Let me go get the camera guy. Get comfy."

Christopher walked like a dancer, graceful but in a way that made him seem delicate. Of course he wasn't, if he was a professional figure skater. A few skaters had been through Valentin's gym over the years, to do acrobatic training that was supposed to help them jump better, so Jake had a rough idea of what their training regimen looked like. It was brutal, nearly as intense as gymnastics.

When Christopher returned, he sat in the other chair, but there was no camera man. "Sorry," he said, "Jim is wrapping up another interview, and we have to wait for Joanna to give the go-ahead. She's helping produce the segment. It should just be a few minutes."

"Okay."

Jake looked Christopher over. He had fine features and rosy skin, but also a square jaw and shoulders that seemed broad for his frame. He was... well, beautiful was the first word that popped into Jake's head. But sexy too. The eyeliner and the pink shirt clashed with his masculine body in a way that resulted in an alluring androgyny that Jake found he couldn't look away from. And Christopher's whole look indicated that he did not give a fuck what anyone thought of him. Jake found that hot too.

"Maybe we can get to know each other a little? I mean, I'm kind of new to this interviewing thing. I have a list of network-approved questions to ask." Christopher pulled a piece of paper from his breast pocket. "So this won't get too scandalous, but it feels strange for me to be asking personal things of a man I met thirty seconds ago."

Well, this was going to be weird. "Sure."

"I mean, Natalie told me a little about you. You know Natalie, right?" Christopher hooked his thumb back toward where Natalie stood.

"I do a little, yes."

"So, basically, the network is spinning this story of you, darling, as this legendary gymnast who still doesn't have a gold medal. But this is your year, right?"

"God willing."

"Great." Then Christopher Caldwell laughed. "God, I'm so sorry. I've been in your seat a billion times, and I know how dumb these interviews are. Still, I'm still trying to toe the network line because I want this job. So let's start over. I'm Christopher Caldwell, but my friends call me Topher. You can call me Topher if you like."

Topher. That seemed right. A name like *Chris* felt too plain for this man. "All right," said Jake.

"I'm here in Madrid doing puff pieces for TBC as a kind of audition for a commentator job. So I want to do really well at this, but I also totally get how awkward it is to be the athlete who just wants to get back to practice. I'm sure the last thing you want to do is this interview."

Something about the lilt of Christopher's—Topher's—voice was really soothing, so Jake nodded. "I mean, no offense. The publicity is nice. But it would have been better to get a few more sets in just now."

"I get it. Believe me." Topher studied his piece of paper for a moment. "Sorry, just trying to memorize these. Give me a sec."

As Topher studied the paper, Jake studied Topher. He was handsome, in a soft way. The hair was a little silly, and that shirt was an eyesore, but the pink also set off the flush of Topher's complexion, his high cheekbones, and his reddish, glossy lips. Jake didn't always find makeup on guys appealing, but Topher's shiny lips really did draw the eye right to them, didn't they? He had freckles across his nose too. And he was built. Thin, yes, with a willowy quality to him, but Jake could plainly see the power in Topher's arms, in his thick thighs, in his broad chest. Topher must have retired a few years ago, but it was clear he still went to the gym regularly and took care of his body.

Once an elite athlete, always an elite athlete.

Jake spared a moment to think on his own retirement. What the hell would he even do with himself?

"God, I can't believe they want me to ask some of this stuff. You don't want to talk about your lack of success."

"That's a question?" Jake asked.

Topher sat up straight and puffed out his chest a little. He leveled his gaze at Jake and then said, in a perfect news anchor imitation, "Why do you think you have yet to really prove yourself on a world stage?"

Fuck. As tickled as Jake was by the imitation, he hated the question. "It's not that I *haven't*."

"No, I know. It's not like I've never heard, 'Gee, Toph, why did you never win an Olympic medal?' 'I don't know, sweetie, I just didn't.'"

"You never won an Olympic medal? That can't be true."

"I think I'd remember if I did."

Something shifted in Jake's perception of Topher, but Jake didn't have time to process it before the frizzy-haired lady and a guy in a TBC T-shirt walked over. "You ready to get started?" she asked.

"As ever," Topher said perkily as he folded and put the list of questions back in his pocket. "Can I modify these questions a little?"

Frizzy Hair frowned. "Well, sure, you *can*. I mean, it's your interview."

So… no.

But Topher seemed to take it as a yes. He crossed his legs and sat up again, looking square at Jake. "Then let's get started."

JAKE MIRAKOVITCH was probably the hottest guy Topher had ever set eyes on.

He had sun-bronzed skin and auburn hair and pretty green eyes. He wore a white shirt that didn't do much to hide his muscles; this was a guy with a tremendous amount of strength. His body's power was evident all over, from his biceps to his thighs. Topher couldn't help but imagine what it would feel like to have those bulky limbs around him.

But he had to push that thought aside. He had to be a professional. He cleared his throat. Joanna counted down and then gave the signal for the camera to roll.

Topher got right into it, because he was filming the interview's introduction later. "How are you feeling?" Topher asked. "You ready for the competition?"

"Yes," said Jake. "I feel really great. We changed the training routine a little at camp this year, so we worked through a lot of possible scenarios to help prepare mentally as well as physically. I don't think I've ever felt so ready for a competition."

"And you're healthy? After the injury at last year's World Championships?" Topher didn't know anything about the injury except that it was on his list of questions to ask.

But maybe it was the wrong thing to ask, because Jake frowned briefly. "Oh. Yeah, I'm fine. I, uh, hit my head when I failed to land a vault correctly and wound up with a concussion, but I recovered well and I've been healthy since. And, you know, everyone tried to blame some setting on the vault table. That does happen sometimes. There was one Worlds where the vault was set too low and nobody landed correctly. But this was just... user error. It was on me. I didn't get off the vault hard enough, didn't rotate fast enough, so I couldn't stick the landing and I hit my head. It happens." Jake sighed. "Sorry. Didn't mean to rant."

"No, I get it. Nobody ran out and tripped me when I missed the quad axel at the Olympics."

Jake looked up and Topher met his gaze. God, those eyes. Mossy green, the most striking Topher had ever met head-on like this. Some unspoken communication passed between them, and Jake said, "Yeah. Exactly." He took a deep breath. "Anyway, I've been working on my self-confidence in training. Working through a lot of strange situations. How do I recover if I mess up? How do I keep myself from panicking if one of my teammates gets injured or misses an important skill? How do I keep a mistake or an injury from derailing my whole meet? That kind of thing."

"But you feel good?"

Jake raised his eyebrows. "Yeah. I feel great, actually."

"So, what do you think of the Americans' chances of winning a medal in men's gymnastics?"

"Good. We're in great shape. I know the men generally fly under the radar because the women get more attention. And that's fair, because they have a fantastic team. The depth of that team—there are women who didn't make the cut who could win medals in their sleep—it's really something. But I think the men's team deserves some recognition too, for all the hard work we've put in."

Topher nodded. He took a moment to recall the next question. "Speaking of the women's team, what's it like being on an Olympic team with your sister?"

"Oh, well. USA Gymnastics is a Mirakovitch family affair these days, I suppose. My whole family is in Madrid. Chelsea and my parents. I mean, my dad coaches the women's team, of course. But they've all been enormously supportive."

Of course. Topher recognize the line for what it was but thought he detected some uneasiness in Jake, an old resentment, maybe, or chafing under the watchful eyes of his family. Topher suspected that would have affected him, too, if his mother had been allowed into the athletes' spaces during competition. Topher liked knowing she was watching, that she sat in the audience, but to have her in the space reserved for coaches would have been unnerving.

Topher was a little dumbfounded by Jake's easy beauty, his strength and athleticism, and he struggled to come up with the next question. In his peripheral vision, he caught Joanna giving him the signal to wrap it up. "Are you unveiling anything new at the Games, or are you sticking to the routines you've done all season?"

"I have a high bar release move I've been working on. I haven't decided if I'm going to do it in competition or not yet. I might save it for the event finals. There are so many amazing athletes here that you really have to go big or go home at the event finals."

"Well, Jake, good luck in the competition!"

"Cut," said Joanna. "That was great, Jake. Thank you."

"You're welcome. Can I have some water?"

"Table behind you. Help yourself."

Topher followed Jake over to the craft services table and watched Jake pour water from a metal pitcher covered in condensation. Ice clinked around in the pitcher as Jake filled a big paper cup. He took a healthy gulp of water, then eyed Topher as he refilled his cup.

"I'm such an idiot," Jake said.

"What makes you say that?"

"Getting upset about the vault at Worlds."

"I wouldn't worry about it. You could barely notice you were upset about it. They'll probably edit your face out of that bit anyway. My segments are supposed to be feel-good pieces, so they'll keep the stuff about how you're prepared and how your family is supportive, because that's what the audience wants to hear."

Jake nodded. "Yeah. Did you have to do things like this when you were competing?"

"Yup. They did this extensive package on me before my first Olympics because I was supposed to win a gold medal. Instead, I fell on my face and lost to the Russians. You'd think I'd started the Cold War again, based on the press I got."

"Don't get me started. Every time I lose a competition, someone writes an article about how I'm such a disappointment to my parents and their great American dream of escaping the USSR and making happy gymnastics triumph over the old grueling system." Jake sighed.

"Oh, the sports news. They really run with their own narratives sometimes, don't they?"

Jake nodded slowly, looking into his cup. Topher tried to get a read on this guy. There was something practiced and elusive about him, probably borne of doing dozens of interviews just like this, wherein he had to pretend everything was hunky-dory when in fact his anxiety was telling him things were anything but.

Or Topher was projecting.

"Does your father coach you as well?" Topher asked.

Jake shook his head. "He coaches my sister. He did coach me when I was a kid, but when I was, I don't know, nineteen or so? I told him I wanted my own coach. Dad wanted to specialize in women's gymnastics anyway. So I work with Alexei, who, incidentally, is an old teammate of dear old Dad's."

"Also a Soviet gymnast?"

"Aren't they all? A good number of the coaches on the elite level came out of either the Soviet or Romanian machines." Jake shrugged. "Look, I gotta get going. It was nice to talk to you, though."

Topher wasn't sure why he did the next thing, but he pulled a card out of his pocket. Probably the network hadn't made these cards for occasions when their commentators developed crushes on interview subjects, but just the same, Topher handed Jake the card and said, "Well, if you ever want to talk to someone who is not affiliated with your family, my cell phone number is on there. Text me. Maybe we can get a drink or something at the America House."

There. That didn't sound *too* much like Topher had asked Jake out on a date. It was the Olympics; circumstances were different than they would have been if Topher had just, say, run into Jake at a coffeehouse. Topher didn't know Jake's status at all; was he gay, straight, bi, single, coupled, married, what? No wedding ring, but that didn't really mean anything. Topher had once had a teammate who took his wedding ring off during competition because he found its presence distracting during his program. Topher kind of thought that was bullshit and the guy was more likely cheating on his wife, but whatever. If Topher had been married during his career, he would have worn the damn ring.

Anyway....

Jake stared at the card for a long moment and then looked up and met Topher's gaze. "I… yeah. Maybe I will. Thanks."

Which was probably the end of that, but it had been worth a shot. Topher smiled and patted Jake's meaty bicep. "And if not, I'm scheduled to be at podium training tomorrow, so maybe we'll run into each other again."

Jake raised an eyebrow. "Maybe."

Chapter Four

TBC HAD a handful of Opening Ceremony tickets available through a lottery for employees. "I never win these," Topher said as he sat in the broadcasting booth and filled in the online form the day after his interview with Jake.

"Your odds are not that bad," Natalie argued. "There are maybe only thirty people, tops, entering the lottery."

"For three tickets."

"Still."

Topher hit Submit on the form and then looked up from his phone. He and Natalie were in the press booth of the Palacio Vistalegre, the official gymnastics venue. The network had decided to pair them up to comment over podium training. They'd be live on the TBC website, not part of the television coverage, but Topher decided to take it as good practice for commenting later. Besides, he could play the gymnastics dummy to

Natalie's expert well enough, giving her plenty of opportunities to show off her knowledge.

"Thanks to flight delays, our third chair, Sam Norton, is not here," said Natalie. "He's another retired gymnast. And he's a hottie. Just saying."

"Are you trying to hook up with a gymnast? Or hook me up with one?" Topher Googled 'sam norton' while they waited for things to happen. It occurred to him that Jake Mirakovitch hadn't been *that* short—within an inch or two of Topher's admittedly not-exactly-towering stature. He looked at his phone. This Sam Norton guy *was* a hottie, but in a bland blond way. "I'm not opposed to this plan, to be clear."

"Just making observations. We'll be on in a sec, so shut up."

Then the producer gave them the signal and they were suddenly on-air.

Nothing was happening in the arena.

"Hi, everyone," Natalie said into the microphone. "I'm Natalie Pasquarella, and I'm here in the booth with former Olympic figure skater Christopher Caldwell. We're live at the Palacio Vistalegre, the beautiful home of gymnastics competition here in Madrid. Welcome, Topher. How are you liking Madrid so far?"

He'd hardly seen any of it, but he said, "It's a lovely city."

"Are you excited for the start of the Games?"

"Thrilled. I'm glad I get to see one of the early events. Can you tell me what we're looking at?"

Joanna gave him a thumbs-up. They'd discussed what to say before he'd sat down at this microphone, and he had a page full of questions to ask if there was a lull in activity.

"Sure," Natalie said. "Podium training is kind of like a dress rehearsal. It's organized in rotations, just like the actual competition will be, and it's the gymnasts' first real opportunity to practice using the apparatuses that will be used during the competition. In most cases, we'll see the gymnasts perform their routines exactly as they will during the team qualifying event tomorrow night, but nothing is scored and these routines don't count. Really, it's a lot of fun to watch."

Topher chuckled. "I certainly can't argue with that. I had the opportunity to talk to some of the gymnasts yesterday. The men's team seems ready to compete. Jake Mirakovitch told me he feels more prepared for this meet than any other in his career."

"That's great. I expect him to do great things this week."

Natalie blathered on for a while about each of the gymnasts on the American men's team while they waited for things to happen. Eventually the athletes started filing into the gym. The Americans, in their official red uniforms, were in a rotation with teams from the Netherlands and Great Britain. Natalie pointed out that both countries were fielding strong teams; the Brits had been on the rise ever since they'd hosted the London Games, and the Netherlands had a pair of Romanian coaches who were doing astonishing things with the program.

"It really is a new era. The Romanians didn't even qualify a team this year," Natalie said, reading off her fact sheet. "Gabriel Antonescu and Petre Sala will be competing in the qualifiers for a spot in the event finals, but that's it for their men's team. Antonescu won a bronze on pommel horse at the last World Championships."

A PA fiddled with the screens in front of them. The official Olympic feed was shown on six screens, one for each apparatus. A seventh screen showed the raw TBC feed, which was a dry run for the official primetime feed later. There was also a window in front of them from which they could see the action on the floor. It was overwhelming and confusing; there were six apparatuses set up with several groups of men at each, fiddling with screws or putting on hand guards or chalking up, and the sheer amount of activity made it hard to know where to look.

"For this broadcast," Natalie said, "we're going to focus mostly on the Americans, and we'll show some highlights of other athletes in between. The Americans are starting on vault, so let's go there first."

The British men vaulted first. Topher didn't have a lot to contribute beyond sounding dazzled when a gymnast stuck a landing or to suck in a breath through his teeth and say "Aw," when somebody missed.

"There's less waiting around now," Natalie added. "There are no judges scoring. This really is a run-through of each vault, each routine. But it's interesting to see who is looking relaxed, who seems tense, which gymnasts are bringing their A game."

"Yeah," Topher said. "It must be nerve-wracking to know these rehearsals are airing on TV, though. We used to do practice skates prior to competition, but we never let anyone except the coaches film them."

"Eh, most of these guys are used to performing with lots of people watching."

Topher couldn't help but think of Jake again. Topher had interviewed a few of the other guys from the men's team, but something about Jake had stuck with him all day. Well, Jake's physical attributes were part of that equation, no doubt, but Topher had sensed something more in Jake. An old pain lingering under the surface, maybe. The curse of being the athlete destined to let everyone down. Of having the weight of expectations on one's shoulders and a history of crumbling under it. To hang on to that nagging feeling that one wasn't really as talented as everyone said, after all. To say Topher related to that on a primal level was understating it.

The American team had sent TBC a list of who would be performing which routines in which order. Topher also had an explanation of the rules, which Natalie was supposed to squeeze into the commentary between other things. She hadn't managed to do that yet, though. So as the last British man chalked up and talked with his coach, Topher said, "The makeup of these teams might look a little different than what audiences are used to."

"Yes," said Natalie. "There's been a rules change since the last Olympics. The top teams can qualify up to six gymnasts. No more than four of them are the all-around gymnasts. They can also bring in two specialists. How many men qualify depends on how the team placed at the last World Championships. The Americans qualified a full six-man team. But the way it works is that four gymnasts compete on each apparatus—oh, let's watch Smithfield vault. It's, oh, that was gorgeous. Little hop on the landing, but that's a tenth. Really nice. Anyway, four gymnasts on each apparatus. During the team competition, the lowest score is dropped."

"So we'll see four American men on the vault."

"Yes. Hayden Croft is their vault specialist. I believe he's going last in this rotation."

"Yes," said Topher, looking at one of the many pieces of paper in front of him.

"Anyway, four compete on each apparatus, the top men on each one qualify for the event finals, and the best overall teams will advance to the team final."

This was all very complicated. Topher had a chart in front of him, and he still didn't entirely understand it. But he said, "Okay."

Perhaps sensing Topher's confusion, Natalie said, "Okay, here's how this will all happen. Podium training today. We'll see all six rotations, so you'll get a feel for how this will go later. The men's qualifier starts tomorrow. The top teams advance to the team final. Only the total team score matters in the team final, but individual scores matter too, because the top individual gymnasts who compete on all six apparatuses will advance to the all-around. There, the best overall gymnast will be crowned. The qualifiers also allow individual gymnasts to qualify for the event finals, which will occur next Saturday. That's a one-and-done kind of thing. Eight athletes compete on each apparatus, the best wins a medal. Does that help?"

"So, wait, the event finals are last? Seems a little anticlimactic."

"Nah. The top gymnasts on each apparatus doing their most over-the-top routines? It's exciting!"

Topher chuckled, enjoying the joy in Natalie's tone. "Well, that does help some. I still may need you to draw me a chart later."

"Well, let's watch what's happening now. The first American up on vault is Jordan Weiss. He's usually a pretty solid vaulter. This is a Tsukahara vault with a half turn. Let's watch."

Topher knew a little about gymnastics. He'd taken some classes as a kid, and he'd had a coach that had used gymnastics-inspired drills and exercises to help Topher build the muscles he needed for jumping. But he didn't know what things were called—he had no idea what a Tsukahara looked like, though he guessed it was named for a Japanese gymnast—so he tried to absorb what he could from the slow-motion replay. The gymnast, Jordan, ran down the... runway... then jumped onto the springboard, did a half twist, pushed off the vault table backward with his hands, and then did a nice layout in the air before hitting the mat with a perfectly stuck landing.

"Not the hardest vault in the program," Natalie said, "but beautifully done."

"Corey O'Bannon is up next," Topher said, reading from the list. A blond guy was chalking up at the end of the.... "That mat they run down? Is it called a runway? That's what I'm calling it in my head."

Natalie laughed. "It's usually just called the run-up area, but I like runway better. Let's call it that. Maybe gymnasts will start strutting down it instead of running."

"Put a little Naomi Campbell in their walk," Topher said. "That's how you vault stylishly."

Natalie giggled. "Anyway, here's Corey."

They paused to watch.

"Oh, little hop on the landing," Natalie said. "But it looked good in the air. Jake Mirakovitch is up next."

Topher's heart skipped a little. From the booth, it was a little hard to see Jake's face, but on the monitor, the camera zoomed right in on him. God, he was gorgeous. His hair had been gelled within an inch of its life, probably so that it wouldn't fly around too much when he was doing these skills, but it wasn't the greatest look for him. Topher wanted to run his fingers through the strands and tease it out, make it wild, make Jake wild....

He cleared his throat. "Jake will be doing a full-twisting Yurchenko," Topher said, reading from the sheet. He was thankful that so many years of figure skating had helped him learn enough Russian, Japanese, and other languages to keep from tripping over some of these terms. *Yurchenko* didn't quite roll off the tongue the way *toe loop* and *Salchow* did, but this wasn't Topher's first rodeo.

"Yes. It's his first of two vaults. Jake is planning to try to qualify for the event final, so he must vault twice and can't repeat the same vault."

"All right. Let's watch."

Jake clapped his hands together once, then stared down the runway at the vault table. He looked determined. Topher didn't have the right vocabulary to describe everything—he assumed every move had a name he hadn't learned yet—but he watched Jake carefully. Jake ran down the runway, then kind of cartwheeled onto the springboard, jumped from it, hit the table with his hands, then twisted in the air before sticking his landing cleanly.

"Wow," Topher said aloud.

"Yeah. That's the best I've seen him do that vault in a while. Let's see if he can pull off the second one, which has a higher difficulty score. This one is actually called the Mirakovitch. It's a variation on a Tsukahara vault, but he's going to somersault in the air. Named for Valentin Mirakovitch, Jake's father."

"That's cool," Topher said, imagining what it would be like to have a skating jump named after someone in his own family, maybe someone jumping a Caldwell instead of a Lutz. He wondered if Jake agreed it was cool or if he found it hard to deal with his father's legacy.

But Jake did the vault beautifully. He got huge height off the vault table, somersaulted in the air twice, and landed with only a little step.

"Nice," Natalie said.

"Yeah, that was amazing," Topher said. "I mean, I am, of course, a total gymnastics neophyte, but that looked really good. Can we see it in slow motion?"

"Yeah, here's the replay. Look at the air he gets off the table. He needs all that to complete the rotations before he lands."

In slo-mo, it was easier to see the flexing of each muscle. Jake's calves were tight as he jumped off the springboard. His shoulders rippled as he pushed off the table. Everything in him seemed to compress into the somersault tuck. Then it all unleashed as he straightened out and hit the mat below. He hit it so hard, it was no wonder he had to take a step.

"It's like landing on one foot," Topher said.

"What do you mean?"

"So, take a Salchow, for example. The skating jump, I mean. You take off from the back inside edge of your skate and land on the back outside edge of your other foot if you do it right. In competition you have to do it perfectly, and judges have those HD slow-motion cameras now, so they can tell if you're not positioned correctly on landing, if you land on one edge, or if the wrong foot gets anywhere near the ice. I was just thinking that sticking a landing in gymnastics is like landing perfectly on the outside edge after a Salchow."

"That is a good way to think about scoring. The judges take deductions for minor errors in skating, right?"

"Yeah, my understanding is that there are similar scoring systems for both sports now. Every move starts with a base score, and deductions are taken for any errors. So landing on the wrong edge of your skate, or in this case, hopping when you land a vault, will cost you."

"Exactly."

On the monitor, Jake grinned at a guy who must have been a coach, and they high-fived each other before the camera moved to look at Hayden Croft.

"Hayden is going to do a vault called the Dragalescu," said Natalie. "That's a vault with a full point value of seventeen, higher than most of these other guys. If he lands it in competition, it'll earn him a huge score. After he hits the table, he'll do two somersaults, then straighten it out and twist around to land it."

"Do you have a gymnastics move named after you?"

"Yep," Natalie said with a grin. "Release move on bars. It's called the Pasquarella."

"They should name some figure skating move after me."

"They really should. Anyway, I saw Hayden do this vault in a vault final a few years ago right after Dragalescu himself did it. Hayden looked better in the air but stepped out of bounds on the landing, which is a mandatory deduction. So he didn't beat Dragalescu with his own vault, but it was close."

"This is a weird sport," Topher commented.

Natalie laughed. "Let's watch."

Topher watched the screen as Hayden did a crazy series of acrobatics to hurl himself off the vault table high enough in the air to roll and twist before getting his legs straight beneath him and landing the vault. There'd been a time in his life in which Topher had been able to make his body do things like that, but those days were long behind him. He still missed competitive skating sometimes, but not the toll it took on his body.

Hayden landed his vault. But if he hadn't, at least he had thick mats to land on, and not a sheet of hard ice.

"Hayden's going to vault again," said Natalie. "The second vault has to be from a different vault family. Hayden is also going to do a Mirakovitch here."

They watched. Hayden... looked good. Topher didn't understand enough to know whether he did the vault better or worse than Jake, but Hayden did stick the landing with no steps or hops.

"That was a hell of a start for the Americans," Natalie said as the Dutch gymnasts got ready to vault.

"Think they can keep it up?" Topher asked.

"I guess we'll see."

JAKE FIDDLED with his arm guards and watched the last British gymnast finish his parallel bar routine as Jake mentally rehearsed his own. Alexei talked to Corey about his skills and then stopped midsentence to scold Jake about holding his handstands long enough. Jake nodded, not wanting to antagonize Alexei, but he knew what he had to do.

They were having a good meet, if podium training could be called that. Everyone had landed their routines so far. Jake's high bar routine had been solid, so he'd thrown in a modified Kovacs, a release move he'd been working on in practice. And he'd nailed it.

On the other hand, Jordan had been a little sloppy on rings and Paul had stepped out of bounds on floor, and everyone had made small mistakes on the pommel horse, but those were minor problems in the scheme of things. With one rotation to go—on one of Jake's best events—Jake felt good.

Corey was up first for the Americans, and Alexei slapped his ass as he went. Jake could do without Alexei treating his athletes like football players, but it was a quirk of Alexei trying to seem more American. Lord knew American men's gymnastics was full of men overcompensating for gymnastics generally being viewed as a girly sport, even though Jake could have easily bench-pressed his detractors.

But Corey looked good on parallel bars now. His landing was a little wobbly, but it was a solid routine. Jordan and Brad were equally solid. No major mistakes. Everyone seemed to feel good after their routines. So Jake went to chalk up. Three above-the-bar skills, three below-the-bar skills, dismount. He had this.

Well, yeah, of course he had this. No one was watching.

He mounted the bars, swung into his first handstand, and mentally counted to five. Then he swung between the bars and threw himself up into a salto, coming out of the tuck in time to land on the bars with his arms. Then he swung again, twisted, and caught the bar with his hands, pushing into a handstand. That was one of his signatures, a move he was hoping they'd name the Mirakovitch, even though there already was a showy release move named after Valentin. Then he swung into another salto, caught the left bar, kept his body inverted, and pirouetted into a handstand on both bars. Three more skills later and he swung himself up and off the bars, doing another salto in the air before landing on his feet. Stuck landing, arms in the air, done.

"We're done," said Alexei after Jake jogged over to the bench. "Viktor wants to have team meeting before we let you go away for the day. Room B in ten minutes."

Jake took a moment to catch his breath; then he grabbed his stuff and followed Corey out of the arena. "Good practice," Corey said.

"It was, yeah. We look great when no one's watching."

"Actually, TBC broadcasted that."

Jake was so startled by this news that he tripped. "Are you kidding? I knew they were recording, but they actually broadcast it?"

"Online, not on TV, but yeah. Commentators and everything. Natalie Pasquarella and some figure skater."

Topher.

Why the thought of Topher watching him should squeeze Jake's chest the way it did was a mystery. But he liked that Topher had seen him on a good day.

And, well, Topher was nice to look at once one's eyes adjusted. Kind of a pretty boy. Attractive in a tall and rangy way.

"I know," Jake said. "He interviewed me yesterday. The figure skater, I mean. Christopher Caldwell."

"The network makes strange choices."

"Not that strange. There are only four judged sports in the Olympics, right? Gymnastics, diving, synchronized swimming, and figure skating."

"And martial arts, kind of. Fencing."

"Okay, fine. Whatever. But figure skating and gymnastics have some things in common. They're both judged sports. Both require absurd amounts of training. Both involve… twisting your body in the air." Jake sighed, realizing it would be easy to lose this argument. "Besides, Natalie knows what she's talking about."

"That's true. I don't know. I just wish they'd take us seriously. Do you know how much airtime men's gymnastics got on TBC during the last Olympics? Twenty-two minutes. In total. I looked it up."

Jake winced. "Really?"

"Yep. Two minutes of that was Jordan's silver medal pommel horse routine. The rest was kind of a highlight reel of our collective spectacular failures. And sure, they've got your face all over the TBC website right now, but you know that unless we kill it in qualifiers, they'll ignore us all again."

"So we kill it in qualifiers." Jake followed Corey into the team meeting.

Corey grunted. "Yeah. No problem. Easy as pie. Gold medals for everyone. Why didn't I think of that?"

Jake rolled his eyes. "Don't make me call Viktor over to give you the speech about attitude."

Corey sighed. "I want to win. I do. I just also want to keep my expectations reasonable. We've fucked this up in the past. Maybe this is the one time we don't. But history is not exactly on our side. Do I think we *can* win gold medals? Yes. Do I think we *will*? That's kind of up to the gods of gymnastics now."

Jake grunted because he didn't necessarily disagree. He kept expecting this meet to feel *different*, but it didn't. It had the benefit of not having really begun yet, so Jake hadn't had the opportunity to fuck up anything so far, but whether he succeeded or failed felt out of his control.

And then Valentin walked into the room.

"I only have short time," said Valentin.

Jake was surprised to see him at all, given there were workers currently changing out the equipment in the arena so that podium training could begin for the women. On the other hand, in addition to being the women's coach, Valentin was the head coach of all of USA Gymnastics, so although Viktor was the head men's coach, Valentin was technically his boss.

"We have opportunities to do something very special here," Valentin continued. "I believe the eight gymnasts in this room are eight best in world. Trick will be not to think too hard." Valentin tapped his temple. "This is Olympics, it is big stage. But use this moment to change expectations. You feel pressure, others think you will follow old patterns, so break patterns. Do gymnastics the way I know you can. Okay?"

Everyone in the room murmured, "Okay."

Valentin never left room for argument, so he nodded once and moved toward the door, patting Jake's shoulder on the way. When he was gone, Viktor said, "I have notes."

Jake sat down. There was nothing like a pep talk... followed by a catalogue of everything he was doing wrong.

CHAPTER FIVE

Day 0

TEAM QUALIFIERS started the morning after the Opening Ceremony, so Jake opted to skip the event in favor of sleeping, as did most of his teammates. Sleep didn't come, though. He lay awake in the room he shared with Corey, staring at the ceiling. Half the time he mentally rehearsed his routines; the other half he just fretted about falling on his face.

Also Corey snored, which didn't help matters.

So Jake got out of bed.

He wandered down the hall of the dorm building that housed the American delegation. Some teams had floors in the other buildings; Team USA was so big, it took up an entire building. So he felt like he walked among friends as he paced up and down the hall a couple of times. He wasn't even the only one pacing; he recognized a female swimmer doing the same thing in another corridor.

He arrived at the lounge set up on the corner of the floor. A man sat on a sofa inside, watching the opening ceremony on TV. He looked familiar, but Jake didn't recognize him until he walked into the lounge and got a good look at his face.

It was Isaac Flood. According to Corey's issue of *Sports Illustrated*, everyone had thought him the second coming—at least in the pool; the second coming of Michael Phelps perhaps—until he'd fallen into a bottle and earned himself a couple of much-publicized DUIs. The article said Isaac had gone to rehab and made an impressive showing at the Olympic swim trials that year. Reading the article had jogged Jake's memory of the last Olympics. Gymnastics and swimming schedules almost always overlapped, but Isaac had received an unavoidable amount of press attention.

"Hey," said Isaac. He was curled up on the lounge sofa, wrapped in a fleece blanket. Although some other athletes lingered in the hall, Isaac was alone in the lounge.

"Hi. I'm Jake. How's it going? Watching the Opening Ceremony?"

"Yeah. Figured, what the hell? I'm swimming tomorrow, so I didn't want to be there, but it's kind of entertaining."

Jake stood beside the sofa and watched the screen for a few moments. An absurd number of dancers seemed to be doing some kind of folk dance in circles that formed the Olympic rings.

"I gotta sleep," Jake said, "but I'm too wound up."

"I know what you mean. I'm Isaac, by the way."

"I know. Everyone knows who you are, Isaac Flood. Wheaties box and all that."

Isaac sighed. "Right."

"I only bring it up because I'm jealous. I want a Wheaties box. This is my second Olympics. Everyone's all 'Jake Mirakovitch, he's the one to beat this year,' but I'm terrified. I've been nailing every one of my routines in practice, but I did four years ago too. And we all know how that went."

"I don't know how that went," Isaac said.

Jake grimaced. What kind of bubble did this guy live in? "Probably best not to relive it. Let's just say the team was a mess. First place going into the team final, and then we all choked. Me especially. Fell off the pommel horse. Whiffed one of my release moves on the high bar. Tenths of deductions here and there add up if you make enough mistakes. We were the gold medal favorites, but we came in sixth. Sixth!"

"I'm sorry."

"Qualifiers are tomorrow, and I want to make at least two event finals and qualify for the All-Around. The women's team has been raking up medals for years, but we're a goddamned joke."

Isaac laughed softly. "Aren't you supposed to be all, 'We're the best! We're gonna win gold!'"

"Publicly, sure. But you get it, right?"

"I do. Nothing you can do, man, but your best."

"Do your best" seemed like odd advice from someone who had once been unambiguously one of the best swimmers in the world. "Yeah," Jake said, a little baffled. "How do you prepare for a race?"

"What do you mean?"

"I mean, how do you keep from choking?"

Isaac pulled his blanket tighter around him and looked toward the TV. "It helps when everyone has low expectations."

Jake scoffed. "When has anyone had low expectations of you?"

Isaac laughed. "Fair. But swimming isn't a team sport. I'm only letting myself down."

"But what about swim relays? That's a team thing."

"I don't know. I mean, it's different. There's some strategy, but at the end of the day, it's about who swam the fastest. If I'm doing a relay, I push as hard as I can for my team. What else can I do?"

Which made a certain amount of sense. Jake nodded. "Sure."

"It's the Olympics. This is the pinnacle, right? I mean, there are World Cups, national championships, all that, but the Olympics is the thing everyone watches. Instead of letting that pressure get to you, you focus on yourself. It's not about proving yourself or whatever. It's about pushing your body to the limit of what it can do. Right? If I'm in a final, I push as hard as I can. I move my arms faster, harder. I put my all into it, until it feels like my body is on fire and I have to throw up. I race until I can't breathe anymore. Because it's not about being safe and comfortable, it's about doing the absolute best that you can."

It's not about being safe and comfortable. Jake had never considered his sport safe, and he had the scars on his body to prove it. But maybe Isaac had a point. Maybe Jake had been pulling his punches in international competition. There'd been such a long precedent of him making major mistakes on the global stage that maybe, subconsciously, Jake had been holding back. He'd been trying not to tear an ACL or get a concussion, trying not to break a bone or take himself out of the competition via injury, but maybe he'd been too safe, had tried to protect himself too much. Maybe he'd tightened up.

Jesus. What a time to have that revelation. In about sixteen hours, he'd have to be in that fucking gym. "Okay," he said, feeling a little overwhelmed.

"I don't know much about gymnastics," said Isaac, "but the whole evolution of the sport is figuring out what the human body can do, right? Each Olympics, the sport has advanced. Sixty years ago, maybe you could win a gold medal by doing a cartwheel over the vault horse. Now you gotta flip in the air three times or whatever. You want to win, of course you do, but the thing to focus on is your training, your practice, doing the best you can within your ability. If you're nailing those routines in practice, they're yours. You know you can do them. So you don't blink, you don't falter, you push the nerves aside. It's a big stage, yeah, but it's also just a meet, you know?"

God. Of course. Jake *could* do those routines. He could do them in his sleep. He could do them flawlessly. The only difference between practice and the Olympics was the audience, which didn't play a role in his performance. This wasn't really any different than a national meet that was only filmed on somebody's mom's phone. "You're totally right. It's just a meet." The rest was nerves.

"And you don't worry about what the Chinese or the Russians or… who the heck is good at gymnastics? The Brits, the Japanese, whoever. Don't worry about what they're doing. You can't control what they're doing. But you can control yourself, and if you're good, that medal's yours. You nail your routine in the meet, it's yours."

Jake nodded. "I never really thought about it that way. I mean, I completely understand what you're saying. But my coach is always, 'you need to do this, Jake, you need to do that.' Hosuke from Japan does this triple layout dismount from the high bar, so I have to do it higher, more perfect. Boskovic from Russia does this pommel horse routine that he once scored a sixteen with, so I have to make mine more difficult."

"Do you love gymnastics?"

"Huh?" What the hell kind of question was that?

"If you know who I am, you know what happened. And my life, it's all swimming. I love swimming. I love the feel of the water on my skin. I love the thrill of racing. I'd spend most of my life in a pool if I could. I got back into swimming after rehab because it made me feel sane again. Anyone at this level has to love their sport. Do you love gymnastics?"

"Of course," Jake said. "I see your face, but I do love it. I love tumbling. I love that thrill of flying over the high bar. Of sticking a landing. And I… I like the burn when I push my body as far as it goes."

"Get that burn back. That's the ticket to winning. Forget about everything else."

"You're one hundred percent right." The burn. Jake had to find the burn again.

"And if you lose, you lose. What happens? The TV network talks about how disappointing it is, and it is disappointing to lose, but whatever, you'll be back in the gym in two weeks doing what you love again, and that's all that's important. I mean, really, fuck everything else. Fuck the gold medal, fuck the Wheaties box, just get out there and do the goddamn best you can do. If anyone thinks it's not good enough, fuck 'em."

Jake laughed. "So that's how you became the second most decorated swimmer of all time? 'Fuck 'em.'"

"Pretty much."

"I'll keep that in mind. It doesn't make for a good postevent sound bite, though."

Isaac held up his hands in a "so what?" gesture. "I don't swim to get good press."

Jake and Isaac watched the pomp on TV for a minute before Jake said, "Does it just go on like this for a while?"

"The host cities are always trying to outdo each other. Hundreds of years of Spanish history distilled into one flourish of artistic expression."

"You know, I think I can sleep now."

Isaac laughed.

Jake went back to his room, turning over everything Isaac had said. This was, in all likelihood, the last Olympics Jake would ever compete in, so why not push himself to the limit? Why not risk broken bones and torn ligaments and concussions? Why not go all out to win that gold medal that by rights should have been his long ago, if he could only get out of his own way?

It was just a meet, yes. It was also the most important meet of Jake's life. But the latter didn't matter. He could get scores of sixteen or higher on every apparatus. He could do some of the most difficult skills in the world, with the highest difficulty levels. He was the reigning American champion. He had gymnastics in his blood—almost literally. This meet was his to lose.

So he wouldn't lose. He would win this time.

So decided, he crawled into bed. He put in earplugs so he wouldn't have to listen to Corey snoring. And he slept like a baby.

TOPHER SIPPED from his third glass of sangria as he and Natalie watched the Opening Ceremony while sitting at the bar in their hotel.

"So we're totally BFFs now, by the way," Natalie said, tossing her long, honey-colored hair over her shoulders. "I had more fun today than on any other broadcast I've ever done."

Topher laughed and fished a cube of apple out of his glass. "I'm glad. I learned a lot." Which he had, although he'd had a lot of fun with Natalie too. They'd probably giggled more during the broadcast than the network would have approved of, although after they'd wrapped, Joanna had told him she'd liked their rapport. Topher wasn't exactly angling for a gig commentating over gymnastics, but he wouldn't turn down the opportunity to work with Natalie again.

Natalie laughed. "You learned which male gymnasts you thought were hot."

"So did you. Let's see how similar our tastes are. I mean that one guy from Russia. Er, what was his name? Boskovic?"

"Yeah. He *is* hot, I'll give you that. But in kind of a Soviet way. I look at him and worry that he and his KGB comrades are coming to kill me."

Topher affected a bad Russian accent. "In Soviet Russia, gymnastics does you."

"Exactly. And then there's the tall blond one from the Netherlands. Ah, Leland?"

"Yes. He was very pretty. It's a shame the Dutch uniforms are so hideous. He doesn't look great in orange."

"The ones they had at the World Championships were pale blue. Maybe they'll break those back out for the team competition. They're a little easier on the eyes."

Topher nodded. "And, of course, we have to talk about Jake Mirakovitch."

"Oh, yeah. I had a crush on him for a long time after we met. He's a total sweetheart on top of being a super hottie. I don't know how anyone gets anything done when he's around."

Topher laughed and thought back to their interview. He hadn't asked any personal questions, but he did wonder a bit about what Jake's deal was. "Do you know his story? Is he single, married, whatever?"

Natalie shook her head. "Definitely not married. Brad's the only guy on the team who is. He'll also tell you *all* about it, if you ask."

"A smug married, eh?"

Natalie nodded and took a sip of her sangria. "The smuggest. But Jake, I don't know. He's gotta be single. Maybe even celibate. His parents keep him on a pretty short leash."

That was bad news. "Just during the season or—?"

Natalie leveled her gaze at Topher. "Jake doesn't get time off. Jake is a part of the Mirakovitch gymnastics machine. He trains year-round. He is occasionally blessed with a few days off, but those are rare."

"I used to take the summers off."

"I trained less during the school year. But Jake... I mean, that guy was bred specifically to be a champion gymnast. Literally. He was never given another choice."

"God."

"So I can't imagine his parents allowed him to date much. There have been rumors here or there, but I don't think he's with anyone now."

Topher was intrigued by these rumors, but not drunk enough to ask about them without shame. "He's so delicious-looking. I'd kill to interview him again. Preferably with no one else watching while we're both naked."

Natalie laughed. "Bless you, Topher Caldwell. I've had that same thought myself."

"I hope this doesn't mean we're going to be fighting each other for men to bang during this Olympic broadcast."

"You really intend to hook up with someone?"

Topher shrugged. "I'm not ruling it out."

"I have a boyfriend back home." Natalie looked off into the distance and smiled, so Topher inferred it was a real deal. "He's great," she said. "I bet he's ring shopping as we speak."

"That's sweet. How long have you been together?"

"It will be three years next month. I met him right after I retired, actually. He... he made my retirement bearable. And he's *not* a gymnast, which is so goddamn refreshing."

"Is he an athlete?" Topher had always theorized it would be hard to relate to someone who hadn't understood his former slavish devotion to training regimens and his continuing diet and gym habits. Topher still cooked for himself most of the time because he knew how to make a meal do its job to fuel his body. He didn't skate every day anymore, but he liked to keep himself healthy.

Natalie grinned. "My boyfriend is a baseball player. Left fielder for the Texas Rangers."

"Get out. Really?"

"No joke."

"Do you live in Texas, then?"

"Yeah. We have a house outside Dallas."

"That's wild. Not that I know anything about baseball. I mean, I know the Rangers are a team. And that the game is played with balls and bats. And that's it, really. Actually, if you'd said Rangers, I would have assumed you were talking hockey."

"Yeah. Well, no. Todd plays baseball in Texas. He made the All-Star Team this year, so he's pretty good."

"Okay." Topher smiled. "Anyway, I *am* single. Haven't even dated much recently. Broke up with the love of my life last year. Or I don't know, 'love of my life' is probably overstating the case. Either way, we ended things in highly dramatic fashion. He took my favorite Prada shoes with him when he left."

"That bastard."

"I *know*. I should sue. But it was for the best. We were both too dramatic. It was like an opera in our apartment every night, with all the histrionics. I miss him sometimes, but I know how poorly suited we were for each other. He was my indulgent post-skating fling, I suppose. He *did* play hockey. Not professionally, though. He was in this hipster hockey league in Brooklyn."

Natalie laughed. "New York is so strange."

"Don't I know it, darling. But, I don't know. I guess a part of me figured I'd be in Madrid, miles from home, and there'd be all these horny athletes around. I'm sure a few of them are on the gay dating apps. I've got three on my phone."

"You do not."

Topher held up his phone. Natalie took it from him and opened one of the apps. "Holy shit. There's a guy very close by." She looked around the bar.

Topher took his phone back. "Oh, that's Mitch. He's a PA. He's staying on the fourth floor. The GPS probably isn't good enough to tell when people aren't on the same floor of a building."

Natalie shot Topher a cocky smile. "How do you know he's staying on the fourth floor? Did you hook up with him already?"

Topher rolled his eyes and fiddled with the app. "No. We flirted a little over the breakfast buffet, though. He's not really my type, and I could tell he kind of thinks I'm ridiculous. Not a lot of other nibbles tonight, though. Well, one, but his profile info is in Spanish, so I assume he's local. And my Spanish is not good enough to make that work. But look at his abs." Topher showed Natalie the photo.

"The horny athletes are all in the Olympic Village, which we are banned from."

"Yeah, but this hotel is but a few hundred feet away. I bet I could coax a fencer or a diver back to my hotel room if I was enterprising enough."

"Or Jake Mirakovitch."

"God, wouldn't that be a coup? I would definitely love to lure him back to my boudoir." It wasn't a lie. Topher had been thinking about Jake since they'd met, although he'd tried not to. Jake was so remote, so untouchable, a gymnastics god with a grueling schedule who might as well have been wearing a T-shirt that said *Straight and unavailable*. Or, even if Jake were available, what would he want with a washed-up figure skater who had proved more than once that he'd never be the sort of athlete who'd end up in history books?

Ugh, Topher needed to get himself out of the shame spiral. He was here to do a job that had nothing to do with his ability to land a quad toe loop. He was stretching out a different skill set. And he wasn't even really here to flirt with men, but they did make for a pleasant distraction.

Back on Earth, Natalie grinned at Topher. "Maybe I'll make some discreet inquiries."

"Oh, please." Topher waved his hand dismissively.

"Or I won't. Maybe your one true love plays an entirely different sport. Maybe he's a swimmer. Or a boxer!"

Topher laughed. "Sure. And maybe I'll pull up one of these apps next time we're near the Olympic Village."

"You're joking, but I know you're thinking about doing just that."

She was right, but Topher only shrugged.

Chapter Six

HENLEY: HERE we are at the beautiful Palacio Vistalegre for the men's gymnastics team qualifying event. This arena in the Carabanchel District just outside Madrid was once the site of a famous bullring. But there will be no bullfighting here tonight. A different, more graceful sport has taken over. Tell me, Eileen, what do you think of the American men's team?

SCHIFFLER: They look strong, Al. They were in good shape during practice yesterday. I'd say this men's team looks great, but we all know how hard it has been for them to maintain any kind of momentum going into the team final.

HENLEY: We do. Four years ago, this men's team was in first place after qualifiers, and then failed to medal in the team final or the All-Around. It was shocking.

O'CONNOR: Some of that men's team is back here. Jake Mirakovitch, Corey O'Bannon, and Brad Porter are all returning for their second Olympics. Jake and Corey look good to make the all-around. But they're competing with their own teammates for all-around spots. Those other teammates include Jordan Weiss, who is Team USA's best hope for a medal on pommel horse. They you've got Hayden Croft, who is a shoo-in for the vault final. And newcomer Paul Petrakis. He has very little international experience, so it remains to be seen what he can do on the world stage.

SCHIFFLER: Jake and Corey are definitely going after that all-around title. What about Hayden? He's also planning to perform on all six apparatuses tonight.

O'CONNOR: He's got a shot. And Jake told me he's trying for as many event finals as his body will allow. Pommel horse is a long shot for him; he's got a solid chance at high bar, parallel bars, and vault. Probably also floor. Corey is their star on rings. His upper body strength is unbelievable.

HENLEY: In other words, this team has the stuff.

O'CONNOR: It really does, Al. This is probably the best men's team the US has put up in two decades. By rights, they should be on the podium after the team final on Monday. What remains to be seen is if nerves or injuries will take them out, as they did four years ago and at every World Championship since. Mirakovitch is the gymnast to watch, but as we all know, he has a habit of coming out of the gates strong and then fading as competition goes on.

HENLEY: He spoke to TBC's own Christopher Caldwell a few days ago. Let's take a look at their interview....

SIX APPARATUSES. Six routines. Just another meet.

Jake stood beside his teammates as they looked up at the vault, their first rotation. Jake had been hoping they'd draw pommel horse first so they could get it over with. Instead, the six of them stood in a row wearing matching uniforms, looking up at the vault table. Jake imagined his five teammates were trying to figure out if that table held the secrets of the universe.

Maybe it did.

They'd had a good warm-up prior to changing into their official uniforms. Jake felt good, generally. He took a deep breath as the announcer droned on in Spanish, French, and English, announcing which team would compete on each apparatus first. Alexei walked over and slapped Jake on the back, telling him to do well in Russian.

Jake, Hayden, Corey, and Paul were up on vault. Only Jake and Hayden were doing a second vault to make the event final. When they got the go-ahead to practice, Jake watched Hayden go first. He hopped wildly on the landing but looked good anyway, no problems in the air.

Paul went next. He wasn't as strong, not as experienced, but he didn't look nervous; he probably didn't have enough experience to understand that he should be nervous yet.

Jake went third. He thought about Isaac's advice to put everything he had into this. It was just a meet, but there was no reason not to put everything he had into this. Pretending the judges were paying attention—and maybe they were—he took off down the run-up area, did a round-off onto the springboard, and launched himself off the table. He felt good in the air and he stuck the landing. So he ran back to the other end of the run-up area and did his other vault. He stuck that one too.

He could fucking do this.

And a half hour later, he did. Small hop on the first landing. He'd felt that one ripple through his legs and had stepped to the side to steady himself. Still in-bounds, though, so it was just a small deduction. The vault had a total potential score of 17.000; the judges scored it 16.655. He'd take it. He stuck the landing hard on the second vault, similar max score, and the judges liked that better: 16.800.

Alexei was apoplectic with joy, which bolstered Jake some.

Hayden's vault scores were slightly higher, even. Paul's and Corey's scores were high enough to put the Americans in first place after the first rotation. Now if they could just keep it up.

Pommel horse came second, and Jake knew they'd lose a little ground here. He'd been doing his pommel horse routine well in practice, but it was his weakest event, no question. Still, when his turn came, he got up there. He pushed all thought out of his head and just did the routine, counting out rotations as he moved across the horse. He wasn't perfect, but he got through it with no major errors and a decent score. Jordan killed it, putting in a nearly flawless routine and smiling when he dismounted. He'd earned a 17.100 for his trouble.

Americans were second going into the third rotation.

Rings were up next. Jake was glad to do rings early in the meet, because doing them last was sheer torture.

By the sixth rotation, each gymnast was tired. His muscles wept as he held those positions. He'd ended up with rings last in a fair number of meets and had come off them feeling like his arms were spaghetti each time. But third was okay. Jake still felt good.

He counted carefully for each held pose as he moved through his routine. The cross was the worst, and his arms trembled through it, but he held the position and later stuck the dismount. His score reflected the fact that the judges probably saw him struggle through the routine.

But Corey killed it. Corey held each position with the same casual ease he might use to lean against a wall. He made it look painless and easy, which was how he was one of the best in the world. He stuck the dismount and got a huge score. Team USA was back in first.

"The rest is cake," Alexei said as they walked to the high bar.

Jake assumed Alexei meant "easy as pie," so he nodded. "Should I do the modified Tkatchev?"

Alexei hesitated, which meant he was likely weighing Jake's options: safely qualify or risk falling to get the higher score. He said, "I think no. Simpler release move. Wait for scores to count before pulling it out."

Safely qualify, then. Jake nodded, seeing the wisdom in that. "All right."

"You look good this meet, Jake. Your father would be proud."

Jake bristled. He didn't know if it was Alexei's less than perfect English or if he meant that Valentin was proudly watching his son triumph over each apparatus, or if Valentin was off somewhere worrying about the women's team, not watching his son compete. Jake glanced at the stands, to the section the American delegation had reserved to watch each other. He saw a few of the women's team members. No Valentin.

So, yeah, maybe Valentin would be proud, if he was watching, which he wasn't. Chelsea was the actual world champion. It was more important to watch her practice than to watch Jake actually compete, apparently.

"Sure," Jake said, biting back a tired sigh.

"You got this. Make me proud too."

"GOOD LORD, his *arms*," Topher blurted out. On live television.

He sat in the commentary booth with Natalie and retired gymnast Sam Norton, who had finally arrived in Madrid. Topher had fallen into this particular gig at the behest of the network, who thought his approach to explaining things was useful. Topher wasn't sad about watching more gymnastics, though they made for a motley broadcasting crew. They were doing commentary over the raw feed that would be broadcast on the app, not during the primetime broadcast, but Topher was okay with the stakes being low for now.

This was it, wasn't it? This was his big audition. He needed to prove that he could talk about sports without sounding silly or without being, well, too much himself. He understood implicitly that a lot of people couldn't see past his exterior and didn't understand that under everything, he was an athlete, and he understood the training, the discipline, the strength, and the inevitable heartbreak of being an elite athlete in the way few others did. He wanted to express himself, after so many years of holding himself back for the sake of others' sensibilities, but he wanted to be taken seriously too, and he sometimes found that tightrope difficult to walk. Could he do both? He was about to find out.

This was an actual scored competition, and Natalie was keeping an eye on the app to see how many people were logged in to watch; the numbers were triple what they had been during podium training. So while this wasn't exactly primetime, it was still a big enough audience that it mattered. And it was still commentating over an actual sport instead of just doing some fluffy piece about the Prado or whatever. He couldn't fuck this up.

Topher focused his attention on the monitor, which showed the feed from the camera that was following Team USA around. And there Jake was on the still rings, his arms bulging as he held his positions.

"It takes a tremendous amount of upper body strength," Sam said. "The rings, I mean. Jake is holding an iron cross, which, let me tell you, is one of the hardest positions. It really takes every ounce of strength you have to hold the position, and you have to do it for at least two seconds."

Jake swung around a couple of times and then moved into a position in which he propped himself up, his arms straight, his body bent into an L.

Jake was... sexy, showing off his strength in this way. Topher began to fantasize about all the other things those arms could do.

Oy, this crush was inconvenient.

A part of Topher knew he had to see Jake again. When Jake dismounted and stuck the landing, Topher was even more sure of it. Jake probably was straight and married to gymnastics and had no interest in an unabashedly femme former figure skater, but Topher almost didn't care. He just wanted to be near the man again. To soak up all that strength and talent and skill. To ask him more questions. To be in his presence.

The American team moved to the high bar shortly thereafter. "The high bar is one of Jake's best events," Natalie said. "We watched him in podium training, and he looked amazing."

"He's got some high-flying release moves," Sam said. "I'm expecting him not to do the real showstoppers until the all-around or the event final, because he'll want to keep it safe here. He's been doing a trick in practice that looks amazing when he catches it right, but I don't think we'll see it until later. This is just a qualifier. The points go away when everyone moves into the finals."

"Doesn't he want to qualify for the event finals?" Topher asked. "Isn't the quals where you'd pull out the triple Lutz triple toe or whatever to get the high score?"

"Yes and no," said Sam. "Jake's about fifty-fifty on completing the move in competition. If he does it well, it'll get him a big score, but if he misses it, it'll be a big deduction. Better to qualify with a solid routine and a pretty good score and get into the event final than to blow it now."

"I get that," Topher said, while wondering if doing a routine with a lower difficulty score would hurt Jake's chances to make the event final. Although the gymnastics scoring was similar to figure skating scoring in some ways, Topher still did not understand the intricacies of it. Then again, when he'd mentioned the changes from the ten-point scale, he'd started an argument between Natalie and Sam, so he'd opted to leave that be.

What he did understand is that there were two schools of thought on scoring: people either liked the simplicity of the ten or liked the nuance of the new system. Under the old system, two gymnasts could get the same score, regardless of difficulty level, if they completed the requisite skills with no major errors. Under the new system, more difficult routines were rewarded with higher scores, to oversimplify. It incentivized gymnasts pushing the sport forward. Same with the system in skating. Whoever landed the most quad jumps generally got the highest score these days, because those difficult jumps raked in the points, so the athletes pushed themselves to do increasingly more difficult skills. Under the old skating system, the athletes received up to six points based mostly on judge subjectivity. The new system was more objective. It was better, as far as Topher was concerned. Sam seemed to disagree.

Sam called most of the high bar routines. He seemed to be the expert, and he did actually have a lot of intelligent things to say. When Topher remarked that a lot of these gymnasts were on their second and even third Olympics, Sam pointed out that because male gymnasts tended to peak much later in life than female gymnasts did, men's careers were a little more sustainable, although they'd be hard-pressed to find a gymnast over thirty on any team. There were a handful of outliers—Brad Porter was thirty-one; one of the Russian gymnasts was an elderly thirty-five—but Jake, for example, was twenty-six and probably anticipating the twilight of his career.

Elite sports were so goddamn tragic that way.

Because Sam pontificated most of the time, Topher was able to sit back and watch Jake swing around the bar. He looked good, although Topher didn't really know what he was looking at.

"These release moves look plenty impressive," Topher said.

"Oh. Yeah, they are a crowd-pleaser," said Sam. "The thing with high bar is that the release moves are the most eye-catching, right? They look impressive to the audience. But everything else is more important. An impressive release move will raise your difficulty level, but you have to hold the handstands for the required amount of time too, and you have to do a certain number of skills with different holds on the bar. So sometimes impressive-looking routines get low scores because the gymnast failed to adequately complete the other elements."

Topher nodded and then murmured, "Interesting," when he realized no one watching the broadcast could see him. "I mean, I understand all about those otherwise invisible deductions. It's like in figure skating if you land a jump but don't complete all of the rotations. There's no double-and-a-half axel, you know?"

"Yup. Luckily, that's not an issue Jake will have," said Natalie. "He did all of his skills well. That tiny step on the dismount will be a mandatory deduction, but that was otherwise pretty flawless. Exactly what he needed to do to help his team and qualify for the event final. We'll see his crazier stuff then. The event finals are always 'go big or go home.'"

"Cool, okay," Topher said.

Topher spent the time during the parallel bar rotation occasionally saying, "Huh," or "Interesting" to things Sam said while concocting schemes to talk to Jake again. Maybe, if Jake finished this qualifier well, the network would let Topher interview him again. Or maybe there'd be some kind of after-party Topher could get himself invited to.

The Americans were in second place going into the last rotation. Natalie and Sam did most of the commentary, because the floor exercise looked like flips and cartwheels to Topher's untrained eye. Natalie seemed particularly impressed with Brad's routine when he finished.

"Okay," Topher intervened, "explain to me how that was different from what Corey O'Bannon did. Because you keep saying Brad Porter will get this huge score, but as a layperson, I can't tell why his routine was better than Corey's."

"Let's look at the replay," Sam said with a grin, as if he'd been hoping Topher would ask exactly this question. "First, Brad's base difficulty score is higher, because he does more complicated tumbling passes. So, like, here he does a round-off into this salto, and he gets his body around twice before landing, then he immediately flips again. His second pass has a specific combination called the Porter because Brad invented it. The other thing worth noting is that Brad is powerful off the floor. The height he gets is just incredible. He can jump higher in the air than anyone in this competition. His only real competition for a medal in the floor final is Daisuke from Japan, who does these incredible twists in the air. Daisuke is the reigning world champion, with good reason."

"So, basically, Brad does a harder routine better."

"That's it, essentially. Jake's pretty good on floor too. He's so incredibly strong. He gets height like Brad, but his tumbling passes aren't quite as difficult. It's the difference between an all-around gymnast and a specialist. Jake does well on all six events, but Brad really shines here."

When they went off the air a half hour later, with the Americans having secured their spot in first place going into the team final and a bunch of opportunities for medals in event finals, Sam said, "Hey, it was fun doing this with you."

"Thanks, yeah," said Topher. "Sorry if I sound silly, but a lot of this is new for me."

"No, it's good," said Natalie. "You asking these questions means we can explain things for the audience. Our audience is probably a good mix of hardcore gymnastics fans or Olympics fans watching the live feed from their desks in the middle of the workday, you know? Some of those people probably only watch gymnastics during the Olympics, so it's good to remind us to explain things."

"Okay. Cool. Just wanted to make sure you didn't think I was a *complete* idiot."

"Nope," said Sam.

"Because I can tell you a lot about figure skating. If you need to know the difference between a Lutz, a toe loop, and a Salchow, I got you."

"Good to know." Sam laughed. "Listen, there's a gymnastics party at the America House tonight. I got a text from Corey saying most of the men's team would be putting in an appearance, plus the coaches and staff and whoever else. I don't think the women's team is coming because they have to compete tomorrow. Still, it should be fun. Want to come?"

Bingo, Topher thought. "I'd love to."

Sam grinned. "Great."

Joanna walked over then and patted Topher's back. "That was great, guys. We got a great response on social media."

Topher took a deep breath, mostly out of relief. "Good. Did everything sound okay?"

"Yeah. I actually liked how you kept relating things back to figure skating. I think having you here could be pulling in part of that audience. Keep it up, okay?"

Topher wanted to ask her a million questions about whether this had helped his chances of getting a figure skating commentating gig or if she was impressed by how he spoke or if he'd always have to be audience surrogate or if this had really been good or not. He had other opportunities on his schedule, and he supposed the "audition" would really be the aggregate of everything he did in Madrid. He didn't want to seem too desperate or needy either. So he just grinned and said, "Yeah, let's do this."

Joanna smiled. "I was hoping you'd say something like that. I know you've got accounts on most of the major social media sites. I think one way we could really pull in younger viewers would be for our feature correspondents to engage with the fans online. Maybe even do something creative. Post photos, talk about what you're doing, that kind of thing."

Topher was a sporadic social media user; he mostly had accounts because his agent insisted. But if it would help him get the job he wanted, he'd do almost anything. "Yeah, I can do that."

"Great. You're done for the day. Check in with me first thing in the morning at the broadcast center, okay? I have a few schedule changes for you."

Feeling a little dazed, Topher said, "Sure, no problem."

CHAPTER SEVEN

JAKE ATTENDED the party at America House under duress. He was tired and wanted to sleep, but Corey
had insisted that their finishing the qualifying event in
first place was reason to celebrate.

"I'll celebrate when I've got medals hanging
around my neck."

"Medals plural?" Corey asked as they walked
across the Olympic Village.

"Yup. I'm winning them all, Corey. Then I'll
relax."

"You're a crazy person."

Jake shrugged.

They arrived at the door of America House, a
one-story structure that housed a bar that was the main
place for the American athletes and their adoring public
to meet and mingle, since only athletes were allowed
in the dorms. The interior looked like every sports bar
Jake had ever been to stateside: lots of wood and brass,

and vintage sports memorabilia covering every available surface.

Corey said, "We did well today, Jake. Stop beating yourself up for bad things that haven't happened yet."

"I'm not." No, he was beating himself up for getting his hopes up that his father gave a shit about how well he performed. Probably dear old Dad was currently with Chelsea in the practice gym, making her do drills and skills. Jake didn't blame Chelsea for that, but he wished Valentin would take some damn time to see him in competition. Jake and Chelsea were both Mirakovitch children. Just because Chelsea had those World Championship titles....

He took a deep breath and pushed through the door.

A party raged on inside; a huge mob of people crowded around the bar. Jake and Corey pushed through the people toward the counter, where Corey ordered them drinks—Jake didn't hear what, but it turned out to be sparkling water—and asked the bartender what all this was for. "Not gymnastics," Corey concluded.

"Four American medals won today," the bartender said, as if explaining was part of his job. "Two golds in swimming, a silver in women's archery, and a bronze in cycling. So everyone's here celebrating."

Corey sipped his drink. "Lucky bastards. Some of them are done competing already."

"Aw," said Jake. "Imagine flying halfway across the world to compete for a couple of hours on the first day of the Olympics. That archer who won a silver medal is done. Full stop. Seems anticlimactic."

"Sure, but now she can just hang back and relax."

"I guess."

Corey slapped Jake's back. "You are constitutionally incapable of relaxing. Come on, let's mingle a little."

The women's gymnastics team was notably absent, since they were competing the next day, although one of the alternates sat forlornly with two people who must have been her parents, probably resigned to the fact that she'd never let go of the hope she'd get to compete until it became clear none of her teammates had suffered a Games-ending injury.

But most of the men's team and their coaches were there. Alexei gave him the "there better not be alcohol in that glass" glare from across the room. Jake shook his head.

Then his gaze settled on someone he hadn't expected to see: Topher Caldwell.

Seeing Topher was jarring, in a way. Most of the athletes gathered in the room—Jake included—wore warm-up suits or casual clothes. Jake was wearing an old pair of jeans and a band T-shirt, having happily changed out of his official clothes. And there was Topher, clad in tight purple pants that had a bit of an iridescent sheen to them and a black tuxedo shirt unbuttoned to his sternum. There seemed to be some kind of foofaraw at his wrists, feathers or faux fur; it was hard to tell from a distance. And despite how ridiculous that outfit would have seemed out of context, Topher managed to make it look sexy. *Really* sexy. That dip of exposed skin under his chin called to Jake. What would it feel like to run his finger along it? His tongue?

"Earth to Jake."

"What?"

Corey rolled his eyes. "There's a table over there with Jordan and Paul. Let's go sit down."

"Yeah, in a sec."

It was against every instinct Jake had. He was in Madrid for only one purpose: to win an Olympic medal. He planned to do everything in his power to achieve that. He didn't need distractions. But there was Topher chatting with Natalie Pasquarella—who wore a little silver cocktail dress—and Jake just *had* to speak with him.

Corey took off for the table with their teammates, and so Jake crossed the room and approached Topher. "Hi," he said.

Topher smiled broadly. "Hi. I was hoping to run into you. There was a ripple through the media that you all planned to celebrate a little for qualifying for the team final in first place."

"Yeah. A *little* celebrating. The only scandalous thing in my glass is the slice of lime."

Topher looked at the glass. "Oh. That's a shame. This is my second martini." He held up his own glass.

Natalie looked between them and said, "Hey, I gotta powder my nose. Be back in a few."

Topher nodded but didn't otherwise shift his attention away from Jake. "I was hoping, actually, to interview you again. The network wants me to do more on social media, so I've decided to make kind of an Olympics video diary. Maybe we could do a segment together? No more than a couple of minutes."

"Could we do it after the team final? That's Monday."

"Yeah, sure."

"I don't want to speculate about our performance until after we have a chance to prove ourselves. Or fail. Could go either way." Jake seesawed his hand.

"I think this is your time." Topher grinned.

"Yeah?" Jake was not at all certain, but he liked Topher's attitude.

"Yeah. So who all is at this party? Your family and friends here?"

"Well, most of my teammates seem to have settled into that corner over there." Jake hooked his thumb toward the table where Corey sat now. "The older guy with brown hair wearing the white windbreaker? That's my coach, Alexei. He won an Olympics all-around gold medal for Russia in the '90s."

"Okay."

"He's a good coach, but he's tough. From the Soviet system, you know?" Jake smiled and shrugged. "Anyway, my family is *not* here. They're all either in the gym or sleeping so they'll be ready for Chelsea to kill it tomorrow."

"Yeah? I've been reading up. She's the favorite for the all-around medal."

"And she deserves it. I'm not just saying that. She's super talented. Does things I've never seen other gymnasts do. And my father is a good coach for her. Loving, but tough. Always challenging her but never pushing too hard. You know?"

"Sure. I had a relationship like that with my skating coach. Also a Soviet, by the way. Magda Kagan. She moved to the States from Ukraine in the '70s. Her family was Jewish."

"Ah."

"She was on a trajectory to be a great Soviet skater before her family defected. Moving to the States took all their money, so she never really competed much after that, but she got into coaching and took me on when I was, gosh, eight? Remarkable woman. Great coach. She was like a mother to me, but she never let me get away with anything. No slacking. I did drills until I thought my feet would fall off. I got kicked in the head by another skater one time and had this huge gash in my forehead. It wasn't that deep, but head wounds can bleed, so I thought I was dying. She basically slapped a Band-Aid on it and told me to keep going." Topher chuckled softly. "I'm so grateful to her, because if she hadn't pushed me, I never would have gotten as far as I did. She was also one of the first people I ever came out to. I don't know why I'm telling you all this."

Jake appreciated Topher speaking, though. He liked the cadence of Topher's voice, felt drawn in by it. He looked Topher up and down. His creamy skin was a little flushed, probably from the martini, and his clothes hugged his body. From a distance, Topher looked willowy, but up close, his strength was more obvious. The round muscles of his arms and chest strained against his shirt, and Jake wanted to run his hands over them. There was a slim line of skin exposed at Topher's throat. Jake wanted to lick it.

What had they been talking about? Oh, right, Topher coming out. Jake cleared his throat and raised an eyebrow. "No offense, but I don't think you'd really fooled anyone."

Topher laughed. "I know, right? But you know how it is. Figure skating is one of the most homophobic sports there is."

Jake knew something about homophobia in sports that were generally considered "girly," but he balked and said, "Figure skating? Really?"

Topher held up a finger. "See, that's exactly it. Everyone assumes that if you don a frilly figure skating costume, you *must* be gay. So all the male figure skaters are always overcompensating and try to prove their masculinity. It's less true now, I think, but when I was skating competitively, the last thing you wanted to be was gay."

Jake slid onto the stool Natalie had vacated because he saw her strike up a conversation with someone near the restrooms, probably to give him and Topher a little more privacy. To what end, Jake didn't know, but he didn't mind her keeping her distance.

Topher also smelled amazing; his cologne had some kind of minty undertone. Jake started to lean close to try to smell him better but caught himself before he did anything inappropriate.

Topher didn't seem to notice. He said, "I used to tamp it down. Try to make myself 'normal.' Tried to make my voice deeper, tried not to move my hands too much, tried not to seem like I was anything but straight as an arrow. That shit is exhausting."

Jake met Topher's gaze and saw the sadness there, the struggle Topher had likely dealt with most of his life. Jake could relate. He didn't think he ever acted like anything but himself, but he still wasn't super eager for his sexuality to be public knowledge. He'd been in situations in which he'd consciously tried to deflect attention or otherwise not stand out in any way, and it *was* exhausting.

Topher smiled sheepishly. "When I retired and came out publicly, I kind of burst out of the closet." He shrugged and pulled at his feathery sleeves.

"Hey, it's all good. You should never have to tamp down who you are."

Topher smiled and nodded. Then his face went serious again. "You compete in a sport that used to be dominated by Soviet Bloc countries, so you must see this. It's changed, of course. A lot of judged sports have. The emphasis in gymnastics now, as I've seen over the last few days, is on strength and athleticism more than grace. Right? Your sister looks like a giant next to some of the Chinese gymnasts, even some of the Russians, who still prize being tiny and pretty over being strong. During podium training, I saw a gymnast fall doing a vault, and Natalie pointed out that she was too small and light to compress the springboard enough get the height she needed to complete the vault." He shook his head. "Sorry, I'm on a tangent. My point is just that the sports have changed as other countries have started to dominate, and I think the American model of praising athleticism over beauty in skating and gymnastics is good because it changes the whole culture of the sport."

Jake was having trouble following Topher now, probably because he was crazy distracted by Topher being all sexy and fragrant. He swallowed and met Topher's gaze, trying to seem casual. "Okay. But men's sports have always been about strength and athleticism."

Topher held up a finger again. "Au contraire, my dear. I think men's figure skating became that in the wake of accusations of it being a girly sport. So you have an Elvis Stojko, who wears leather on the ice and does a quad jump before anyone else. In some ways that's good, because it pushes the sport forward. But in other ways, that's bad, because it becomes the standard. And, look, I wanted to win, but my willowy ass was never going to be an Elvis Stojko. You know?"

Jake shook his head. "I'm not sure I follow. Like, I get the gist of what you're saying, and I understand it, but it's just so… dumb. Classifying sports as masculine or feminine, I mean."

"Sure, but didn't anyone in your school make fun of you for being a gymnast?"

"I was homeschooled." That was an oversimplified way of explaining the long series of tutors and private teachers Jake's parents had hired to shove some learning into Jake and Chelsea's heads between tumbling passes.

Topher rolled his eyes. "Of course you were. You spent hours every day in the gym, didn't you?"

"I've been doing gymnastics so long, I can't remember if it was my idea or my parents'."

Topher's eyebrows shot up, but then he relaxed his face. "That's something we can unpack later. But you have to admit, men's gymnastics *are* about strength and athleticism. You don't play music during floor exercise. You don't spray your hair with glitter. It's a wholly different sport from women's gymnastics, from what I can tell. And yet gymnastics is traditionally seen as kind of a girly sport."

"I suppose."

Topher leaned forward a little. "Do you mean to tell me there's no homophobia in gymnastics?"

"No, not at all. I've seen it. I've witnessed it." Jake had experienced some of the same overcompensating as Topher had described, although in gymnastics it tended to manifest itself in a lot of testosterone-shaded masculine grunting and yelling when the gymnasts failed or succeeded. And, well, it didn't hurt that a lot of male gymnasts looked like weightlifters.

"There you go."

Jake wrestled with whether he should come out to Topher. If it was worth mentioning. It wasn't really a secret; it had just never come up in an interview.

Instead he said, "My parents own a gym in Texas."

"Yeah, I know. Like I said, I've been reading up."

"Right." And apparently Jake was going to tell this story as a way to do the exact kind of deflecting Topher had just been talking about. Too late, he was talking again. "So you know, we accept gymnastics students at all levels. We had this kid who joined an after-school beginner class. Matt was his name. He was maybe nine? And I knew as soon as he walked onto a mat that he was gay. He pinged the radar, I guess. And he loved gymnastics. I worked with him a little when I was re-covering from an injury last year. He loved tumbling especially. His mother encouraged him, but his father, you could tell, wasn't totally sold. What made matters worse is that the older brother of one of the female gymnasts would stand around and make fun of him."

"That's awful," said Topher.

"Yeah. Apparently kids were teasing him at school too. He quit at the end of this school year. I'm still try-ing to talk him into coming back, but I think he feels too much shame. And I hate that. I never really had to deal with it, because look at who my parents are. I was either going to embrace or run away from gymnastics. Nadia Comaneci and Bart Connor have a son who is really into BMX biking, I heard."

"Yeah, I watched an interview with Nadia in which someone asked her if her son would do gymnastics, and she was like, 'God, no.'"

"Right. My parents had different opinions."

Topher took a sip of his martini. Jake was suddenly mesmerized by the bob of Topher's Adam's apple.

"What were we talking about?" asked Topher.

Jake laughed, hoping beyond hope that Topher was similarly distracted. "Uh, homophobia in our sports?"

"Right. I dunno. I feel like we understand each other."

"Yeah. Maybe more than you think."

TOPHER CAUGHT sight of Natalie chatting with one of the swimmers across the room. He appreciated her keeping her distance while he talked to Jake, although it was sort of moot since it wasn't like he and Jake would be hooking up.

Jake was nice to talk to, though. His voice had a friendly lightness to it. And he seemed genuinely interested in what Topher had to say. He was breathtakingly gorgeous, even in a faded T-shirt and jeans. What would it feel like to be wrapped up in those arms? Topher had to curl his fingers into his hand to keep from reaching out to touch him.

"So if all your friends are over in the corner, what made you come talk to me?" Topher asked.

"I don't know. I feel like.... So, I'm always awkward talking to media because I don't love doing it, but I think during our interview the other day, we gained some understanding for each other. It's rare for me to meet someone other than a gymnast who understands what my life is like. All the training. The long hours. The injuries. Did you ever have to do one of those interviews for a morning show where some reporter decided she could do your sport too?"

Topher nodded vigorously. "Oh, yeah. What's her face, the host of the TBC morning show? Before the last Olympics I competed in, she did a segment with me where she put on figure skates and said, 'Okay, teach me how to do a jump,' before we went on-air. She'd barely ever skated before."

"Yeah. I know who you're talking about. She came to my parents' gym and did a couple of cartwheels on the mat and declared herself a tumbling champion. I know she was joking, but there's this assumption sometimes that what we do is easy or worthy of mocking, and it gets tiresome. Because it is so fucking hard."

"It really is."

"My point is, what do you even say to that? Like, ha ha, yeah, that was a swell cartwheel. I tore my ACL while learning a particularly tricky tumbling pass, but sure, that's the same."

Topher smiled and wondered the real reason why Jake had come to talk to him. He liked the idea that they might become friends after all this was over. Well, what he *really* wanted was to push Jake against the nearest wall and have his way with him, but he knew better than to wish for such things. "Would you seriously be game for another interview? Not now. Whenever you're ready."

"Yeah, sure. I'm happy to talk about any of this on camera. After the competition is over. I don't want to jinx anything."

"No, I know. I understand that. You looked great today, though."

Jake sighed heavily. "Qualifiers are usually not our issue. It's not until the medals are on the line that we start to fuck up."

Topher let out a breath. "At the US Championships before my first Olympics, another skater crashed into me during the warm-up before the long program. I didn't think I was injured, but it turned out that he'd nicked me with his skate. I was so high on adrenaline and nerves that I skated the long program and came in first, but when I got back to the locker room, I saw I had this huge gash on my leg and had bled into my boot. I ended up needing stitches."

"Oh God."

"Once I got home and the adrenaline wore off, it hurt like a mother. But I thought it was an omen. Like, okay, you won a US Championship with this injury. You can do anything. And I held on to that through the short program at the Olympics. Actually, the profile TBC did of me included footage of the injury and a couple of gory pictures of blood oozing out of the stitches. It was super gross."

Jake scrunched up his face. "So gross. Nobody needs to see that."

Topher laughed. "Well, the stitches came out right before I got on a plane for the Olympics and the injury was basically healed, but I rubbed the scar for luck before the short program. And I was in great position going into the long program to win a medal. But I don't know…. Something about being the favorite was my undoing."

Jake frowned and nodded like he completely understood. "You choked."

"Yeah, I choked. Fell doing a jump I landed all the time. I got the yips."

"I know all about the yips," Jake said. "I tripped over my own fucking feet on the floor at the World Championships one year."

"You can train yourself into being an elite athlete, but competition is mental. When I was younger, it was one thing. Finishing out of the medals at my first Olympics? It sucked, but I figured I had another shot. Finishing out of the medals at my *second* Olympics, when I knew my retirement was creeping up on me? It was…."

"Heartbreaking." Jake closed his eyes. "I'm already preparing myself."

"No, don't do that." Without thinking about it, Topher reached over and touched Jake's shoulder. Jake leaned into the touch a little, so Topher left his hand there. "Listen, it *was* heartbreaking. That moment when I realized I'd never achieve my dream of winning a medal? I mean, I went back to my room and just sobbed. I thought my life was over. But the thing is, it wasn't." Topher dusted some invisible dust off Jake's shoulder and lowered his arm. "I mean, it sucks, and I miss skating competitively with an ache I'll probably never shake off, but life goes on. I've gotten to do a lot of fun things since retiring. I got to have a personal life that my training schedule never allowed for. Good things are ahead for you, I know it."

"I guess."

"Listen to me, Jake. My time is over. I'll never have the opportunity to try for a medal again. But *you* do. And I know that winning a medal is easier said than done, but I saw what you could do today, and it's within your reach."

Jake ducked and shook his head.

"I know that me telling you that you can do this is meaningless. I *know*, okay? I know a hundred people and all your coaches and your parents and half the known universe telling you that you can do it is meaningless. I wish I had the answer for how you can get out of your own head and win that medal, but I don't. I do know that you shouldn't count yourself out yet, though. You're amazing, Jake. I'm not just saying that. You did things today that defy laws of physics. Your team is well positioned to win the team final."

Jake pursed his lips. "Sure, the parts are all there...."

"You have to believe you can do it, though."

"Did I tell you I talked to Isaac Flood?"

"No."

Jake nodded. "Last night. I ran into him in a dorm lounge. His advice was basically to give it everything I have, to leave nothing on the table. So that's what I'll do in two days. I'll give this competition every last bit of strength I have. I won't pull my punches or second-guess myself. I'll go for it. That's all I can do. I think that even if we don't win, if I can leave Madrid with no regrets, that will be enough."

Topher nodded. Right. No regrets. Topher had a lot of them, especially regarding his last Olympics. He wondered if things would have been different if someone had said something that hit him in just the right way before he approached the long program. Well, he couldn't linger on it now, but he could try to help Jake. "Good. Do that. Leave everything you have on the ice. Er, mats."

Jake smiled. "I will."

Topher looked around the room. The conversation was getting heavy, and he wanted a segue out of it. A couple—Topher thought one or both of them were swimmers—was playing tongue hockey in one corner. The men's gymnastics team was in another, although a couple of them stood as if they were getting ready to leave. Topher said, "Besides your family, you have anyone else here? Friends? A girlfriend?" He figured he might as well throw the fishing line out.

"Oh, no. I don't date a lot, which is probably obvious. And pretty much all of my friends are gymnasts too."

Topher looked at Jake's pretty green eyes and his smooth skin and the way he filled out his clothes, and his hands itched to reach out and touch him, but he shoved them in his pockets—which probably looked silly in a pair of pants this tight—and put his focus back on the conversation. "That's been one of my favorite things about retirement. I have other interests beside figure skating. I finally get to talk about them to other people."

Jake laughed. "Yeah? Like what?"

"Cooking, for one thing. I've been playing around with some recipes. I might write a cookbook or something. I took a couple of classes because I wanted to be a better cook, but I really enjoy it. I also still eat really healthy. Lots of greens, lean proteins, moderate portions. But eating like an athlete doesn't have to be just sustenance, you know? You can cook a really good, healthy meal that tastes amazing." And one could cook for one's gentlemen callers as a prelude to sex, although Topher didn't dare say that aloud.

"That's awesome."

"Thanks. I even went on one of those competition shows on the Food Channel. They did a special celebrity episode, and I had to compete against a bunch of other athletes to cook the best three-course meal. I came in second." Topher shrugged. That had been another one of those suggestions from his agent to get some good press so TBC would notice him, but it had been a lot of fun too. "Turns out that female boxer who won two gold medals also knows how to cook a steak perfectly. Who knew?"

Jake laughed. He had a great laugh, bright and natural. Topher grinned in response. But he knew he couldn't keep Jake here forever, no matter how much they enjoyed talking or how much Topher wanted to see if he could get away with more flirting. With great reluctance, he said, "Looks like your friends are leaving."

"Oh. I should probably get some sleep."

"Yeah. I don't want to keep you." Topher met Jake's gaze again and thought maybe he saw something there, regret or sadness maybe, or else he was projecting. They stood only a few inches apart; it would be so easy to…. He coughed. "Uh, it was great talking to you. You still have my number, right?"

"I do, yeah. I'll text you, I promise. I've just been busy."

"Yeah, I get it. Competition and all. Qualifying for four event finals. No sweat, really."

Jake grinned and winked at Topher before he walked across the room to his friends. Topher was sorry to see him go. He figured it was probably time to call it a night rather than try to interpret that wink. He wasn't feeling any of the alcohol he'd consumed anymore, but he did have to piss like a racehorse, so he walked in the direction of the men's room, thanking Natalie on the way.

America House had American-style restrooms—stalls instead of separate enclosures, urinals instead of a trough—which was kind of charming, so Topher closed himself in one of the stalls. He heard another man come in and use the urinal. As the guy washed his hands, Topher emerged and was surprised to see Jake standing there at the sink.

"Hello, again," Topher said as he washed his hands.

He looked up and met Jake's gaze in the mirror. They stared at each other for a long moment. There was some kind of kinetic energy in the room, swirling around them, perhaps pushing them together, and Topher didn't think it was all in his head.

Jake leaned back and flipped the lock on the main restroom door. Topher was alarmed for a moment until he recognized the look in Jake's eyes.

Lust.

Of all things.

Topher swallowed.

"I lied before, a little. I keep wrestling with myself about saying anything. But I'll just put this out there. I'm crazy attracted to you. More so the more we spend time together."

That was a shock to Topher's system. His heart pounded. He didn't even know how to respond. He would, of course, take Jake in a heartbeat, but for Jake to actually say it?

After opening and closing his mouth like a fish a few times, Topher managed to say, "Yeah? I... well. You are smoking hot. You must know that."

Jake smiled ruefully. "I don't have time for anything right now. I have medals to win and I don't want the distraction. But honestly? I've been thinking about you since the interview."

"Same."

Jake walked closer to Topher, closing the space between them. "Before we... I kind of just want to... I mean, tell me to stop if you—"

"Good Lord, don't you dare stop."

Their lips collided.

Jake's hands framed Topher's face as he deepened the kiss. Topher snaked his tongue into Jake's mouth. He tasted clean, and Topher savored that, enjoyed it. He loved the way his lips fit with Jake's. This was a crazy dream come true.

But he pulled back and said, "I'm not your first—"

"I'm super gay, Topher. You're not my first anything. Well, I've never made out with a figure skater before, so I guess there is that."

"Oh, okay." Topher's head spun. So he did the only thing he could think to do, which was kiss Jake again.

Oh, yeah. He could just imagine how this would progress. Maybe Jake would hoist Topher up on that counter and have his way with him. Topher could already feel his bare skin against the cool marble of the counter. He slid his hands up Jake's T-shirt, over his skin, and Lord, he had *muscles* there. Muscles on muscles. He had—

Someone rattled the door.

Jake pulled away. "Shit. I really do have to go. My coach got us time at the practice gym first thing in the morning, and I gotta sleep or I'll be useless. But, um, hold that thought?"

"I… yeah." Topher stared at Jake, feeling dazed.

Jake smiled. "I'm glad I did that. I wasn't going to, not tonight anyway, but I'm glad I did."

"Me too. Good luck at practice."

"Thanks. Good luck with… whatever you're doing tomorrow."

Topher laughed. "Yeah. Thanks."

Jake nodded and undid the lock on the door. Before he could open it, Topher said, "Sweet dreams, darling."

Jake winked. "They will be." Then he walked out, making a big show of explaining to whoever was out there that he'd accidentally hit the lock on the way in. Topher retreated to one of the stalls, hoping to get his heart to stop pounding before he rejoined the public.

Chapter Eight

Primetime Broadcast
Transcript: Men's Gymnastics Team Final

HENLEY: The Americans look good after the first two rotations. Don't you agree?

SCHIFFLER: They look great, Al. They vaulted with very few errors. This particular vault from Hayden Croft was nearly perfect. Let's look at it again.

O'CONNOR: He gets a ton of height on it. He flies off the vault table.

SCHIFFLER: Jake Mirakovitch had a good rotation too. This vault was also great. Just a little wobble on the landing, but it still earned him a high score.

HENLEY: Jake made a bunch of event finals, didn't he?

O'CONNOR: Yeah. High bar, P-bars, vault, and floor. Which is not really surprising. Pommel horse and rings are his weaker events.

HENLEY: But he has the potential to leave this Olympics with six gold medals.

O'CONNOR: That's true. The odds are against him, though. I mean, we've been covering gymnastics for years together, so you know the most likely thing to happen is that he'll make a mistake somewhere. He doesn't often hold up to scrutiny in international competition.

SCHIFFLER: Still, he's shown no sign of nerves here today. This was a great parallel bars routine for him.

O'CONNOR: Yes. He gets great height above the bars, even manages to catch himself gracefully. And this dismount—it's one of the harder ones in the competition, but he manages to get his body over the bars, he does that perfect layout in the air, and then he just nails it. Perfectly stuck landing.

HENLEY: It's worth noting that the Chinese basically took themselves out here. Here's Chieng on the bars. He looked so great in the qualifiers, and this routine could have easily earned him a high score.

O'CONNOR: Oh, yeah. He's the reigning world champion. His work on the P-bars is, well, unparalleled, if you'll excuse the pun. This should have rocketed the Chinese to the top of the leader board, but then this happened.

SCHIFFLER: Gymnastics 101. You gotta stick the landing.

O'CONNOR: This fall is a mandatory deduction. And that's a hard thing to recover from.

HENLEY: So let's take a look at the leader board. It's currently the Americans in first place, Japan in second, South Korea in third.

O'CONNOR: This South Korean team is weak on some of the apparatuses, so I think it's likely that

Russia or the Netherlands will overtake them. But I have to say, if the Americans keep performing the way we all know they can, they may be the team to beat.

HENLEY: But still, they have to keep it up. And it could all unravel here. Third rotation is pommel horse. Their nemesis.

O'CONNOR: Yeah, this is going to be a tough one....

Day 3

JULIA MOSS was a photogenic skier hired by TBC to run around Madrid reporting on the Summer Olympics from a Winter Olympian's perspective. Like Topher, she was angling to get a commentator job, and with her bubbly personality and pair of gold medals, she seemed like a shoo-in. Topher had been paired with her on Monday with the goal of compiling a report from the stands. The network wanted more of a "casual spectator" point of view in their coverage to help new viewers relate to the sports. There were four events on the agenda: fencing, synchronized diving, gymnastics, and swimming, in that order.

Fencing had been more fun than Topher had anticipated. For one thing, Julia had coincidentally been a fencer in college and actually knew a little about it, so she was able to explain what the moves were. Otherwise it kind of looked like the two fencers were just poking at each other with long sticks. But as Julia explained the equipment and why the helmets lit up red or green, Topher got really into it. It helped that one of the competitors was a twenty-two-year-old kid from the Bronx with one of those super-inspiring stories—he grew up in poverty, discovered fencing at an after-school program, and had a natural aptitude for it. Topher delighted in cheering for him. Well, and also yelling at the refs when they made a bad call was a great deal of fun.

"I've never even watched fencing before," Topher told Julia as they took a bus to the next venue. "That was amazing."

Julia grinned. "It's only going to get better. Time for men's diving."

Topher supposed his role here was to pontificate on the merits of judged sports, although diving seemed a lot more straightforward than gymnastics or even figure skating, for that matter. Each diver completed the dive or he didn't—and it was easy to see when something went wrong. Then the score was multiplied by the difficulty level. Or something like that. It wasn't Topher's job to know the rules.

Julia had a giant smartphone that she used to record their reactions to events. So, while on camera, she said, "Can we talk about all this male flesh on display?"

"Lord Almighty," said Topher, playing along. He used a hand to fan himself. "I'm having heart palpitations."

He wasn't exaggerating that much. The divers were all but naked. The American pair, Timothy Swan and Jason Evans, were both really hot, albeit on the small side. Topher generally liked his men a little bulkier. But there was no denying that a pair of handsome men prancing around in only tiny bathing suits, then hurtling off a diving platform before getting out of the water again and hugging a lot, was a hell of a lot of fun to watch.

"Timmy Swan was the subject of some gossip," Julia explained when she put her phone away.

"Oh, yeah. He dated some actor, didn't he? Came out in a big splashy way. Then they broke up, right?"

Enough sports-related gossip had seeped into the media he consumed that he recalled that story now. The story itself didn't interest Topher as much as watching an out gay diver perform well.

"I heard the actor was stealing money from him."

"Ugh. That's the worst." Topher hadn't heard that rumor, but whatever happened certainly didn't seem to be fazing Timmy Swan much.

When the Americans won the bronze medal, Topher and Julia went ballistic cheering.

Then the bus took them over to gymnastics. They'd missed the first rotation, but they settled into their seats in time to see the second. In truth, Topher had been looking forward to this event all day, and he was a little upset that he wouldn't able to see the final in its entirety.

It was difficult to see Jake across the huge expanse of the gym, but Topher's heart sped up anyway. He touched his lips, remembering the kiss from two nights before. They'd sent volleys of texts to each other in the intervening thirty-six hours, and Topher enjoyed the hell out of flirting with Jake. Maybe nothing would come of it, but Topher felt like there was potential here.

Now they were in the same room again—or at least the same cavernous sports venue—and Jake probably had no idea Topher was even there.

Through a couple of rotations, Topher tried to explain what he knew about gymnastics to Julia and her giant phone.

"I watch just enough gymnastics to know that the pommel horse is basically a mechanical bull," Julia said as the Americans chalked up in preparation to take their turn.

"That seems true," said Topher. "The American gymnasts I've spoken to all basically hate this apparatus."

"Well, let's watch some guys fall off the bull, then."

But then something amazing happened: the Americans didn't falter.

Well, Corey wobbled on one of his elements and Paul's dismount could have been cleaner. But no one fell. Then Jake got up on the horse.

Topher held his breath through the entire routine.

He watched on the Jumbotron so he could actually see what was happening, because his seat in the stands was too far from the floor to see Jake's movements. Jake's legs seemed to helicopter over the horse. But on the big screen, there were moments when Topher thought Jake might lose control. He seemed to be hanging on precariously. But he did an impressive series of maneuvers, traveled the whole length of the horse in a handstand, and then dismounted cleanly.

He'd gotten through it with no major mistakes. And got a big score.

"Is fifteen and a half good?" Julia asked.

"Hell yeah."

Jordan, the pommel horse expert, flew through his routine and never once looked like he didn't have complete control over the apparatus.

Thus the Americans were still in first place going into the fourth rotation.

They might just pull this off, Topher thought.

The next rotation took the Americans to the high bar, which was the apparatus closest to where Topher and Julia sat.

And it was incredible. The three Americans who preceded Jake did well, but Jake got up on that bar and just flew. He bent his body and threw himself around the bar, in the air, as if it were the easiest thing in the world. He did a trick he hadn't done in the qualifiers, one that was probably incredibly difficult, but Jake did it as easily as he breathed. He didn't *quite* stick the dismount, but his small hop would only be a small deduction, hopefully.

Julia got out her giant phone again and put it in selfie mode. "That Jake Mirakovitch is a dish, isn't he?" she said as the rotation wrapped up.

Topher sighed and batted his eyelashes. "He sure is dreamy."

"This has been a whole day full of eye candy. And we still have swimming to go."

"I may not survive."

Julia laughed. "God, this is the best, isn't it? No stakes for us, except that we want Team USA to win. We get to just relax and watch the sports."

Topher was a little irritated that they were dumbing this down so much for the audience, and he wanted the opportunity to talk about athleticism and skills and flips and dismounts, but he couldn't do much in a thirty-second video, so he said, "It is really fun. I'm learning a lot about these sports too. I almost know the names of some of the gymnastics moves now."

Julia laughed. "I almost understand what the scores mean."

JAKE WAS tired and worried for his arms as Alexei helped him jump up on the rings. But he mentally rehearsed his new mantra: put everything he had into this. Get the burn back. He pushed himself into an iron cross and counted to five as he held it, though his arms shook through the whole thing.

It was the last rotation. He had not made any major mistakes. Paul had stepped out of bounds on the floor exercise, which had definitely affected their team total, and in this last rotation, they were basically tied with the Japanese. Those athletes were now on parallel bars, an event they excelled at, so the Americans were going to have to ask a lot of their tired bodies in this last rotation if they wanted the team gold.

But they could do it. It was in their grasp.

Jake focused on the task at hand, tightening and loosening his body as he flipped and moved into the next pose. His muscles howled. His whole upper body screamed. But he refused to give up or submit to his body's weakness. He would not be the reason this team fell off the podium.

He heard Alexei shouting, "Come on! You do it, Jake! Come on!" from the sidelines.

He maneuvered into his last pose and tears sprung to his eyes from the effort. No doubt he was pushing himself to his very limits. He counted to five anyway.

Then he swung around the rings twice and dismounted.

He landed on his feet, which took all of his effort. He refused to move once his feet connected with the mat, but after a pause, he raised his arms and saluted the judges.

He wanted to collapse as he jogged to the sideline. He'd been putting in his maximum effort all day. He'd thrown an extra release into his high bar routine, he'd held the handstand longer than he needed to during the pommel horse routine, and he'd put as much power as he had into the floor exercise. He hurt everywhere now and his arms felt like spaghetti, but he'd done it.

He couldn't collapse yet. The cameras were still on him.

Alexei walked over and slapped his back. Viktor did too. "Good job, Jake," said Alexei. "You did good."

"Your father watched from practice gym," Viktor said. "He says he's proud. Look?" He thrust a cell phone at Jake.

Indeed, Jake saw a text from Valentin. *Tell Jake he flew today. I'm very proud.*

"Oh," said Jake, surprised by the rare congratulations from his otherwise perpetually stoic father. Jake knew somewhere deep in his soul that his father loved him, but it was an easy thing to forget for a son who constantly let his parents down.

Viktor pat Jake's shoulder. "You did not choke."

Well, no, he hadn't, and he was happy for himself but having trouble feeling anything past the pain that was sinking into what felt like every muscle in his body.

"It's not over yet," Jake said, gesturing with his head toward the rings, where Corey currently prepared to mount. But he absorbed the praise from his father. He let it fill his chest and hold him up as he waited for his score.

A 15.833. He'd take it.

Corey looked tired too as he launched himself at the rings. But if anyone had it in him to get this done, it was Corey.

Viktor said, "Japan just finished on bars. If math is right, Corey needs seventeen for us to get gold."

Jake's heart sank. Corey was good, but he was tired, and his arms shook in the iron cross nearly as much as Jake's had. A single mistake, and it was all over.

Or it wasn't, since math was on their side. They'd still medal, which was better than any American men's team had done in a very long time. But they'd come so close to the gold that Jake had practically considered it his.

"Use that," said Alexei, leaning close and speaking in a whisper, in his heavily accented English. "That fire you feel right now, the disappointment? You take your silver tonight, then you take that fire to all-around. You can win it, Jake. You are best all-around gymnast in whole competition. Even Japanese team, they have flaws. It is team of specialists, not all-around gymnasts."

Jake nodded, though he felt too tired to absorb that.

And Corey got it done. He held all the poses he needed to, he stuck the dismount, but he wasn't perfect, which showed in his score: 16.155. They were just tenths of a point out of first place.

Still, they'd won a silver medal.

They'd won a silver medal!

And Jake could take that success, and the fact that he'd gotten through finals without any major mistakes, without injuring himself, and without doing anything embarrassing, to the all-around final. And then it would be entirely in his hands; he'd no longer be reliant on his teammates for success.

A silver medal, his first Olympic medal ever—hell, his first international competition medal ever—was his. All six exhausted teammates came together in a sweaty group hug that involved a lot of grunting and sighing and "Holy shit we did it!" and "Thank God it's over!"

Cory reached over and ruffled Jake's hair on the way out of the hug.

"We did that," said Corey.

"Can you feel your arms?"

Corey grinned. "Nope. Totally worth it, though."

And it was. Jake let out a breath. He had a silver medal. And the gold had been within his reach.

"I don't know what you did today," Alexei said, "but do it again in two days."

Jake nodded. Jesus. Was any of this real? "I will."

CHAPTER NINE

TOPHER WAS wiped out as he returned to his hotel room. He flopped on the bed face-first and just lay
there for a long moment. Then his phone buzzed in his
pocket, so he had to shift and maneuver under himself
to get it.

Text from Jake: *You have a few minutes?*

Topher rolled over and called Jake immediately.

Jake laughed when he answered. "I meant to text.
How much is this call going to cost?"

"Eh, who cares? The network is paying my cell
phone bill while I'm here."

"How much will it cost me?"

"Do you care? I'll hang up now."

"No, I don't care. It's nice to hear your voice."
Jake laughed again. "I suppose I can afford it. Before
I flew to Madrid, I shot a bunch of commercials. I got
asked to do ads for the randomest shit. Not just athletic stuff. I mean, I did an ad for a gymnastics apparel

company, but I also did commercials for laundry detergent, a bank, a cell phone company, and one of those companies that sends meal ingredients to your home for you to cook yourself. I also got asked to do an ad for a candy bar, but that felt weird and I turned it down. I hardly ever eat candy during the gymnastics season. Or, well, ever."

"Ah, the pressures of stardom." Topher chuckled. "I made a few ads during my heyday. But when I came out, that all dried up. I was a little too flashy and controversial for most endorsement deals." Topher sighed and then whisper-shouted, "That means I was a little too gay."

"Well." Jake paused. "I mean, you should know, I'm not in the closet. My family and friends all know I'm gay. It's just not public, I guess."

"That… good." So Jake lived in a glass closet. In truth, that was a relief. Topher didn't like the idea of dancing around someone's closet door.

"And not even for any specific reason. It never comes up in interviews," Jake said. "The bigger story is always my perpetual failure."

"You certainly didn't fail today. I saw it from the stands."

Jake made a soft sound that might have been a gasp. "You did?"

"I did. How does it feel to be an Olympic medalist?"

Jake sighed. "I don't even know how to process it. I still don't believe it's real."

"Did you all celebrate tonight?"

"A little. My mother snuck me a glass of champagne, even. But everyone was so tired, the party didn't last long. You really came to watch?"

"Yeah. Today I was shooting a video diary about what it's like to view sporting events as a Winter Olympian spectator. Julia Moss, who won a bunch of skiing medals two years ago, came with me. It was a whole thing. I had to duck out of the gymnastics arena before the medal ceremony to make it to some swim finals, but I did see your last rotation. You looked great."

"Thanks. I didn't know you were there."

"I didn't think to mention it the other night, and I didn't want to text in case you were busy."

"I probably was." Jake sighed. "God, I'm tired."

Topher shifted his weight on the bed. He was no stranger to hotel beds—he'd been traveling to skating tournaments his whole life—and he imagined that this room was far more spacious and comfortable than the Olympic Village where Jake was staying. "Do you have a roommate over there?"

"Yeah. Corey O'Bannon. He's soaking in the tub right now. I did the same earlier. I'm still pretty sore from today."

"That sucks."

"No, I like it. It feels good. It feels like I really tried today. I put everything I had out there, you know? I walked away with no regrets. If I wasn't sore, I'd be worried I didn't try hard enough."

"You deserve that medal, Jake."

"It was a team effort, but I'll take it. I... I'm surprised by how much I want the all-around medal. Like, this is nice, and we worked better as a team than we ever have, and I'm really proud of it. But an individual medal? That's... I mean, it's not the icing. It's the whole fucking cake."

"I understand what you mean. Well, not that figure skating is a team sport, or it wasn't in my day, but I've gone to international competitions when my teammates medaled but I didn't, and I was always proud that my friends did well, but winning my own medals was always sweeter. Of course it was."

Jake chuckled. "If anyone eavesdropped on our conversations, they'd think we were the most selfish people."

"I disagree. What do we do this for besides aspiration? I dreamed about winning an Olympic gold medal from the first moment I strapped skates on my feet. When I was a kid, when my coach made me do school figures, and I'd pretend I was skating at the Olympics so that skating a dozen figure eights in a row didn't feel too much like repetitive drudgery. I mean, yes, some people take up a sport for the athletic challenge, or to get into better shape, or just for fun. I worked with a woman at my old training facility who wasn't very good and she knew it. But she loved skating. She was never going to make an Olympic team, but she came to training every day anyway for the joy of it. But those of us at the elite level are always working toward those medals. And the kids watching at home, they dream about those medals too." Topher let out a sigh and sank into the pillows. He felt a pang of disappointment. He'd never have a chance at a medal again. He'd mostly made his peace with that, but every now and then it hit him like a gut punch that he'd never compete again.

But Jake would.

"Get that gold medal, Jake."

"I will certainly try." Jake paused, then asked, "Can I ask, what exactly are you doing in Madrid?"

"It's kind of a long audition for the job of calling figure skating in primetime in two years. I'm making friends with the network and proving how good I am on camera."

"Oh, I bet you'd be great at calling figure skating."

Topher laughed. "You barely know me."

"No, but I can tell you know the sport and you understand what the athletes are going through. I was out of competition with a concussion for part of last year, and I watched a lot of sports on TV while I was recovering. One of the guys they always send out to call gymnastics, Al Henley? His only job has been as a sportswriter and sportscaster. He's never been an athlete, at least not professionally. Most of the time he sits back and lets the experts make the call, or he acts as an audience surrogate to ask the questions that only gymnastics insiders would really know the answers to. But every now and then he says something really boneheaded, or he chastises a gymnast for screwing up something without understanding how truly difficult it is."

"Yeah. Natalie Pasquarella was telling me about that. Natalie's trying to replace him, by the way. Henley's a million years old. He was on my flight over here, and we chatted a little. He's a really nice guy, but he doesn't have a good understanding of how sports have evolved even in just the last ten years. Gave me a lecture about how the end of the perfect ten is a black mark on the sport."

"Eesh. But I've heard that plenty. What people need to understand is that nothing is stagnant. As long as there are barriers to break, athletes will keep breaking them."

"Yeah. That's the thing with Olympic athletes. Never tell them they can't do something. They'll find a way. Did you say you had a concussion last year?"

"Yeah, I hit my head in competition. At the World Championships, actually. Wiped out landing a vault. The network made you ask me that question about it in my interview, remember?"

"Oh God."

"That's the Jake Mirakovitch story, isn't it? Best gymnast in the world. Always bites it when it counts."

"Not anymore. You were great today."

Jake was silent for a long moment. Topher was content to let him stew over whatever he was going to say. Eventually Jake said, "I know it's within my ability to do this. What might do me in is my fear I'll screw this up."

"You won't."

"One of the commercials I shot was contingent on my not falling on my face. Like, I shot the commercial and got paid for my time, but if I didn't win at least one medal, it wouldn't air and I wouldn't get the rest of my money. You can't have the dude who failed selling your product, can you? The endorsement only matters if I win."

"That's awful."

"It's insurance. TBC wanted me to be the golden boy of this Olympics, but it wouldn't be the first time they'd backed the wrong horse."

Topher sighed, his stomach dipping again. "Case in point right here."

"Sorry, I didn't mean you specifically."

"No, but the whole system sucks. You know, the year after my last Olympics, I skated in an exhibition tour. It was fun, but in some ways it felt harder than competition. Like, if I fell on my ass at the Olympics, which I did more than once, I was disappointing myself, my coaches, my team. But falling at an exhibition—which I did once—was worse because I was disappointing fans who had paid money to watch me land that jump." Topher could feed off a crowd sometimes, but having the expectations of hundreds of spectators piled on triggered his nerves like few other things did, and he'd been completely miserable on the tour. It had been one way to hang on to skating as he felt his body giving up. And yet that ache grew in him now, the heavy realization that the thing he'd worked toward his entire life was no longer something he could participate in. "I hated letting audiences down, so I got out. No more skating in front of crowds anymore."

"Retirement is going to blow," Jake said.

That was an understatement. Topher had found solace in cooking, in fashion, in trying to get this commentary gig. He still got on the ice sometimes when the ache got particularly bad, and just gliding around often eased him. But Lord, he missed competing. "No one really thinks about that, huh? You were homeschooled, you said. So you've basically trained your entire life for this week. And when it's over, what do you do?"

"My body can't take a lot more. I know that. I have maybe one more season in me. But I'll fall to pieces if I try for another Olympics. Too many old injuries. My body fucking hurts right now."

"So you retire at… how old are you again?"

"Twenty-six."

"Right, so you retire before you hit thirty, and then you've got the whole rest of your life to figure out what else to do with yourself."

"That's the tricky thing. It's why I shot all those ads. I don't want the attention. I want a nest egg, money I can live off while I figure out what to do next."

"That's smart. You have any ideas for what that will be?"

"Nope. I mean, I'll probably work at my parents' gym for a while. I like working with the little kids, actually. They're so cute, and they're always really excited about what they're doing."

"You have your own place in… where are you from again?"

Jake chuckled. "Houston, Texas, baby."

Topher laughed too. "We're from different planets, babe. I live in New York City."

"I do have my own place. It's an apartment in the suburbs. Easy drive to the gym." Jake sighed. "I love my parents, but I couldn't live at home and also train with them all day."

"I can't even imagine. My mother can barely skate. Her main role in my training was driving me to and from the rink. I don't remember exactly what sparked my interest in skating, actually." Topher let out a breath. He'd been skating since before memories had started recording themselves in his brain, it seemed. Likely he'd seen skaters on TV and wanted to try it. "So you want to coach?"

"I don't know. I can't picture my life past gymnastics. I guess I always figured that after I retired, I'd finally have time to really date and fall in love and get married and all that. Maybe I'd coach. Maybe I'd wait tables for a while. I just don't know."

Topher opened his mouth to respond to that, to appreciate the sentiment behind the words, but Jake said, "Oh, I hear Corey draining the tub. I should probably go in a minute so he can sleep."

"I want to see you again. How do we make that happen?"

Jake was quiet for a moment. Topher almost worried he'd get turned down, but then Jake said, "Well, for now, I can try to meet you at the America House tomorrow night. Odds are pretty good our women's team will win gold. I can't stay out late because I'll have to get up the next day for the all-around, but I could hang out a little."

Topher frowned at that. He wanted time *alone* with Jake, to explore the burgeoning attraction between them. "What about somewhere more private?"

"I don't know. The logistics of that are tricky. The press isn't allowed into the athlete dorms, and it's hard for me to get away right now. I don't know how I'd explain my absence."

"Another interview, at least."

"I know I said after the team competition, but I'm wiped. How about after the all-around? But… yeah. Understand I'm not turning you down. I want to see you again too. Somewhere private."

Jake's meaning wasn't lost on Topher. "After the all-around. We'll figure something out."

"Okay. I hope so."

JAKE SAT on his bed with his phone in his hands as Corey walked out of the bathroom wearing shorts and a T-shirt.

"Who were you talking to?" Corey asked.

"How much of my conversation could you hear?"

"Hardly any of it. I had my earphones in until I drained the tub. I could only hear that you were talking."

Jake nodded. "So, okay, I want to tell you something, but it cannot leave this room."

Corey's eyes flashed. He'd always loved gossip. He tossed his toiletries bag in his suitcase and then settled on his bed. "Tell me."

"That was Christopher Caldwell."

"The figure skater?" Corey's brow furrowed in confusion. "Does he want another interview?"

"No. Well, yes, but that wasn't why he called. He, um, well, I kind of kissed him the other night."

Corey's eyebrows shot up. "You what?"

"It's crazy. Something is wrong with me psychologically. Because I should be focusing on this meet, and I am, but I also haven't been able to stop thinking about him since we met doing that interview, so when I ran into him at the party after the qualifiers, I kind of, well...." Jake held out his hand in a fill-in-the-blank gesture.

"So are you guys, like, a thing now?"

"Hardly. We've been texting since that night, that's all."

"But he called you."

"I kind of asked him to."

"So, you want something to happen?"

Jake closed his eyes and thought about it for a moment. Topher hadn't been much more than a pleasant distraction from the overwhelming pressure Jake had been trying not to think about, but Jake also could not shake the idea of them together. Preferably naked. With a bed nearby. "I do, yeah. Which is insane because I should be focusing on the competition. I don't normally get crushes like this, not during a meet. But, I don't know. He's fun to think about. Do I think anything will come of it? No, not really. I like him, but he lives in New York."

"He reminds me a little of Bryan."

"Yeah?" Jake considered. Bryan was Jake's most recent ex. They'd met while Jake was recovering from the concussion, so they'd been able to spend a good amount of time together, but once Jake went back to training full-time, things had fallen apart. Bryan loved fashion and liked to play around with gender, which was something that had drawn Jake to him initially. Jake admired people who were comfortable enough in their own skin to express themselves so boldly. Topher had that going for him as well, although his personality was really different from Bryan's. Bryan hadn't understood the life of an elite athlete, not the way Topher did.

"I guess I can see that," Jake said. "They do have some things in common. But Topher has also been an Olympic athlete, so he understands. We were just bemoaning the fact that logistics will keep us apart, at least until the competition is over."

"That's the dream, isn't it? An Olympic fling?"

"It's not *my* dream. It's fun to think about it, but planning it is a bit of a buzzkill, actually. But didn't you hook up with that fencer four years ago?"

"She was a fan. What can I say?" Corey laughed. "I am weirdly happy for you. I hope things work out. And I promise not to tell a soul."

"It isn't because I'm ashamed or anything. I just don't want to deal with press attention—or my dad—if it's the kind of thing that fizzles before we fly home."

"Believe me, I understand. Especially now that we have to do real press. I'm hella nervous about going on *Wake Up, America!* tomorrow. I think I liked it better when we were losing and everyone ignored us."

"I'd rather have the medals."

"Seriously, though, if you didn't come back here one night, I wouldn't tell Valentin."

Was that something Jake could pull off? Could he sneak into Topher's hotel without being noticed by anyone? Could they hook up without anyone knowing? It seemed so unlikely, and yet it was incredibly tempting. If Jake hadn't been sore all over, he might have called Topher back to ask where he was staying. "Don't tell me things like that. You really think I could pull that off?"

Corey laughed. "Sure. Why not? You're a grown adult. But now we should get some sleep. The van to the TV studio leaves promptly at eight. That's what Viktor said, right?"

"Yeah."

Corey fiddled with his covers and flipped off the light, so Jake got under his own quilt and glanced at his phone one last time. Topher had texted, *Sweet dreams.*

They will be, Jake texted back.

CHAPTER TEN

Day 4

TUESDAY MORNING was bright, sunny, and warm, which happily coincided with the network's plans for Tourism Day. Topher stood with Julia, Natalie, and a retired soccer player named Keith in a green room with Joanna, who held a stack of papers in her hands.

"Okay, I'm sending you off in pairs. I've got an itinerary for you, and you'll each have a car and driver as well as a camera guy. If you want to take cell phone video and post it on social media, we'd love that too. Let's see. Topher and Natalie, I like the chemistry with you two, so I'll pair you off. Keith and Julia, are you okay working together?"

Everyone nodded. Topher knew Julia had a little crush on Keith, and she grinned as she hooked her arm with his. Keith smiled bashfully. So they'd be fine. And this was ideal for him. Topher liked Julia, but he felt like he and Natalie made a more natural pair.

"Good," said Joanna. "Here are your itineraries. We basically divided a list of ten major tourist attractions in Madrid in half, so you'll each see five today. I know that doesn't give you a lot of time at each spot, but the point is to create kind of an overview of what there is to see in Madrid. Each of your spots will probably be less than ten minutes. Got it?"

Keith asked about how much walking there would be—he had a bum knee, it turned out—so Topher looked over the itinerary while Joanna and Keith chatted. Both pairs were starting at El Retiro Park, just south of the broadcast center building, and then Topher and Natalie had a central section of the city, basically: the Prado, the Palacio de Santa Cruz, the Plaza Mayor, the Casa de la Villa, and then they'd wrap up at the Basilica of San Francisco el Grande.

"Mostly we're going to comment on architecture," Natalie said, looking over Topher's shoulder. "I mean, these are all beautiful buildings, I assume. I've only seen pictures of most of them. But we're not going to have much time to tour them."

"Oh, that's the other thing," Joanna said. "We've arranged for each of you to have an expert in Spanish architecture with you. We're just waiting for them to arrive here at the studio, then I'll send you on your way. I think it'll be another ten or twenty minutes, so if you want to hang out or go watch *Wake Up*, you're welcome to do so."

The meeting broke, and Topher stalled, a little hungry and wanting another cup of coffee before they left. He considered heading toward craft services when Natalie hooked her arm around his. "Let's go see which poor athletes they're interviewing on *Wake Up*," Natalie said.

A big white sofa sat just off set; the crew sometimes pulled it onto the primetime set for evening guests, and it was soft and comfy. After Topher snagged a cup of coffee and half a sandwich, he and Natalie sat there. According to the chyron on the monitor, *Wake Up* reporter Nikki Kenmore was wrapping up an interview with swimmer Isaac Flood.

"God, he's hot," Natalie said. "In kind of a bad boy way, you know? I bet he has a scandalous tattoo under his Speedo."

Topher chuckled. "We're just going to spend our entire time here objectifying the male athletes, aren't we?"

"Is that a problem?"

"Nope." Topher grinned, glad he had someone to ogle guys with. "Flood is the one who got the DUI a couple of years ago?"

"Yeah, but he went to rehab. Now he has a gold medal. It's wild."

The show broke for commercial. It wasn't live; some of these interviews were being recorded to air later in the day, so as not to interfere with the athletes' schedules too much. It was currently about 10:00 a.m. local time, but 4:00 a.m. in the States.

"Quiet on the set!" yelled a PA, glaring at Topher and Natalie.

Natalie mimed zipping her lips, though it was clear from the way she hunched over that she was holding in a laugh.

Then the men's gymnastics team walked out.

Topher hadn't been this close to Jake in two days. He wanted to keep his distance so he didn't distract

Jake during the interview. But Lord, Jake was just so incredibly handsome. Especially all cleaned up. His hair wasn't gelled to death the way it had been during competition, and instead he looked clean and put together. He wore the official Ralph Lauren warm-up suit that the athletes were required to wear for medal ceremonies and appearances like this. It was cute: red raglan sleeves on a blue zip-up fleece jacket, paired with a nice white T-shirt with blue piping at the neckline. All six team members had the matching warm-up pants too, which were probably comfortable but looked a little stiff. Nothing groundbreaking, design-wise, but they needed to look like athletes, not models.

Topher had applauded himself on not being a label whore as he'd gotten dressed that morning, but he'd put together an outfit that was Thom Browne-esque, modeled after the collection from a few seasons ago of suits with shorts. So Topher wore a pair of dark tan shorts that fit very precisely and went to his knees, a white short-sleeved button-front shirt, and a bow tie the same color as the shorts. He had a royal blue cardigan in case things got chilly later, and he'd opted for a blue-and-yellow paisley belt and his Gucci loafers to finish off the look. Okay, he was a little bit of a label whore, but he loved these fucking shoes. They were light brown, but the tongue of the loafer had some elaborate yellow stitching, and a blue leather strap spanned over the top to keep them interesting.

Natalie looked good too, in a Jenny Packham day dress. Topher had guessed the designer immediately when he saw her. That Natalie also loved fashion was a delightful surprise. It really was fate that they'd been paired up.

Jake looked over and made eye contact with Topher. He looked startled at first, but then he smiled.

Okay, then.

Nikki did a fairly standard interview with the team, congratulating them on their silver medal and asking how they'd overcome adversity to finish on the podium for the first time in twelve years. Topher couldn't hear their responses very well, but the gist seemed to be that they'd trained a lot. Nikki zeroed in on Jake for a few questions, asking how felt about the all-around, which was kind of bullshit considering Corey had also made the all-around and the rings final. Then she wrapped up and they broke for commercial again.

"Take five, guys. Lori, the one over there with the purple polo shirt, will tell you how to get back to your van."

"Ooh, let's go talk to them," Natalie said.

She was off the sofa before Topher could protest. She ran over to Jordan and said, "Hey, congrats, guys! I didn't get to tell you before."

"Hey, Natalie," Jordan said. "What are you doing here?"

"The network is sending me out to see the sights today. This is my partner in crime, Topher. Do you know him? He used to be a figure skater."

He'd met everyone at least once now and had watched enough gymnastics to remember everyone's name, at least. He shook hands with each team member, letting his hand linger in Jake's a little longer than was probably necessary.

"You all were great yesterday," Topher said. "I watched from the stands. Congrats on the silver."

"Thanks," said Paul, beaming. "This is so exciting. I've never been on TV before."

Lori of the purple polo shirt said, "Hey, you just need to proceed down the same elevator you came up. The one down there at the end of the hall. Your driver will be waiting for you in the lobby."

"Can I use the little boy's room first? I'll meet you guys in the lobby," Jake said.

Lori directed Jake to the restrooms while the rest of the guys got in the elevator. Topher knew exactly what Jake was doing, so he turned to Natalie and said, "Excuse me a sec," and then followed Jake to the bathroom.

Before he'd even finished pushing through the men's room door, Topher found himself folded up in a pair of strong arms. Jake laughed softly and said, "Thank you for being psychic."

"Are we alone?" Topher asked.

"Yeah. I checked. And I only have a minute, but I couldn't let this opportunity go to waste."

Then Jake was kissing Topher, so Topher went with it, opening his mouth and snaking his arms around Jake. God, Jake could kiss. His lips were soft, but he applied just the right amount of pressure, and he tasted like the butter mints the network had in bowls around the studio.

Topher was never going to be able to eat one without thinking of this. And Topher loved those butter mints. He'd love them more now.

He pulled away gently but didn't loosen his grip on Jake. "We'll get caught," he whispered.

"I'm going in a sec. But I was thinking... it's the all-around tomorrow. Then I get two rest days, and the event finals start Saturday. Then I'm done. Chelsea and I decided to stick around next week, though. I'd really like to spend some time with you, if I could."

"Do you think you could get to my hotel? It's only about three-quarters of a mile from the Olympic Village."

"I'll walk if I have to. Corey promised to cover for me if I sneak out."

Topher smiled. His heart raced; they were really going to do this, weren't they? He gave Jake a peck on the nose. "We'll text in the meantime. And call anytime. I mean it. I love talking to you."

"Yeah, me too." Jake sighed. "I better go join my team. I've got time in the practice gym scheduled for this afternoon. It took us almost forty minutes to get here this morning. Traffic in this city is bonkers."

Topher backed off. "Okay."

"I'd rather spend today seeing the sights with you and Natalie."

Topher smiled. "Don't say that. Go train and win a gold medal. For me."

Jake smiled back. "Yeah? You want me to win it for you?"

"I mean, if you need extra motivation. It could be like a knight winning a tournament to win the heart of the fair lady. Except instead of a fair lady, you have fair me, and instead of jousting against a guy on a horse, you have to fight with the pommel horse."

Jake laughed. "I like the sound of that. Okay. I'll win a gold medal for you." He kissed Topher's cheek, gave him another quick hug, and left the men's room.

Topher tried not to swoon.

JAKE WATCHED Chelsea vault from the monitor in the practice gym. She'd totally nailed her balance beam routine—she'd executed all of her skills cleanly and stuck the landing. Chelsea was the best gymnast in the field, and Jake didn't think anyone could dispute that.

Viktor walked over with his arms crossed over his chest. "Your sister will win gold."

"She'll win the team medal single-handedly if she has to lift her teammates over the vault table herself."

Viktor chuckled. "Go back to the high bar. I want you to be comfortable enough with the modified Tkatchev to do it in competition tomorrow."

"All right."

Jake finished practice forty minutes later and changed into street clothes so he could watch the rest of the women's competition from the stands. He and Corey had seats in the designated section reserved for Team USA personnel. Jake's mother sat there now, and she seemed particularly excited to see him. "I've barely set eyes on you since we landed, *rybkah*," she said, using his childhood nickname—it meant little fish. Not his favorite term of endearment, but he let his mother slather kisses on his cheek.

"I know, Mom. But you and Dad have been with Chelsea."

"Valentin, yes. Me, no. I'm watching both of my babies from the stands. How was your practice? You win gold medal tomorrow?"

"It was okay. I feel pretty good."

"Alexei is not pushing too hard?"

"No, Mom. It was a good practice."

"Will you do modified Tkatchev in all-around final?"

"I'm not sure. Event final, yes. Depends how I feel tomorrow. If I think I can do it without falling on my face, I'll do it."

Jake's mother tilted her head. She switched to Russian and said, "Do you think you'll fall on your face? Did you fall in practice?"

"Once," Jake replied in Russian.

"It was practice. It doesn't matter. But only do it tomorrow if you feel safe. I don't want you to get hurt."

Jake nodded. "Thanks, Mom," he said in English.

She put her arm around him, hugged him, and slobbered on his cheek some more.

"I adore you, Mrs. Mirakovitch," Corey said with a grin.

"Ah, you too, darling. You win medal tomorrow too. Gold for my boy, of course, but silver for you?"

"I will certainly try. And I forgive you for favoring Jake, even though I'm better-looking."

Jake's mother clucked her tongue. "No one is more handsome than Jakob." She ruffled Jake's hair. "But Corey, you know you are like son to me."

"I know." Corey smiled.

In the arena, Chelsea prepared to go up on the uneven bars. Like Jake, Chelsea soared on the bars. Valentin had gotten his start as a bars coach, applying men's skills to the women's event, which meant Chelsea also did the modified Tkatchev Jake had been working on, and she usually caught hers. It wasn't even that people reminded him of this; no one ever rubbed it in. But Jake couldn't help but notice that often, where he failed, Chelsea succeeded.

Women rarely even attempted the Tkatchev move on the bars, which required the gymnast to launch him or herself over the bar and catch the bar between his or her legs, but it was becoming more common. The modified one Jake had been working on had a twist in it, requiring the gymnast to turn 180 degrees in the air before catching the bar, and it was enormously difficult. Chelsea launched herself off the lower bar, did two turns on the higher bar, and... did a regular Tkatchev, not the modified one she'd been practicing.

So apparently he wasn't the only one with competition jitters.

Still, it lowered her difficulty score by only a few tenths, and everything else in the routine was flawless, so she'd still do well.

"Plain Tkatchev," Jake's mother said.

"Yeah. She switched grips instead of doing the twist."

"It's fine. Still best bar routine I've seen today."

"You're biased," Jake said in Russian.

"I'm a gymnastics expert," she replied.

"Are you guys talking about me when you slip into Russian?" Corey asked, even though he knew better. Lana Mirakovitch had lived in the States long enough to speak English almost fluently, but she was usually more comfortable in Russian.

"Yes," said Jake.

"Thought so," said Corey.

Chelsea's score was indeed huge, a 16.255.

"I dislike new scoring system," Lana said. "The ten, I understood."

"You know the issues with the ten." They'd had this conversation many times.

"Yes, but why choose system with added difficulty level. Hard to tell if seventeen is good or fourteen."

"Mom."

"I'm saying."

The additive score system was a good for the sport, Jake had always thought. Under the old system, Chelsea could have been given the same score as a gymnast who did an easier routine but completed it cleanly. The new scoring system allowed Chelsea to push the sport forward and rewarded her for it.

But Lana was old school. She liked the old system.

"Americans will win gold medal," she asserted.

A quick glance at the scoreboard indicated this was a foregone conclusion. The American women's team was a solid fifteen points ahead of their closest competitor. The rotation wasn't complete, but the last American gymnast, their bars specialist, Jessica, would have to not do a routine to lose the lead. She could just do a loop around the high bar and call it a night and they'd still win.

Which maybe highlighted the difference between the men's and women's teams, since the men had lost the gold by so little.

It didn't matter now. Jake vowed to cheer on his sister and then do everything in his power the next day to make that gold medal his. It was all he could do. He had no control over other gymnasts who might suddenly excel or fail, who might unveil new skills and shatter previous scoring records. He could only control himself.

He thought of Topher suddenly, of the lost gold medal.

In Russian he said, "I've met a man."

"In the romantic way?"

"Yes. Here in Madrid."

"An American?" Lana asked. "A gymnast?"

"An American, yes. Not a gymnast. Retired athlete. He's in Madrid as a reporter for TBC. I really like him."

"You do not need a distraction."

"I know." Jake braced himself for the lecture.

"But you should have a future after gymnastics."

That answer surprised Jake. He turned to look at his mother directly and said, in English this time, "Really?"

"Yes." She reached over and ran a hand through his hair, smoothing it off his forehead. "All I ever want for my children is happiness."

It was something Lana had said to Jake many times, but for whatever reason, it really hit him then. He nodded slowly and considered what would make him happy. He couldn't quite wrap his head around the concept; doing what was expected of him was his modus operandi—pleasing others calmed him—and he didn't often stop to think about what would make him happy.

Would being with Topher make him happy? Who knew? It was too soon to say for sure. Gymnastics made him happy, insofar as it gave him his greatest highs and most terrifying lows. He loved the sport. He hated the way his gut churned before a meet. He loved the high of nailing a routine. The broken bones and torn ligaments and concussions and everything else had not been picnics.

Who was Jake outside of gymnastics? He didn't know. Gymnastics was practically his whole identity. And that was something no one he'd ever been with had ever understood.

But Topher did.

Maybe that wasn't the strongest foundation for a relationship, but then again, maybe meeting Topher was like opening a door into a world for Jake to inhabit after he finished gymnastics.

"We've flirted," Jake said in Russian, "but that's it. And he doesn't live in Texas. But... I don't know. There's something there, maybe."

Jessica's score flashed up on-screen, which sealed the deal: the American women's gymnastics team had won the team gold medal, and by a wide margin.

Everyone in their section lost their minds cheering, Lana and Corey included, so Jake cheered along, standing with everyone and yelling "USA!" when the crowd started chanting.

As the gymnasts started filing out of the arena, Lana patted Jake's shoulder. "Focus on the competition first. Then find your happiness."

Jake couldn't help but smile at that. "All right, Mom. Thanks." And that was sound advice. Jake could do that. Win the all-around gold medal first. Then win Topher.

CHAPTER ELEVEN

"SEEMS QUIET," Corey observed as he and Jake walked into America House.

"Everyone's at the Aquatics Center," said Chelsea, walking up to greet them. "That Flood guy is swimming again, and everyone wants to see him win more medals." She rocked on her heels. "Did you know that I can legally drink in Madrid?"

"I bet Valentin has opinions about that," said Jake.

"No drinks, *solnyshka*. Rest and practice." Chelsea puffed out her chest and spoke in Valentin's accent.

"What does that endearment mean?" Corey asked.

"Sunshine," said Jake. "Are you celebrating with mineral water?"

Chelsea held up her water glass. There was a paper umbrella in it. "I asked for the bartender to make it *look* like a cocktail. I won a gold medal today. I deserve *something*."

Corey laughed. "We gymnasts really know how to live."

The celebration was definitely more subdued than it had been for the men's team, but Jake suspected that this was in part because the men's victory had been less... expected. The whole women's team was here, clustered around a big table with smiles on their faces for their hour of permitted group social time, but the air didn't feel quite as electric as it had the night before. Or maybe that was just Jake.

Jake and Corey were *supposed* to be sleeping in preparation for the all-around the next day, but most of the rest of the men's team was here celebrating with the women, and Corey couldn't resist a party.

"Okay," Jake said. "We stay thirty minutes, we don't drink anything more exciting than Diet Coke, and then we go to sleep so we can get up at the crack of dawn for Viktor's crazy pre-meet training extravaganza."

Corey raised an eyebrow. "I'm going to tempt fate and order a ginger ale. Let Viktor come for me. Also, don't look now, but your man is at the bar."

Jake slid his gaze toward the bar, where Topher was indeed sitting and chatting with the bartender. Jake tried not to feel jealous... and failed.

"Revised plan," said Jake. "I go over and congratulate the women, then go to the bar to order a Diet Coke as a pretense to talk to Topher, and you be all charming and distract the women's team so that no one notices I'm talking to him."

"No problem. But, geez, Jake, live a little. Order a regular Coke."

Jake walked over to the women's table. All the women hugged Jake—he was a constant presence at the women's training camp since he trained on the same equipment, so they'd all gotten to know him pretty well that spring—and he congratulated each in turn. But he'd done this dance before, and he could practically feel himself being pulled back toward the bar. When Corey arrived with a ginger ale in hand, Jake excused himself to go get a drink.

He sidled up to Topher at the bar and asked the bartender for a Diet Coke.

"Hello," said Topher. "Of all the gin joints in the Olympic Village, you just had to walk into mine."

Jake grinned. "I did say I'd try to meet you here."

"And I heard you, which is why I am here." Topher let out a breath. "In the meantime, I've been trying to figure out how to get more airtime talking about sports instead of Spanish architecture. Because I spent most of today being escorted around Madrid with an architect who used a lot of big words that I could *not* care less about learning."

"Why would they have you do that?"

"TBC thinks that having athletes from the Winter Olympics who have their own fan bases doing feature stories to add color to their coverage will pull in new viewers. I'm trying to be game for anything and show I'm a team player so that TBC thinks I'm personable and easy to work with, but I'd much rather talk about sports than flying buttresses. So I thought maybe I could pitch a story, but I got nothing."

"Gymnastics scoring?"

Topher laughed. "Half the commentary staff will shank me. That's like bringing up the grassy knoll to a room full of conspiracy theorists. I dunno. I was just randomly Googling things to see if anything struck me as particularly interesting, but I can stop." He gave Jake a once-over. "Are you ready for tomorrow?"

Jake smiled. He took in the whole picture of Topher, from his high hair to his bow tie to his crazy shoes. "You still look cute at the end of the day."

Topher laughed. "Thanks. Seriously, though."

Jake slid onto the stool beside Topher. "I want twenty minutes of no gymnastics speak. Am I ready? Sure, as ready as I'll ever be. Now let's move on."

"Okay. Deal."

The bartender plopped a soda in front of Jake, so he took a gulp. Topher sipped from a martini glass. Jake said, "So, you want to be a skating commentator?"

"I do. I want a job where I put all of my extensive knowledge to good use. I can't skate the way I used to anymore, but I can talk about skating all day. Plus, I'm told I have a, um, big personality."

Jake laughed. "Is that a euphemism?"

Topher smirked. "Maybe."

"Did you see anything interesting today?"

"I liked the Prado. They had an exhibit of El Greco paintings that was pretty spectacular. I like the sculptures too. All those burly men carved into marble."

The bartender left a basket of fries between them. Topher looked up. "I didn't order these."

"On the house," said the bartender with a wink. "They're good for sharing."

"Well, well," Topher said when the bartender moved on. "I think he's onto us."

Jake reached over and took a fry. As he bit into it, he met Topher's gaze. "So burly men. Is that what you're into?"

"If you're asking if I'm into you, I think I've made that abundantly clear."

HAD TOPHER said that aloud?

Jake's smile in response was radiant.

Topher wasn't sure what to do. He wanted to flirt with Jake, to touch him, to kiss him, to haul him off to the nearest private place and have his way with him.

He sensed that Jake wanted the same. But with most of the gymnastics team sitting twenty feet away, he had to basically sit on his hands.

He wanted to honor the deal not to discuss gymnastics, though, so he said, "If you had the night off, what would you be doing?"

"You."

Heat flooded Topher's face. "I... no, really."

"If I was home? Corey and I would probably go out somewhere."

The spike of jealousy that went through Topher was fierce. He glanced at the gymnastics team, where Corey was gesticulating grandly while telling some story, probably. "You and Corey are...."

"What? No, no. Not what you're thinking. Corey's straight. He's one of my best friends. He and I go out together when we have time. We're kind of each other's wingman. I'm not mad that you got jealous, though."

"I'm not jealous," Topher said, in a way that totally made him sound jealous.

Jake laughed. "Anyway, there are some bars in Houston we like. Every now and then Corey lets me drag him to a gay bar."

"So if someone caught you with a guy, you'd be okay with it?"

Jake shrugged, but his face tightened up. It looked to Topher like he was, in theory, but would probably find the reality uncomfortable. Topher didn't want to poke at that, so instead he said, "There are a couple of places near my apartment that I like, pretty much all of them gay bars. It's weird, though. As you may have noticed, I stand out in a crowd a little." Topher gestured to himself. "Which means I get recognized sometimes. That can be fun, but then they want to talk to me about figure skating, which inevitably turns back to 'Sucks that you didn't win a medal' and then all my old wounds are just sliced right open." Topher hadn't meant to go that far, so he cleared his throat and added, "Not to be graphic."

"I don't get recognized really ever. I think the audience for men's gymnastics is pretty narrow, especially since the American team hasn't been so successful lately."

Topher nodded. "I'm not sure which I'd prefer. I like the attention. I don't like reliving my past failures."

Jake gave Topher an appraising look. "Can I ask you a question about that, though?"

Topher's heart squeezed. He didn't want to talk about it, but he still hoped that maybe he could draw from his experience to help Jake in some way, so he said, "All right."

"You don't have to answer, but… what did you do the night before your long program?"

"What do you mean?"

"Well, you've said, in both of your Olympic performances, you did well in the short program but fell in the long program. That's… it's a pattern I'm familiar with. Doing well in qualifiers but choking in the final. So I'm curious what you did to prepare for your final."

"As a cautionary tale?"

"No. No, not at all. This is not a judgment on you! I just wondered."

Topher took a deep breath. He was still bitter about his fate, and being at the Olympics certainly was making him remember it more acutely than he had in a while. It wasn't exactly pleasant to go farming into his memories. But he said, "At the last Olympics, I practiced. There was a practice rink in the adjacent building of the main rink. I think short track was happening that night, so I couldn't practice on the main ice. I thought that if I practiced my routine until I knew I could do it with no mistakes, I'd be fine going into the final. Then, once I'd worn myself out, I went back to the dorm and slept. Nothing exciting."

"Viktor wants me at practice first thing in the morning. I'm supposed to be sleeping now. But, I don't know. Maybe it's time to try something different."

That piqued Topher's interest. "What did you have in mind?"

"Drinking soda and eating french fries with a guy I really like." Jake smiled. "I really do have to get a good night's sleep, but please know that if I wasn't competing tomorrow, I would totally follow you back to your hotel."

Topher nodded. He figured they'd make something happen after the all-around. Jake had a longer break before the event finals anyway.

"I just... I'm stressed," Jake said. "There's this churning in my stomach. I want that gold medal tomorrow more than I've ever wanted anything, and I know I can easily lose it. There are so many things that can go wrong, or that I can do wrong, and, I don't know, I can almost feel it slipping out of my fingers already."

Topher knew that feeling. But he didn't want Jake to give in to it. "You haven't lost it yet. Tomorrow hasn't happened yet. You already have a medal, so you know you can do well when it matters. I know what it's like to be in your position. You know what I would have told myself before my last long program if I could?"

Jake looked up and met Topher's gaze. "What?"

"None of it matters. What your coaches want, what the public wants, what everyone expects of you...."

What matters is you, your training, and your sport. For-get about what anyone else thinks. Just go out there, try your hardest, and do what you know you *can* do."

Jake nodded. "Everything on the mats."

"Exactly. Whatever magic you worked in the team final, do it again if you can."

"Sure. But you're not going to give me that speech about how one meet means nothing and I'll still have my friends and family when it's over, will you?"

"Nope. Because you know what? Losing sucks. Training your whole life and getting a shot at two Olympics is something so few other humans ever do, and when the gold medal is in your grasp but it slips from your hand? That's… it's the worst feeling—one of the biggest regrets of my life. But it's also not the end of the world. And honestly? I got in my own head and I held back. I don't think I did leave everything I had on the ice, and it eats at me." Topher let out a sigh. "I bled and broke bones and tore ligaments for my sport. I've got scars on my legs, on my wrist here." He pointed to the scar from the surgery to reset his broken wrist when he'd landed badly catching himself from a fall in prac-tice. "If I had it to do over, I'd bleed and break bones and tear ligaments during the final if it meant I could have that medal. Will you win a gold medal tomorrow? Who knows? None of us have any control over that. But what you *do* have control of is what you do on the mats, whether you give the competition everything you have. So do *that*. Give it everything. And walk away with no regrets. That's all you can do."

Something on Jake's face changed. His brow stiff-ened and his eyes narrowed. "I will," Jake said. "Every-thing on the mats."

"Good."

"Thank you. I didn't come here for a pep talk, though. Don't get me wrong, I appreciate that you understand this experience. I'm so glad I have someone to talk to about it. But… I also really like you. I bet we'd have fun together in a non-Olympics setting."

"Naked fun?" Topher raised an eyebrow.

Jake laughed. "Sure, but I meant generally. Do you like dancing?"

"I love to dance."

"See? And you liked the Prado, so you probably like art museums generally?"

"The Metropolitan Museum of Art is my favorite place in New York City."

Jake grinned. "Those are two of my favorite leisure activities. I'm not much of a party boy. I mean, I'll go get a drink and dance with a stranger, but I'd much rather dance with someone I know and like."

Topher leaned close. "Same."

Jake leaned close as well. "I like naked fun too."

"Babe. I love the way you think."

"Unfortunately, I should probably make a show of returning to my teammates and then go get some sleep. Will you be able to watch me tomorrow?"

"I want to. I'll shell out the money for a ticket if TBC won't send me."

"You don't have to do that."

"I want to. I'd love to see you do your thing on the mats again."

"Do my thing?"

"You know."

"You make gymnastics sound sexy."

"Oh, honey. Gymnastics *is* sexy. Watching you… uh… do tricks? On the apparatuses? So sexy."

"Good to know. I'll file that away for later. But they're called 'skills.'"

"And I knew that. But you're a little distracting."

Jake picked up his soda glass and gave the basket of fries a rueful look. "I should get back."

"No making out in the men's room this time?"

Jake slid off the stool. "I would love to, but I'm trying not to arouse suspicion. See that over there? That is a whole table of spies. And the last thing I need is the 'romance is distraction!' lecture from my father."

"Was that his accent?"

"Yeah. Soviet gymnast, remember?"

"Ah, yes." Topher laughed. "We had different childhoods."

"And anyway, I think a little distraction is a good thing. Maybe I'll think about you tonight instead of release moves and tumbling passes."

"Hey, whatever helps you. I'm glad to be of service."

"And maybe I'll service *you* in a different way after the all-around."

Topher's heart rate kicked up. "Please do. Actually, I have an idea. Follow me for a second."

Topher had been at the America House for about forty minutes before Jake had arrived. It was a slow night since most of the fans were at events, so Topher had walked around and explored the place. He knew there was a patio out back with picnic tables and a couple of dart boards. The overhang above the patio also created some shadowy spots where people could not be seen unless someone else was outside. And as luck would have it, it was so hot out that the patio was deserted.

So Topher led Jake into a shady area and smiled. "We're alone."

"And yet outside. You're not thinking…."

"Probably not what you're thinking, but I did want to do this."

Topher leaned in and pressed his lips against Jake's. Jake giggled a little and pulled Topher further into the shadows, throwing his arms around Topher's shoulders. Topher snaked his tongue into Jake's mouth and put his hands on Jake's waist. Jake groaned into Topher's mouth, a sure sign that this could go too far, too quickly. Topher leaned away slightly.

"We're trying *not* to get caught. 'Romance is distraction,' remember?" said Topher.

"You do a decent Russian accent."

"I participated in a sport dominated by Russians. I'm serious, though."

Jake sighed. "I know. I should get back inside. God, I like the way you kiss, though." He touched his lips, which Topher found endearing.

"You've got a big day tomorrow. But seriously, any time you want to make out more, I'm game. Just tell me the time and the place."

Jake grinned and stole one last kiss. "Let me win that gold medal first."

CHAPTER TWELVE

Day 5

CHELSEA STARED doubtfully at some of the offerings at the buffet in the cafeteria.

"You have to eat," said Jake.

"Fine. There's just so much garbage on the menu here. You'd think having this many athletes in one place would inspire them to put in a juice bar instead of a fast food place."

"Eggs and toast won't kill you."

Chelsea charmed one of the chefs into making her a breakfast sandwich while Jake stacked his plate high with breakfast meats and cheeses—not to mention the thinly sliced Iberico ham that was everywhere in Madrid, so salty and delicious. While he waited for Chelsea to sort out her breakfast, he found a table in the corner, surrounded by unoccupied tables. At this early hour, hardly anyone else sat in the cafeteria anyway.

Chelsea slid into the seat across from him after he'd eaten a couple of bites of his breakfast. She handed him a plate full of toast, probably realizing he needed to carb load even though toast wasn't his favorite. Too bad nobody served spaghetti for breakfast.

"Thanks," he mumbled.

"You feel ready for today?"

"As ready as I'll ever be. Viktor wants me and Corey to report to the gym in about forty minutes, as though more practice time will make any kind of difference in our performance today."

"It might help you warm up and shake off the nerves."

Jake sighed. "Don't take his side. Sleeping in could have helped too."

"Just be thankful it's Viktor and Alexei, not Dad. Did you see that tabloid story about how Dad, as the women's coach, clearly favored me over the other gymnasts, and that's why I was so good?"

Jake scoffed. "Whoever wrote that story has clearly never met Dad." If anything, Valentin was harder on his daughter than any other gymnast on the American team. Although there were times that Jake was a little jealous of Chelsea for earning so much attention from their father, he was enormously glad Valentin wasn't his coach.

"Anyway," Chelsea said, "I'm thinking about doing that modified Cheng in the all-around."

The Cheng was a vault named for a (male) Chinese gymnast. "Are you joking?"

"Is that crazy?"

"Has any woman ever even done a Cheng?"

"Simone Biles."

Jake frowned. He worried for his little sister sometimes. He appreciated Chelsea's adoration of Simone Biles—had there ever been a better female gymnast?—but he also worried about Chelsea under-rotating and breaking her neck. "Modified how?"

Chelsea rolled her eyes. "Don't you pay attention in practice? Dad and I changed the landing. It ends with a layout so that I'm more likely to land on my feet."

"Sorry, Chels, but I also have medals to win. I don't sit in rapt attention whenever you're in the gym." It came out sounding more bitter than he intended, but at the same time, Chelsea sometimes forgot the world didn't revolve around her. She might have been the best gymnast in the world—male or female—right then, but even if she was only the best gymnast in their family, she could acknowledge that Jake was also competing.

"Oh." Chelsea shook her head. "I'm sorry."

Jake took a deep breath. "Just be safe, all right. Don't break any bones."

"I can do the vault. I've landed it in practice a hundred times. I've just never done it at a meet, so it's still a little bit of a question mark. But if I feel like it's not gonna happen, I won't try it."

"Okay."

They ate in companionable silence for a few moments. Jake looked around. He didn't recognize anyone in the cafeteria, and no one was sitting close enough to overhear, so he said, "You ever think about life after gymnastics?"

Chelsea pointed a fork at him. "Shut your damn mouth."

"No, I'm serious. You've probably got another Olympics in you, but I don't. I'm going to have to do something else with my life."

"You could coach."

"I might do that, actually. I like working with little kids."

Chelsea grinned. "Grooming the elite gymnasts of tomorrow."

Jake nodded, but the reality was that he genuinely enjoyed being around children. He didn't necessarily want to groom young gymnasts into the life he'd led. He didn't really wish his grueling gymnastics schedule on anyone. But the kids were often just happy to be there, and Jake liked their unbridled enthusiasm. It *was* a lot of fun to tumble on the big mats. Jake sometimes forgot that gymnastics was supposed to be fun, but those kids reminded him. So coaching was a strong possibility. "But I wasn't just talking about a job. What about family?"

Chelsea shrugged. She was only nineteen; she probably didn't care much about starting a family yet. "I'll date when I retire."

"Yeah. But that's what I mean. I dunno. Mom and Dad keep saying they're okay with the gay thing, but what do you think they would do if I brought a boyfriend home?"

Chelsea narrowed her eyes at Jake and put her fork down. "Do you… you don't have a boyfriend, do you?"

"No. But I… well, I've met a guy here in Madrid. I mentioned him to Mom, actually. She seemed happy for me."

"You met a guy!"

Jake waved his hands. "Shut up. There are ears everywhere. And I don't even think it has the potential to go anywhere. Maybe we'll hook up a couple of times before we fly back to our separate lives, and that's it.

But I keep imagining introducing him to Dad, and Dad losing his mind."

"Romance is distraction!" Chelsea said in a good imitation of Valentin's Russian accent.

"Well, that. But… I don't know. I never felt like he was totally comfortable with having a gay son."

"Dad loves you." Chelsea waved a hand dismissively and then picked her fork back up. "I wouldn't worry about it. And he never has to know about your Olympic fling." She ate a bite of egg. "Who is it? Someone I know?"

"Retired athlete doing commentary for TBC."

"Ooh. Is it Sam Norton? He's dreamy. I didn't know he was gay."

"I don't think he is. Also, this guy I… well, he's not a gymnast."

"I do know him, don't I? That's why you won't tell me."

Jake trusted Chelsea, but he suddenly felt nervous, afraid she'd judge him. His stomach flipped over. But he swallowed and said, "You know that figure skater, Christopher Caldwell?"

Chelsea's eyes went wide. "You're hooking up with Christopher Caldwell?" she whisper-shouted.

"No. Not hooking up. Yet. We've run into each other a few times and I like him, but that's it so far. But I think we might hook up. He likes me back."

"Okay." Chelsea tilted her head as if she were trying to solve a math problem. "He's kind of over-the-top, don't you think? He interviewed a few of the women's gymnastics team members a few days ago, and he was wearing a sheer white shirt with feathers on around the collar. In certain lighting, you could see his nipples. It was a lot of look."

"I mean, yeah, he dresses a little strangely, but he's really sexy and he… he gets me. He knows what it's like to have all that expectation on your shoulders and then to let everyone down. Do you have any idea what I've gone through? To be labeled the best gymnast in your generation and then to fail? Repeatedly?"

Chelsea went pale. "Come on." Her voice was soft.

"Sorry. It's just that he understands that. He was in the same position I was at the last Olympics. In the same position I could still be in, because I could still fall off something at the all-around."

"You won't. You can do this."

"I know… I'm just saying." He hadn't intended to make Chelsea feel bad, though it was clear she did now. He sighed. "It's nice having someone to talk to who knows how all this feels. Can you guess how many people there are in the whole world who get that? It's a minuscule number."

Chelsea frowned. "Just be careful, Jakey."

"I will be. But I'm not even saying that, like, I'm gonna marry the guy. He'll probably lose my number once he gets back to New York."

"You've exchanged phone numbers?"

"We've been… texting."

Chelsea shook her head. Jake didn't like that she was being judgmental, but he could also already hear the entire coaching staff of USA Gymnastics yelling at him for even thinking about sex when the Olympic all-around title was on the line. And Jake was most definitely thinking about what sex would be like with Topher.

Still, he said, "It's nothing. Forget it. I'm just saying, *someday*, I'd like to get married, which means *someday*, I'll have to introduce a man to Dad, and I don't know how he'll react."

"I think he'd be okay with it, but I honestly don't know either." Chelsea polished off her breakfast sandwich. "Eat the toast."

Jake laughed. "Thanks, lil sis. You're so helpful."

"You know, Georgia has a boyfriend back in Houston who she's been texting with nonstop, and Dad keeps confiscating her phone."

"But, see, it *is* possible to date and be an elite gymnast."

"I mean, it's *possible*. For Georgia."

"Not for you?"

She waved a hand and nudged the plate of toast closer to Jake. "I have medals to win."

"Well, you can check Olympic team gold off your list."

"Yup. But I'm just getting started."

TOPHER SPENT the morning recording introductions to some of the pieces he'd done so far, and when Joanna approached him to ask if there were any events he'd like to see that day during the hole in his schedule, he maybe got a little overexcited when he said, "Men's gymnastics."

Joanna seemed unfazed. "If I get you a ticket in the TBC section, can you do some stuff on social media for us? Short videos, photos, that kind of thing?"

"Absolutely."

On his way to the venue, Topher texted Natalie, and she told him to come to the press area. He slid into the TBC staging area, grateful for the magic of his press pass, and found Natalie chatting with Chelsea Mirakovitch.

Chelsea and Jake were unmistakably related; they had the same coloring, the same slightly pointed nose, the same arch to their eyebrows. Chelsea was like a miniature version of Jake, maybe five feet tall on her tiptoes, her features delicate where Jake's were harder and more masculine. As Topher approached, Natalie said something that made Chelsea laugh, and the sound rang out over the din of conversation in the room.

"Oh, hey, Topher, let me introduce you to Chelsea."

Topher held out his hand, and Chelsea gave it a squeeze. He couldn't help but think about how this was the sister of the man he currently most desired. But he smiled and said, "Nice to see you again," because he'd actually met her a few days before at a women's gymnastics press event.

"Nice to see you too."

Topher smiled at Chelsea. "Do you plan to watch the competition today?"

"Yes, part of it. Not from the stands, though. My father thinks watching from the stands will make it look like I'm not training every possible minute. I tried to argue that it showed confidence, but he thinks I need to intimidate the competition. So I came down here to see if I could watch the TBC feed."

"What do you think of your brother's chances?"

"Good, if he doesn't blow it."

Topher stepped back, surprised. Did no one in Jake's family actually have faith in him?

"Sorry, that was harsh," Chelsea said. "He has it in him to win gold, but he gets so nervous in competition that it makes him tighten up, and he makes mistakes."

"He looked great in the team competition," said Natalie. "You'd never know he was nervous."

"I mean, I *want* him to win the gold medal. We had breakfast this morning, and he said he felt good." She gave Topher a once-over. "This outfit seems… subdued for you."

Topher looked down at his outfit. He had changed at the International Broadcast Center after filming his bits that morning, hoping to blend into the crowd better at the venue. But, still being himself, he wore a blue T-shirt with silver stars on it and a pair of charcoal gray trousers with red pinstripes—like a deconstructed American flag. He'd combed his hair away from his face into a pompadour atop his head and worn ruby earrings. "I can't wear hot pink every day."

Chelsea gave him an odd look he couldn't interpret. Then she said, "There's still, like, an hour before the competition really starts, right? What time is it?"

Natalie pointed to the wall clock. Chelsea excused herself and stepped away to fiddle with her phone. Topher hoped she was wishing her brother good luck.

Topher turned to Natalie. "So, I had an idea, if I can get access to some of TBC's archival footage. I want to pitch it to Joanna. Tell me what you think of it."

"Shoot," said Natalie.

"Before the women's all-around, I think it might be interesting to do, like, a brief history of the sport. I was Googling stuff last night. Did you know that women's gymnastics is relatively new? I saw this video of the first women's gymnastics competition in the Olympics in the 1952 Games, and it was just, like, women twirling batons with pompoms on them."

"I know. I think that would be fun. Look up Larisa Latynina. She was the pioneer of women's gymnastics as we know it, and she was dominant. She was the most decorated Olympian of all time until Michael Phelps broke her medal record. Then look up Věra Čáslavská. And Ludmilla Tourischeva, another Russian gymnast. She's legendary in part because she did a routine once that was so powerful that after her dismount, the bars collapsed behind her, and she didn't even blink. The clip is online. It's amazing."

Topher laughed. "You should write all these names down for me."

Natalie pulled out her phone and started writing a text, probably sending him the names of all these gymnasts. She talked as she typed. "Even Nadia Comaneci won her perfect tens with skills we don't even do anymore. The sport is so different. In the old days, it was a lot of prancing around and looking pretty. Now you need real strength to win championships. Chelsea may look tiny, but she's built like a tank. Hell, Chelsea's doing men's skills on some of the apparatuses."

"Really?"

"When you got here, we were bemoaning the fact that there are a handful of moves called the Mirakovitch on different apparatuses. I think two are named for Valentin and one is for Jake. Chelsea wants a move named after her too, but how many Mirakovitch moves can there be?"

Topher couldn't even fathom what living with these people would be like. "I'm starting to think that whole family is insane."

Natalie shrugged. "I think the trick today will be for Jake to compete against everyone else and not himself. And if he's at the top of his game, his main competition is Hosuke from Japan, one of the few men in the whole competition who is legit good at every apparatus. But Hosuke had knee reconstruction surgery at the end of last season and may not be one hundred percent."

"Oh. Okay, I'll look for him. But what about—?" Topher's phone chirped in his pocket. "Hang on."

He pulled out the phone and saw a text from Jake: *Go to the men's room just outside the press area.*

Well, Jesus. "Be right back," he told Natalie. "Gotta take a call."

How did Jake even know Topher was here? Topher's heart pounded as he slipped out of the press room and walked to the men's room down the hall.

Nearly as soon as he entered the room, Jake pushed him against the door and flipped the lock. Then he kissed the bejesus out of Topher.

"Um. Hi," Topher managed to get out when they came up for air.

"Hello."

"Other men may need to use bathrooms, you know."

"I know, but this was the best I could do." Jake panted. The look in his eyes was hungry. "Chelsea texted me that you were here, so I snuck out of practice. I have to be back in, like, thirty seconds, but… I have not been able to stop thinking about you since last night."

Topher felt dizzy, not believing what was happening. "Uh, Jake? It's not that I don't want to see you—because I definitely do, and I haven't been able to stop thinking about you either—but you have to be on the floor in an hour. And you're competing for an Olympic medal. What in the name of Michelle Kwan are you doing here?"

Jake took a step back. "So, okay, you know how everyone's always like, 'No distractions during competition. You must focus on your sport.' Well, it occurred to me that a little distraction might be good for me. I tend to get in my own head during competition, and that's when I fuck up. But if I have something else to focus on, that might keep me from overthinking things. And…."

Jake kissed Topher again, and Topher was grateful that his body responded quickly, because he was having trouble getting his heart and mind to catch up.

"You are a welcome distraction," Jake concluded.

"Um, okay."

"I had to see you. Are you here to cover the all-around?"

"No, I have a ticket to watch so I can make dumb videos for the TBC social media accounts. This is all a very, very lucky coincidence that I happened to be in the press area at a moment when you could get away. Very lucky."

Topher finally gave in and kissed Jake, pulling him into his arms and running his hands over the smooth skin of Jake's back, down to his ass. He felt Jake grow hard against him; Jake's warm-up pants were not enough of a barrier to leave anything to the imagination. Topher could probably rip those pants right off and have Jake right here. No one would miss Topher… but someone might miss Jake.

"We can't do this here," Topher whispered.

"I know, but…." Then Jake kissed Topher again.

Topher pulled away. "No, really. If we keep going, I won't want to stop, and things could get messy. We'll have to answer questions neither of us is ready to answer."

Jake sighed and stepped away. He took a deep breath. "You're right."

"To be clear, if you didn't have to compete in"—Topher looked at his watch—"fifty-three minutes, I'd keep this going, but you have to get ready. I will not be the reason you don't take full advantage of this opportunity. And you promised to win a medal for me, you may recall."

Jake looked at the floor for a moment, his chest rising and falling with his slowing breaths. "You won't be the reason I don't win. There's nothing I want more than this medal. I just… I couldn't miss the opportunity to speak to you for a few moments either."

Topher leaned against the door and looked Jake up and down. His sandy brown hair was disheveled, not gelled into place yet. He wore a white T-shirt that seemed glued to his body; it said *Miracle Gymnastics Houston* across the front. His black warm-up pants were slung low on his hips. Jake's body was… something else. He might have been short, but his body was powerful, and he still managed to have long arms and graceful fingers. Topher could easily picture those fingers wrapped around his….

"Tell you what," Topher said after clearing his throat. "You owe me an interview."

"That was a pretense so we could see each other again. Just so you know."

Topher grinned. "I do know. Forget the interview for now. Here's all I want from you."

Jake raised an eyebrow. "You better say good loving."

"Sweetheart. We barely know each other and already we're like this." Topher gestured between his temple and Jake's. "But no, actually. Look, I had my opportunity to win gold and I blew it. I was never a great quad jumper, but I landed them in practice well enough that I could put at least one in every program and then make up the points with my artistic score. But then all these skaters came up behind me who could get those artistic points *and* land four quad jumps in a program. And they'd made it look easy. It's like gymnastics, I guess. Each year, new skaters try new tricks that no one has ever landed in competition before."

"Sounds right."

"I fell in my long program. Shit like that happens. It's sports. Nothing is a given. There are athletes warming up for today who have been doing skills you've never even thought about, skills no one has ever done in competition before."

"Is this supposed to be a pep talk?"

"Those are the up-and-comers." Topher put a finger on Jake's chest. "*You* are the best. I want for you to go out there and give it everything you have and win a fucking gold medal, okay?"

"I can do that." Jake pumped his fists.

"If you want further motivation, I can threaten to withhold kisses until you bring me a medal."

Jake laughed. "You wouldn't."

"It would be an interesting test of my willpower. And this conversation we're having kind of screams, 'Topher has issues and is projecting them on Jake.' But I'm here for whatever you need."

"Thanks. You'll be on my mind, then."

"Really?"

Jake grinned. "Well, no. Probably tumbling passes and vaults will be on my mind, but maybe I'll try to think of you if I start psyching myself out."

"Then let me give you something to think about."

Topher couldn't help himself. He leaned close to Jake's face and smiled before giving Jake a soft, slow kiss.

He pulled away gently and gave Jake a wink when their gazes met. "I gotta go, and so do you, but text me later. Or not, if you're partying to celebrate your gold medal."

"Don't jinx it."

"Perish the thought." Topher flipped the lock on the door. "I'll be in the stands, sexy. Think of me fondly."

"I will."

Topher slipped back out of the bathroom and returned to the press area, hopefully before anyone noticed he was gone. Chelsea had disappeared, and now Natalie was chatting with a few crew members. Topher stood just inside the door and collected himself.

This thing with Jake... he had no idea what to do with it.

CHAPTER THIRTEEN

AFTER KEEPING Natalie company until she had to go to the booth to record her commentary, Topher fell into conversation with Eileen Schiffler, one of the primetime gymnastics commentators. She was a nice woman in her sixties who had done some work on previous Winter Games as well, so they knew each other a little. Topher decided to play nice even though he knew Natalie hated that these older commentators were still doing the call most Americans heard.

After all that, he managed to make it to the stands when the all-around was already in progress. The all-around was a chance for the best gymnasts in the world to compete directly against each other. No more teams to add or subtract points—just each individual gymnast proving his mettle on each apparatus. The best cumulative score on all six apparatuses won.

He found his spot in the TBC section of the stands, which was basically several long rows of seats peppered

with various personnel from the network. Topher sat between two empty seats and got out his phone. Flipping
on the video selfie camera, he posed, smiled, and softly,
he said, "Hello. It's time to take in the spectacle of men's
gymnastics, which is fast becoming my favorite event
at the Olympics. The women's team has been getting so
much publicity that hardly anyone is paying attention to
the men's team, despite the fact that they won *silver* at
the team competition. Jake Mirakovitch, whom I think
we can all agree is absolutely dreamy, could win a *gold
medal*, and I know everyone at home is rooting for him.
Right? Now look at this." Topher rotated the camera so
that it captured the vast gymnastics battlefield below,
where men flipped, flew, and fell.

While he panned the camera, Topher spotted Jake
chalking up near the high bar. "Excellent timing," Topher told his phone as he zoomed the camera in on
Jake. "Let's watch Jake kill it at high bar. I have it from
the horse's mouth that this is his best event."

Jake walked below the bar and clapped once,
sending a chalk cloud into the air. He hopped up and
grabbed the bar and swung back and forth a little before jackknifing his body and swinging all 360 degrees
around the bar. Topher still hadn't learned the names
of all the moves, but he watched Jake swing around
the bar a couple of times before launching himself into
the air, twisting his body around, and then grabbing the
bar again. Jake flew a good two feet above the bar as
he twisted. Then he launched himself into the air again
and caught the bar facing the other way. The move had
happened so quickly that Topher hadn't even seen the
twist. Jake swung around a couple of times again before
holding a handstand and doing some kind of trickery by
bending his body and ducking around the bar. Then he

rotated around the bar again, launched himself in the air, and did a somersault before catching the bar again. The audience seemed to be with him now, oohing and aahing with each completed element.

Topher was sure each of these tricks—each one bigger than the last—had an official name, probably after some legendary gymnast of the past. But all Topher really knew as an observer was that Jake looked great as he completed each move, completely in control, like spinning around a bar was an easy thing everyone could do every day and not something that required a great deal of skill, strength, and training. Topher was in excellent shape, if he did say so himself, but he had no idea how to make his body go around a bar like that.

And then came the dismount. Three quick rotations around the bar, and Jake launched himself in the air, twisting in two different directions simultaneously before straightening out and landing on the mat. No stumbles, no steps, just Jake sticking the landing, posing for a moment, and then pumping his fist in the air.

Topher couldn't really tell much about difficulty level or which skills the judges might deduct points from, but he had the sense that he'd witnessed something special.

"That was *spectacular*," he said to his phone.

He turned off the camera and posted the video while the next gymnast—a British man—mounted the bar.

The rest of the rotation went by in a blur as Jake's crazy high score distracted Topher and reminded him of what had happened in the men's room before the competition. If this rotation was anything to go by, Jake wasn't psyching himself out at all. Topher glanced at the leaderboard. After two rotations, Jake was in first place.

Would Jake pull this off?

Rings were Jake's next station. Topher sat forward in his seat. He wanted this for Jake so badly, his heart beat in his throat.

And though Jake's arms shook a little during his rings routine, it looked really solid. It wasn't the highest rings score in the group, but his other scores kept him in first place.

Topher hoped for Jake's sake that whatever magic was happening now kept going.

FLOOR AND vault had gone well. His high bar routine had been nearly flawless. Rings and pommel horse had… happened. He'd gotten through both without any major mistakes.

And now Alexei stood beside Jake as they waited for his turn on the parallel bars, his hand at the nape of Jake's neck. Jake currently sat in second place, mere tenths of a point behind Hosuke, who right then took off down the run-up area to vault.

Viktor walked over. "You win medal" was all he said.

"I'm trying," said Jake.

Viktor nodded. "Do Toumilovich third."

Jake nodded. He'd kept his high bar routine safe, something he regretted in retrospect because he could have used the extra points, but he could pull out all the stops on the parallel bars. He could swap in a Toumilovich, which involved using the bars to propel himself into the air to flip and twist at the same time, instead of the easier kip skill he usually did as the third element in his routine. They'd been doing some more difficult tricks in practice, and he could beat Hosuke with the routine he'd done in the team competition if Hosuke was less than perfect on vault, but having the higher base score would give him a little bit of a point buffer.

Six years of international competition had taught him how to mentally calculate scores. Some complicated math was involved in strategizing for which elements to do; sometimes a few tenths of a point could tell him when to take risks. But the points only really counted if he did the skill correctly.

Some fanfare in the arena drew Jake's attention to the scoreboard, where Hosuke had posted a high vault score. That meant Jake needed a score over 15 on the P-bars. No pressure.

He felt his heart rate kick up.

But no, he couldn't let that happen. His nerves had caused him to tighten up and under-rotate at Worlds; that was why he'd hit his head and gotten a flipping concussion after performing a vault he'd done probably a thousand times without error.

"You can do this," said Alexei. "Don't be nervous."

Easier said than done. It hit Jake quite suddenly that only a ninety-second routine stood between him and a gold medal. That this was all a matter of him nailing it or him completely fucking up and losing the medal again. And there were so many ways to fuck up—not holding a handstand long enough, losing his balance on a pirouette, not getting enough height on his tricks, and of course, whiffing a landing or falling off the bars. He'd done that last thing a few World Championships ago—just totally lost his balance and couldn't save it—and it was such a stupid amateur mistake that the moment was burned in Jake's brain forever. It was Olga Korbut hitting her feet on the mat while mounting the lower bar at the 1972 Olympics. At the time he'd been so shocked that he'd made a mistake on such an elementary skill that his whole body had gone numb. It was like he'd forgotten how to do gymnastics entirely.

So it was of course entirely possible for Jake to fuck this all up, to have spent the entire meet near the top of the leaderboard and blow it in the last rotation. The odds were in favor of that happening, since it had happened so often before.

Except he *could* do this. He could deliver a 17-point P-bars routine if he did the trickier skills.

"You win medal," Viktor repeated. He slapped Jake on the back before walking over to the vault, where Corey, currently in fourth, probably needed a pep talk.

Jake watched Smithfield from the UK complete his P-bars routine.

"I'm freaking out," he told Alexei.

Alexei nodded. "I know. Forget Olympics. Forget medal. Pretend we are in gym in Houston. You do routine the way you do thousands of times."

Jake nodded, but he'd gotten this pep talk before. It didn't prevent him fucking up. Nerves, growing exponentially, often did him in. There were six cameras trained on the parallel bars, and all those cameras made him nervous. The fact that there was so little room for error made him nervous. Hosuke nailing his vault made him nervous.

Then Topher popped into his head. He'd hardly thought of Topher at all once competition had started, despite what he'd said, but... Topher. Something to think about that wasn't gymnastics. He pictured himself and Topher hanging out after the competition ended. Getting drinks at the America House. Making out like teenagers in a men's room. Sneaking into Topher's hotel room and having sex. Yeah, that was all...

definitely not gymnastics. And now his heart raced for an entirely different reason.

Jake glanced at Alexei, who watched Boskovic's turn at the P-bars with pursed lips.

Topher sat somewhere in the stands. Jake knew about where the TBC section was, but he didn't dare look toward it. Still, knowing Topher was watching, that Topher was rooting for him, was weirdly calming. Thinking about Topher and what might happen excited Jake, but in a way that didn't make him feel like he needed to vomit, unlike the looming parallel bars. Maybe Topher was not exactly a life-after-the-Olympics plan, but he was definitely something. Thinking about him made Jake happy.

Maybe that happiness was exactly what he needed. He took a deep breath and let warmth spread across his chest.

Alexei slapped Jake's back. "You're up."

Jake already had his armguards on, so he stuck his hands into the little cauldron of chalk and rubbed some all over his hands while Alexei did a cursory check of the bars.

Ten skills. Ninety seconds. Gold medal.

Jake shook out his limbs, trying to stay loose. He ran each hand over one bar and gripped it a couple of times, making sure the chalk gave him the right amount of grip. He had the muscle memory to do this routine. He'd done it twice today in practice, in fact.

He walked between the bars, grabbed both, and pulled himself into his first skill.

He followed Viktor's instructions, thinking about the first three skills and doing the trickier one third. He could tell, as he sighted the bars, that he got good height on that third one. He caught himself on his arms and moved into the handstand. He counted, felt his arms shake a little and tried to mentally push aside the stakes.

Just another meet… just another meet… push into the burn…. Topher.

He thought of Topher watching him from the stands, and it made him feel warm and tingly instead of nervous, and he launched himself into his next element. And the next. And soon he'd completed everything except the dismount, so he set himself up for it, launched himself in the air, somersaulted twice, and put his feet down.

Bam! Stuck landing.

It was over.

Alexei combusted, laughing and cheering as he ran over and threw an arm around Jake before Jake had even properly finished saluting the judges. "You stuck… I can't believe you stuck landing! Oh, Jake, that was amazing! Almost no mistakes."

"Did I… do that?" Jake asked, feeling a little dazed. He was conscious suddenly that there were several cameras on him, but it didn't matter. If he fell now, no one could deduct from his score.

"You do great gymnastics, Jakob. The Toumilovich—I've never seen you get height like that. Very, very good."

Viktor stood waiting when Jake got back to the bench, and handed him a towel. Jake wiped the chalk off his hands and the sweat off his face and turned toward the scoreboard. He wished he had a calculator, but he knew he needed about a 15.5-something to beat Hosuke.

The score flashed up on screen. 15.738.

Jake's bones liquified. Alexei had to catch him. But he'd done it.

He'd fucking *done it*.

Jake Mirakovitch was the best male gymnast in the world. And now he finally had the gold medal to prove it.

Suddenly he was pulled into a manly embrace with a lot of back-slapping and realized Corey was hugging him, then half the coaching staff.

And... holy shit, Valentin was running toward him. Where had he even come from?

"My son, my son," Valentin cried as he pushed everyone else aside and pulled Jake into his arms and put a hand on his head. "Oh, my son, you won all-around. I'm so proud. *So* proud."

Jake closed his eyes and leaned into his father's embrace. Valentin Mirakovitch had been a legend in his day, and now he was a legendary coach. And Jake....

Jake had finally lived up to all that.

Valentin was basically the only thing holding him up, though, because Jake was suddenly exhausted. All that pressure, all the tension he'd held in his body, all the strength he'd needed to get through routines on six apparatuses and twentysome years of gymnastics.... He felt all of that in his bones, which felt like they'd just turned to jelly.

But he'd done it. He'd won an individual medal. And it was gold.

He started crying. And once he started, he couldn't stop it, so he pressed his face into his father's shoulder so as to not let all the cameras trained on him know that he was anything other than elated to have won this medal. But they didn't know... no one knew. No one knew what it was like to be the son of one of the greatest gymnasts the sport had ever seen and to compete for that attention with his talented sister. No one knew what it was like to train at a gym with his family's name on it, to deal with concussions and busted knees and shattered wrists and a torn Achilles that one time, to have a body covered in scars, that ached on bad weather days. No one would ever know what the weight of all that expectation felt like, nor the strength it took to throw it off.

So he cried, because he was happy, but he was exhausted. And it wasn't even really over, because he still had the event finals. But holy shit....

He'd done it. Jake Mirakovitch was the best all-around gymnast in the world.

Valentin steered Jake toward the bench and helped him sit down. Jake kept a hand over his eyes so it wouldn't be clear that he was crying. Valentin sat beside him.

"I know what this cost you," Valentin said softly in Russian. "And I know I am hard on you. I know those tears, and I know the relief they show. And I know you probably think I care more for Chelsea because I am her coach, but I'm very proud of you, Jakob. You work harder than any gymnast I have ever seen, harder than your sister, and you deserve a gold medal." He let out a sigh. "I hope you know, gold medal or no medal, I am still proud, and I still love you."

That only made Jake cry harder. Jesus Christ. He wasn't going to be able to look at a camera.

He took a deep breath and tried to get himself under control.

"Thank you, Dad," he said.

Valentin patted his back. "I knew you could do this. You had this in you. The real fight was mental, not physical."

Jake laughed and shook his head, trying to shake off the tears. He mentally cursed Valentin's coach pass, wishing he wasn't here so that Jake wouldn't lose his shit on camera, but such was life and here he sat, so he wiped his eyes, waved at the TBC camera, and stood back up. He looked around, and half the equipment had already been moved to make way for the medal stand. The medal stand Jake was about to stand on top of.

"How?" Jake asked aloud.

"Do not question," said Valentin. He hugged Jake again. "Go get your medal."

CHAPTER FOURTEEN

JAKE STOOD in the middle of the huge crowd packed into America House. It had been a great day for Team USA, who would also be taking home medals in swimming, cycling, and fencing. Jake wore his medal over his official Team USA warm-up suit and kept touching it, not believing it was real. It was heavier than he'd expected.

Corey had finished the all-around in fifth, which was still a better showing than any American male gymnast had managed in the previous Games.

The entire American gymnastics team had gathered here, including the women, including Chelsea, who, ever the disciplined one, drank water out of an officially branded Team USA bottle. She stood beside him and kept making comments about people in the crowd.

Jake really wanted a beer. He hadn't been able to get to the bar yet, because every time he stepped toward it, some other person appeared to congratulate him. He'd basically given up on getting anything from the bar, but he took another step toward it anyway.

Then Topher appeared.

Jake's heartrate sped up. He hadn't seen or heard from Topher since those kisses in the men's room before the all-around. Conscious of his audience, Jake said, "Hi," instead of jumping Topher on the spot.

"Congratulations! You did something truly amazing today."

"I… thank you." Jake's instinct was to wave it off and downplay the compliment, but he *had* actually done something pretty amazing. "It still hasn't really sunk in."

"Hey, Jake, want something from the bar?" Chelsea asked.

"Yeah, I want a…." But she vanished before Jake got all the words out. "Beer." He let out a breath. "So close."

Topher laughed. "Would you like me to get you a drink?"

A woman Jake didn't recognize hovered behind Topher and gave Jake a we-can-talk-when-he's-gone gesture. Jake tried to give Topher sad puppy-dog eyes. "Yes, please."

Topher winked and pushed his way toward the bar. Jake reluctantly turned his attention toward the woman who wanted to congratulate him.

Four other people had come up to talk to him by the time Topher returned with his beer. The crowd was starting to overwhelm Jake, and though he wanted to celebrate, he wanted to go hide somewhere with equal fervor.

Topher looked around and then met Jake's gaze. "If you wanted to step out of the crowd and further discuss our interview, it's a little less crowded on the terrace out back. I think everyone's only inside because it's pretty muggy out and the AC in here is pumped up cold enough to freeze Miami."

"But the interview was just a… oh." Jake smiled. He could see "discuss the interview" quickly becoming a private joke, perhaps a euphemism for making out in a bathroom, since they seemed to be good at finding ways to do that. "I mean, yeah, I would love to get out of here, but people keep trying to talk to me."

Topher smiled. "It's so hard winning gold medals."

"It is, but I see you're making fun of me, so I'll let that slide."

Topher looked around again. "All right. The crowd is thinning a little, probably because all these swimmers have to swim again tomorrow and the shuttle back to the press hotel left already."

"Really? How are you getting back?"

Topher waved his hand. "There will be another one in an hour, or Natalie and I can get a cab. I'm not worried about it. But we can break right through this nonsense. Follow me."

Like Moses parting the Red Sea, Topher raised his arms and suddenly the crowd gave way for him. Jake scrambled behind him, trying to use his body language to convey that he didn't need anyone to talk to him right now, thanks.

It *was* muggy and gross outside, hotter than Jake had remembered, but the terrace behind the America House was nearly vacant. Topher pointed to a little table, so Jake grabbed a chair and sat, grateful to be out of the crowd.

"Dear God, it's hotter than Satan's asshole out here," Topher said, waving his hand in front of his face.

"But there are so many fewer people. I'd still take this over that." Jake gestured back toward the door.

"I am a creature of the cold," said Topher. "I can't deal with the heat. I spent most of my life on ice. Almost literally."

Jake smiled and settled into his chair. He was conscious that prying eyes and ears were everywhere, but he was too happy to be chatting with Topher to care much beyond keeping a safe distance between them.

Then Topher produced a fan from his pocket and unfurled it. It was teal and had light pink cherry blossoms on it, with black lace trim along the top. It was quite a feminine fan, but also very Topher. Topher fanned himself and looked a bit relieved. "My hair gel is probably melting."

"You look fine," Jake said. "I mean, you look *fine*. In both senses of the word."

Topher laughed, then glanced around. "Let's not get caught," he said softly. "This is a friendly business meeting."

"Sure it is."

"So how does it feel? Winning a medal for me, I mean."

Jake wasn't quite ready to confess how exactly Topher had helped him out today, but he fingered his medal. "I won it for you in a symbolic way, just so you know. I'm never taking this thing off my neck."

"Fair." Topher reached across the table and ran a finger over the ribbon. "It's so pretty."

Jake didn't want Topher to move away—he liked that Topher was close enough to kiss now—but he said, "We don't want to get caught."

Topher backed away and looked around. "No, I know. Actually, let's film something for the TBC social media account. Come here."

Jake slid his chair around to sit next to Topher as Topher got out his phone. He fiddled with the camera, said, "Smile!" and hit the record button.

"Hey, America! I'm here at the America House in the Olympic Village with *gold medalist* Jake Mirakovitch, fresh off his win today at the individual gymnastics all-around. Say hi, Jake."

So Jake waved at the camera and said, "Hi!"

"How are you feeling, Jake?"

"I feel great! I still can't quite believe it!"

"What are you going to do now that you've won? Please say 'I'm going to Disney World.'"

"I mean, yeah, I think I should go to Disney World. I've never been, actually."

Topher scoffed. "Really? Oh, my God, you have to!"

"Well, let me get through the event finals first."

"Think you'll win more gold?"

"I hope to keep this streak going, yeah. I've never had a competition like this before. I feel like I'm in the best shape of my life!"

"I'll be rooting for you, and I know our TBC viewers at home will too. Thanks, Jake!"

"Thank you!"

Topher stopped recording and lowered the phone. Then he grinned. "There. Plausible deniability."

JAKE WAS all smiles now that they were outside. He'd looked distressed as the crowd closed in around him, so although Topher wanted some time to chat with Jake uninterrupted, he was also happy to get Jake to a place he felt safer.

"But seriously, though," Jake said after Topher tucked his phone away again after posting the video. "My coach has gym time booked for many hours tomorrow, and then the event finals are Saturday. Most of the team is flying home on a chartered flight Sunday night, but I told my family I wanted to stay behind and see some events."

"And they're letting you?"

Jake rolled his eyes. "First of all, I'm twenty-six. Second, Chelsea is sticking around too, to do some stuff for TBC. Well, assuming she wins tomorrow, which she probably will. But she had so much buzz coming into these Olympics that she's already kind of a media darling. So they're paying her to do some fluff pieces."

"Oh, great." Although Topher was a little irritated—why was Chelsea horning in on his gig?

"My parents are flying home on the charter too," Jake said, "but they want me to stick around Madrid to babysit Chelsea, basically. She's an adult, though, so I'm just saying, I'll have some time free."

"Interesting." Topher leaned forward and waggled his eyebrows.

"I had been planning to stay in the Village, but Chelsea wants to move to the press hotel, and I'm starting to think that might be a good idea."

"Why, Jakob. Are you implying that you have an entire week in Madrid in which you might be staying in the same hotel as a certain retired figure skater, and that you intend to sneak into his room at night?"

"That is exactly what I am implying," Jake said.

Well, that was delightful news. "I like this plan a great deal, but you do realize that the hotel is crawling with press."

"I know." Jake sighed. "I thought of that when Chelsea started trying to persuade me to move to the hotel. But I figure if we're not caught in the common areas together, we'll be all right." He sat back in his chair and looked at the sky. "Or, I don't know. This is clearly the peak right here. I don't have a lot of years left in my career before my body falls apart. Definitely not another Olympics. Maybe I should retire on top and come out of the closet publicly. Or just not freak out about potentially getting caught."

Topher shook his head. "Let's not be hasty. I waited until I retired to come out."

Jake raised an eyebrow.

"I mean, I wasn't kidding anyone, obviously. All this fabulosity is too much for a straight man." Topher gestured at himself. "But I was dating this ice dancer from Calgary shortly after my retirement, and we wanted to go public. That relationship didn't last, obviously, but the cat was out of the bag. Or the homo was out of the closet, as the case may be."

"Your family took it well?"

"Oh, they all knew. Again." Topher repeated the gesture toward himself. "And it was really just my mom anyway. Losing the gold medal was the tougher thing for her to deal with—it's not cheap raising an elite figure skater. By the time I told her I was gay, she was basically like, 'Oh, is that all?'"

Jake nodded. "My father was weird about it at first, but he came around. He had this orthodox upbringing, but I think gymnastics exposed him to enough of the world that nothing much surprises him. And he essentially defected from the Soviet Union when he moved to the US permanently, so he's got a rebellious streak in him. My mother was fine with it—she's always been very supportive. She… oh, shit, here she comes."

"There you are, Jakob!"

Svetlana Nikolaeva was a strikingly beautiful woman with long, light brown hair the same shade as Jake's and a graceful, petite body. Topher had researched her a little; she'd been a rhythmic gymnast from the USSR before marrying Valentin Mirakovitch and giving birth to the two best gymnasts in the world. Interviews with various USA Gymnastics team members indicated she was kind of the team mom, always very encouraging and friendly.

She gave Topher a wide smile now. Then she turned back to Jake. "We thought you went back to dorms."

"I needed some air. Mom, this is Topher Caldwell. He's a retired figure skater doing some work for TBC. Toph, this is my mother, Svetlana Nikolaeva Mirakovitch." Jake's Russian enunciation was perfect, and Topher liked the way his mother's name rolled off his tongue.

Acting on a hunch, Topher said, "Nice to meet you," in Russian.

Svetlana squealed with delight. She said something back rapidly. Topher knew some Russian but not enough to follow what she was saying now.

"She's thanking you for greeting her in her native language," Jake explained.

"You're fluent in Russian."

"Da. Of course he is," said Svetlana. "You may call me Lana."

"Thank you, Lana," Topher said in Russian.

She smiled. "Jakob, please do not stay up very late. There is car coming at ten o'clock to bring you to broadcast center."

"I'll head back to the dorm soon."

"We were just filming a little video for the network," Topher said. "I can let him back inside to meet his adoring fans again now."

"Not necessary. I only needed to know where he was. Take your time." She gave a little wave and went back inside.

"That's probably the sign I should go," said Jake with a sigh.

Topher nodded, feeling sad. "I may melt if we stay out here much longer anyway. Is my hair flat?"

Jake looked at it and smiled. "No. It looks great."

"Good. Well, I—"

"Text me," Jake whispered. "Often. And if I can get away, I'll meet you somewhere."

"There's a men's room at the broadcast center, you know. I'll be there in the morning too."

Jake grinned. "I want to kiss you so bad right now."

"Hold that thought, sweetheart."

Topher looked around. No one was outside, and it really was face-melting hot out. Still, Topher stood and grabbed Jake by the shirt, then led him into the shadowy area under the overhang. One quick glance around verified again that they were alone. So Topher kissed the hell out of Jake.

He wanted to take this further right now. Jake smelled like chalk and sweat, which was somehow totally doing it for Topher, and his clothes were soft over his hard muscles. Topher wanted to push Jake against the wall, rip his clothes off, press against him. Topher darted his hand to trail down Jake's spine and over the curve of his ass; then he lifted Jake's leg and moved to push Jake back, and—

"Woah," said Jake. "Not here."

Shit. It was too easy to let things get out of hand.

"Which hotel are you at again?" Jake asked with a sly smile.

"Are you serious?" asked Topher.

"As a Soviet gymnast."

So Topher told him the name of the hotel, but he didn't dare hope that anything would happen tonight.

"I'll see if I can sneak away, maybe wear fake glasses or something. Pull a Clark Kent."

Topher laughed, even though he was still uncomfortably aroused and half convinced he was dreaming all this. "I mean, only if you want to."

"Good Lord, I want to. I'm tired of just imagining what it would be like. I don't have to compete tomorrow. Now is the time."

"I'll understand if you can't, but I'd love to have you tonight. And I mean that in every sense of the word."

Jake nodded. He gazed at Topher with lust in his eyes. Then he stole another kiss before returning to the America House.

Topher sat outside for a few more minutes, trying to calm down, sipping his wine and looking at the night sky. Madrid may yet hold some magic, he thought. He smiled to himself. Then he pulled out his phone and texted Jake.

I miss you already.

It took a minute, but Jake texted back. *Same*. Then a minute later, he texted an eggplant and a peach emoji.

Topher laughed. *Was that a sext?*

Jake responded with a wink emoji.

Then Natalie appeared. "Jake said you were out here. Are you… sitting here by yourself?"

"I was with Jake until a few minutes ago. It's unbearably hot out here, but I wasn't quite ready to rejoin the masses."

"Most of the masses have gone back to the dorms to rest up for tomorrow's competition. Are you ready to go? The shuttle back to the hotel leaves in about fifteen, so if we head out to the parking lot now, we should make it in plenty of time."

"Sure. Let's blow this popsicle stand."

CHAPTER FIFTEEN

WHEN HE walked back into America House, Jake was thrilled to discover that nearly everyone had left. Unfortunately his immediate family was still there. And although he couldn't deny that he enjoyed being showered with praise by his parents and ate it all up with a spoon while Chelsea stood by looking a little put out not to be the center of attention, he was distracted by Topher and Natalie walking through the restaurant, likely toward the cab stand or shuttle stop. Jake really wanted to be leaving with them.

After the elder Mirakovitches finally left, Corey emerged from the men's room and offered to walk Jake and Chelsea back to the dorm. Unwilling to disclose anything about his sex life to Chelsea just yet, Jake had no choice but to go along.

When he and Corey got back to their room. Jake shoved a change of clothes and a toothbrush into his backpack and said, "Well, I'm leaving."

"Hey, Jakey. I want you to have sex tonight, I do, but you do recall that you won a gold medal today and therefore have to go on TV first thing in the morning?"

Shit. Jake *had* forgotten. He pulled out his phone. According to his schedule, he didn't have to meet the car until ten in the morning. "As long as I'm back here by eight, I should be okay."

"All right. But for the record, if you lose track of time and are a no-show for the car, I'm not responsible."

"Of course not. Why would you be?" Jake started to slide his backpack onto his shoulders but paused. "Wait, do you think I shouldn't go?"

"No, I think you should. I'm a little jealous, even, because I haven't met any ladies I'd like to invite over since I'll have the room to myself for the night. But go. Get yours."

Jake laughed. "Uh, thanks. Um. I'll try to get back here early tomorrow morning. Please don't… tell anyone. Not even Chelsea."

"No, I won't. Have some fun, Jake. You deserve it."

Jake pulled a hoodie from his closet and brought the hood up to obscure his face.

His heart pounded the whole way down to the lobby. He looked around when he got outside. He was terrified of getting caught, but it turned out Topher was staying at the same hotel as his parents, which meant Jake had a logical reason for going there. If he ran into Lana and Valentin, he'd have some explaining to do, but since Valentin was the type to go to bed early and usually woke with the sun, the odds of that happening were low.

Still, he looked around as he asked the security guard to hail him a cab. A group of young men—swimmers, Jake guessed, based on their body type—were goofing around near the entrance to the building, but they seemed absorbed enough in whatever they were talking about that they didn't seem to see Jake. So Jake slid into a cab when one arrived for him.

He texted Topher: *Please be in your room.*

The reply came slowly, but when Jake's phone buzzed, he saw Topher's response: *I am. 305.*

Jake took a deep breath. *I'm in a cab.*

Topher responded with a gif of some actor dancing excitedly.

The hotel was on a busy block, the entrance sandwiched between two restaurants. Plenty of people were around, but they seemed to be locals or tourists, not athletes or the press. Happily, no one seemed to recognize him. He walked right through the small lobby and followed the signs toward the elevator without making eye contact with anyone.

His heart raced and his skin tingled as he boarded the elevator.

They were really going to do this.

He looked both ways when he stepped off the elevator and was relieved that no one was in the hall. He found Room 305 and knocked on the door.

Topher answered the door wearing a deep blue robe, likely something he'd brought from home and not from the hotel. The material looked soft, and it parted at Topher's sternum to reveal he wasn't wearing a shirt. His skin looked smooth and touchable.

"You going to come in or are you just going to stand there gawking?" Topher asked.

Jake blinked a few times to refocus and looked up to meet Topher's gaze. Then he walked through the space Topher made when he opened the door wider.

Doubt crept in, not for the first time that day. Oh, he wanted Topher, but how could this ever be anything more than a quick, athletic bout of sex? They had so little in common, at least on the outside. Topher had *high maintenance* written all over his body, but Jake could barely maintain himself during training. There was just enough of an age gap between them—five years, if Jake's math was right, but that was an eon in sports—to give Jake some pause.

And yet they understood each other. Jake had worried, as he'd lain awake in bed the past few nights, that Topher might resent him for finally getting the medals Topher had probably thought he'd deserved. Jake could no longer call himself the greatest gymnast in the world without an Olympic medal. He was the greatest male gymnast in the world, full stop, and had a medal to prove it now. He didn't feel much ego about that, though.

No, his greatest triumph had been finally breaking through whatever bullshit had held him back in international competition. The medals were nice, but that was the thing he was most proud of. And Topher had never had that opportunity. That was the thing with elite athletics—a competitor burned bright for a very short period of time, and then he or she was just the ashes of a promising career.

That was grim.

"I think a whole opera just played out in your head," said Topher, gesturing Jake into the hotel room.

"Sorry. Lots on the brain."

"Ah."

Jake looked around the room. It was nice, albeit small, and was dominated by a king-size bed that took up most of the space. And then there was Topher's luggage. So much luggage. Jake generally liked to travel as light as possible.

What was he even doing here?

"Oh, honey," Topher said, "I see the look on your face, and I recognize that you're wondering if you made mistake in coming here. And I will just tell you two things."

Jake looked at Topher, who stood a few feet away, standing with his hip cocked.

"First, I'm not asking you for any kind of commitment. I like you a lot, but I'm a realist, and I know what your training schedule must be like. And I know that I'm not moving to Texas, so let's call this what it is—two men who like each other and want to bang."

Jake laughed despite himself.

"Second," said Topher, "you're really hot, and I think you think I'm pretty sexy, so let's just roll with that and not make it more than it is."

"Okay," Jake said. "I can do that."

He'd done it enough times. He made it very clear to the men he went home with that he didn't have time for commitment. He was no stranger to one-night stands. He viewed it as a release, an outlet, a place to put the sexual energy that burned through him, especially after a particularly good meet. This was something he knew, something familiar.

Then why did it feel so different?

"Do you have doubts?" Topher asked.

"About you? No. About sex? No."

"Then what's the issue?"

Jake sighed. "I don't know. It's like I've forgotten how to do this. How do we even get started?"

"Okay, I got you there." Topher walked over to Jake and cupped his cheek. "You're just confused because we're not in a men's room trying to squeeze all of our pent-up attraction into a thirty-second kiss. We have lots of time now, no?"

"I have to be back around eight in the morning. The car to the broadcast center is coming to fetch me at ten."

"Ah, your star continues to rise. Still, that's perfect." Topher smiled, and it was so warm and genuine—and, wow, his teeth were really straight and white—that it did a lot to calm Jake's nerves. "Okay, let's start here."

Topher was not the tallest man Jake had ever been with, but he was still a few inches taller than Jake. So Jake turned his face up in anticipation, and Topher dipped to meet him, pressing his lips against Jake's. Warmth spread instantly across Jake's chest, relaxing him, reminding him what he wanted and what he was doing here. He reached up to cup the back of Topher's perfect head and pulled him closer; then he opened his mouth to take in more. They nipped at each other's lips, sliding against each other, and then Jake closed his eyes and licked into Topher's mouth. Topher groaned in response.

Jake moved his hands and put them on Topher's waist, pulling him close. Topher was already hard, his erection pressing against Jake's belly. If Jake needed a reminder of why he was here, it was that.

Because Topher was so fucking sexy. The way he played with gender turned Jake on, there was no denying that, and Jake admired how Topher expressed himself, not seeming to care about what anyone thought of him. And he loved Topher's body, graceful but strong—the body of an athlete who had once been at the top of his game.

Jake wanted to strip Topher of all his makeup and hair gel and frills to see the man underneath.

"Is it wrong," Jake asked between nibbles at Topher's jaw, "that I'm worried about messing up your hair."

Topher barked out a laugh. "It's fine, darling. Please mess it up. I want you to."

"Can it even be messed up? How do you get it to poof up like that?"

Topher took a step back and reached up to fiddle with his hair. He extracted a little pad from the pompadour; then he grabbed a spray bottle from a dresser and spritzed his hair with water. There was a towel nearby that Topher grabbed and rubbed over his head. His hair tumbled down around his face, the strands in front a few inches long, falling near his cheekbones.

"I honestly don't mind if my hair gets messed up. It's for a good cause."

Jake couldn't help but smile at that. "I like your hair."

"Good."

Jake reached over and ran his fingers through Topher's damp, slightly sticky hair. He had a ton of questions about how Topher managed to style it that way, but now didn't seem like the right time to ask them.

Topher kissed Jake again and nudged him toward the bed. Jake took the hint and let himself tumble back onto it. He lay on his back, propping himself up on his elbows.

"Take off your clothes."

Jake didn't need to be asked twice. He hated the sound of the fabric of his warm-up pants rubbing against the bedspread, for one thing, but also, he was eager to get naked with Topher before he lost his nerve again. He toed off his sneakers, pulled off his hoodie, and shucked his pants, leaving him in just a pair of blue briefs.

Topher stood staring for a moment, which felt gratifying.

Then Topher, with his eyes on Jake at all times, undid his robe and let it slide off his shoulders. It pooled at his feet and revealed the only other thing he'd been wearing—a pair of black briefs that weren't doing a lot to hide his excitement.

Topher climbed onto the bed. Jake smiled and took Topher into his arms.

"Your body is killing me," Topher said. "I've never been with a gymnast before."

"I've never been with a figure skater."

"This old thing?" Topher gestured at himself.

Jake leaned back and took a solid look at Topher in his seminude glory. His body was as lean and strong as Jake had surmised. He wasn't in peak condition anymore, nor should he have to be this far from his retirement, but he still had a solid chest, defined pectoral muscles, six-pack abs, and sturdy thighs. Topher likely still worked out regularly—it was hard to quit cold turkey—and his body showed it. But Topher had a grace too, long limbs and piano-player fingers, smooth gestures and those crazy long eyelashes. He also had an angry-looking scar near his rib cage, a surgical scar on his knee, and who knew how many old injuries that weren't even visible. "What happened here?" Jake asked, drawing a finger along the scar on Topher's torso.

"Oh. It looks worse than it is. There was a tussle during a warm-up at my training rink. Another skater whiffed a landing and kind of fell on me, then I tumbled into another skater, and the three of us got all tangled up on the ice. One of them got me with a toe pick. I needed a few stitches, but of all my sport-related injuries, that one was pretty minor. Ironic that it left the worst scar."

Topher ran his gaze along the length of Jake's body. "I'm surprised you don't have more scars."

"Broken bones and concussions, mostly."

"Jesus."

"I have mats to land on. I don't want to think about falling on ice."

"Lesson one is learning how to fall so you don't injure yourself too badly. But I also bruise like a peach. I think part of the reason why the women wear such thick tights is to hide all the bruises on their thighs. I certainly always had a few during the season."

Jake nodded. "You have to put everything you have into it in order to be the best."

They stared at each other for a long moment. Jake didn't want to talk. They were both naked and close to each other. The heat from Topher's body warmed Jake. So why were they talking about old injuries?

"I'm sorry we're not having sex right now," Jake said, running a hand over Topher's shoulder. "I don't know why I'm so up in my head. I've got a mostly naked man in my arms and it's like my body forgot what to do."

"Let me help you with that, then."

Topher leaned over and kissed Jake, then ran a hand over Jake's chest, sliding his palm over Jake's nipples. He moved that hand along the side of Jake's torso, over his ass, then pulled at his thigh to drape his leg over Topher's hip. Their still-clothed cocks lined up, rubbed together, and a zippy thrill went through Jake. He felt like his body suddenly came online, like his reptile brain was finally starting to take over from his more logical brain.

Jake ran his hands down Topher's back. It wasn't all smooth skin; Jake's fingers found bumps from old

scars there too. Just here and there, reminders that Topher had participated at the top levels of what could be
a dangerous sport. Jake cupped Topher's asscheeks and
pulled him close, grinding against him, their erections
rubbing together. Topher growled somewhere low in
his throat and thrust his fingers into Jake's hair. He nib-
bled at Jake's lower lip, then pressed their lips together
fully again.

Jake surrendered to it. He tried to shut off his brain
and just be in this moment with Topher. His body tingled with arousal, and Topher's pale skin was flush
with it too. Jake loved kissing Topher, loved the pressure and plumpness of Topher's lips, loved the way Topher tasted.

"I want to see all of you," Topher murmured
against Jake's skin.

Jake slid back, hooked his thumbs into his briefs,
and slid them off. He spread his legs for Topher as
he tossed the briefs on the floor. Topher's expression
looked like that of a man who'd just been served a
gourmet meal. He took Jake's cock in his hand and
stroked it a few times. Arousal zipped through Jake,
and his hips jumped off the bed as he leaned into Topher's touch.

"My, my, Mr. Mirakovitch. This is quite
impressive."

"Let me see you," Jake said, grabbing the waist-
band of Topher's briefs. He could feel the heat of
Topher's skin, the smooth hardness of Topher's cock
where it pressed against the fabric. And when Jake revealed it, he was not surprised to see that Topher's cock
was as long and thin as he was.

Jake had to taste it. He peeled Topher's briefs off and
kissed the tip, then took Topher's cock into his mouth.

Topher made a noise that was somewhere between a hiss and a sigh. Jake pinned Topher's hips to the bed and sucked as much of Topher's cock into his mouth as he could, relaxing his throat. Jake might not have had great amounts of sexual experience, but he knew what he was doing, and he wanted to pull out all the stops with Topher, make him feel good, make this night unforgettable.

If this was the only night they had together, he wanted it to be amazing.

Jake wrapped his hand around Topher's balls and ran a thumb over the skin there, making Topher writhe. He started to snake his finger toward the entrance to Topher's body, but then Topher jerked and said, "No, wait."

Jake pulled away and looked up at Topher. "Too much?"

"You are *quite* good at all that. But if you touched me there, I would have come immediately, and I don't want that yet. Because then I might be done for a while. I'm not as young as I used to be."

Jake grinned and slid up to lie beside Topher once more. He grabbed Topher's face and pulled him in for a kiss. Topher moaned into Jake's mouth and put his hand on Jake's hip, pulling Jake closed despite what he just said.

"I want you inside me," Topher said.

"I want that too. I, uh, brought a few condoms."

Topher smiled and looked delighted by that. "Look at you."

Jake laughed. "They pretty much hand them out like a coach gives out criticism in the Olympic Village. I've been collecting them in case I got this opportunity with you."

Topher smiled, probably remembering his own past experiences in Olympic Villages. All those young people in peak physical condition sharing a space meant there were bound to be sexy times. Jake smiled back at Topher, then bent over the side of the bed to grab a condom from his pants pocket.

Topher climbed over him and pulled something from the nightstand drawer. They briefly tangled, which gave Jake a moment to taste the skin on other parts of Topher's body. His hip was right there, that scar near his rib cage, then his armpit. Jake pressed his nose there and inhaled. Topher smelled amazing.

And hey, Jake was an athlete. He figured growing up in a gym had probably wired him to find the smell of men's sweat particularly alluring.

Topher wriggled away from Jake and stretched himself out on the bed. Then he handed Jake a bottle of lube.

"Good thinking," Jake said.

"It's from my in-case-of-emergencies stash."

"This is definitely an emergency."

"*Definitely*. I want you inside me right now. Urgently. Siren dot gif."

So Jake didn't waste any more time. He took the lube from Topher and smeared some on his fingers. Then he did what Topher hadn't let him do before—slid his fingers behind Topher's balls to the entrance to his body. Topher kept his legs spread wide and tilted his hips up to give Jake better access.

Topher seemed beside himself with arousal, unable to keep his hips still as he thrust back against Jake's hand. His cock was hard and red, already leaking. Jake bent his head to lick the tip of it again, and Topher made an incoherent noise. Jake loved how responsive Topher was, how he was already coming apart, but he needed Topher to last long enough for Jake to do what he really wanted.

When Jake was satisfied Topher was ready for him, he rolled on the condom, smeared more lube on himself, and got on top of Topher. He positioned himself, then pressed forward. Topher hissed and threw his head back.

"Tell me to stop if you need me to," Jake said.

"Don't you fucking dare stop," said Topher, putting his hands on Jake's ass and pulling him further into Topher's body.

Topher was ridiculously tight. His body squeezed against Jake's cock, and the sensation was exquisite, perfect. It had been long enough since Jake had had sex with anything but his hand that he didn't think he'd last very long. But maybe that was okay, because Topher made some otherworldly noises as Jake bottomed out in him. Then Jake began to move, and Topher clutched at Jake's shoulders and said, "Oh God."

"That's what I want to hear," Jake said. He dropped his head and kissed Topher, who returned his kiss with enthusiasm and slid his hands up Jake's back. Jake thrust in and out, the tightness and friction of Topher's body making him feel like they might make a fire. And maybe that's exactly what they were doing. Sweat dripped from Jake's hair, and Topher's skin was becoming slick, and all they could do was rut against each other and moan, pressing each other to find their releases.

"Holy…," Topher said. "I don't want to… but I'm… gonna come…."

"Yes," Jake panted. "Come for me."

Jake grabbed Topher's cock and stroked it, pressing his thumb into that spot right below the head that caused magical things to happen. Topher bucked against Jake, squeezing his muscles and making Jake worry about embarrassing himself by coming too fast.

But then Topher's eyes rolled back in his head and he cried out. And suddenly he was spilling all over Jake's hand and Topher's own belly. His body clamped down on Jake, and that was it. Jake surrendered to it, clutching at Topher as he came, shooting into the condom and letting out a long moan.

As he came back down, he found himself lying on top of Topher and feeling slightly sticky.

"Christ," said Jake.

"You mumble in Russian when you're really worked up," Topher said.

"I do?"

"Has no one ever pointed that out to you before?"

"I'm guessing no one else I've been with recognized it. How good is your Russian?"

"I can hold my own in a simple conversation."

Jake lifted his head and met Topher's gaze. In Russian, he said slowly, "That was amazing, and I can't wait to do it again."

Topher grinned. In Russian, he said, "Same."

Jake rolled off Topher and onto his back. Now he was covered in sweat and lube and cum and whatever goop Topher put in his hair, and he had not a single regret, but he was a little uncomfortable.

Topher let out a happy sigh. "When my limbs resolidify, let's hop in the shower, eh?"

"It's like you read my mind."

CHAPTER SIXTEEN

Day 6

JAKE ARRIVED back at the dorm just as Corey was waking up, and he felt tired but refreshed. He certainly hadn't slept much the night before, but a deep satisfaction had settled into his bones, and he had enough excitement and adrenaline pumping through his system that he was wide-awake.

Valentin insisted on tagging along to the interview at the TBC studios, which Jake thought was a little strange. Chelsea was warming up at the practice gym for her own run at the all-around, and Valentin should have been there. And yet here he was, in a limo with Jake.

The drive to the International Broadcast Center felt surprisingly long. Jake gazed at the Madrid architecture while Valentin fiddled with his phone, probably texting with the coaching staff to find out how Chelsea was doing.

"I know you think I care more about Chelsea," Valentin said.

"I don't think that."

"You do, and I cannot blame you for that. But I want to show you I love my children equally. I would love you if you never won medals."

Jake sighed. He didn't want to have this conversation. "I know, Dad."

Valentin nodded. Then he said, "When I was boy, my father sent me to gym. I train with Soviet system. I live in gym. I love gymnastics, but that was hard. Some days I hated gymnastics. You and Chelsea, you spent so much time in gym as babies, I think gymnastics got in your blood. But I wanted you to have easier training. Gymnastics should be fun, not like army drills. I worry I still have too much Soviet in me."

Jake stared at his father. Valentin's accent was heavy, but Jake was so used to it, he understood every word. Yet he still had trouble gleaning the meaning of this little speech. Training had been hard, but no harder than for any other elite gymnast, from what Jake could tell. Jake fingered the ribbon from which the medal hung around his neck. Gymnastics required some innate talent, and it helped if one was short and had a certain build, but at the elite level, the difference between even gold and silver often came down to training. And maybe Jake's childhood had been challenging, but it had gotten him where he was now. And he planned to give everything he had to gymnastics until his body gave out.

Which would be soon. Then he had early-onset arthritis to look forward to.

But even as he'd spent hours every day on grueling drills, he'd never wanted for anything. He had two loving parents who were financially comfortable. It had never really occurred to him to want something other than a gymnastics career, and his parents had done everything in their power to support that dream.

"I wouldn't have changed anything," Jake said.

"No?"

"I love gymnastics too. All I've wanted, since I was a little boy, was to win this medal." Jake lifted it and turned it toward Valentin.

"I am so proud of you, Jakob. The most proud a father could be."

Jake wasn't used to this level of praise or emotion from his father, and it made his eyes sting. He wasn't sure how to process this or what to say. He looked out the window and pressed his hand to his forehead. He didn't want to cry again, so he swallowed and said, "Thanks."

"Do you wish sometimes you became skateboarder or runner instead?"

"Skateboarder?" Jake laughed. "No."

"All right. I worry."

"I know. Don't. I'm good." Jake sighed. "I keep thinking about what I will do when I retire."

Valentin nodded. "A few years away yet."

"Maybe."

"You coach juniors. You're good with little ones."

Jake smiled. He appreciated the endorsement, if not the tone in which Valentin delivered it.

When they got to the studio, Jake was on the lookout for Topher, hoping to at least say hello, preferably not with Valentin around. But Jake and Valentin were herded into a greenroom with a few other medal winners from the previous day. Valentin fell into awkward conversation with a fencing coach who had been a fan in the eighties, but she had a hard time understanding him through his accent.

Jake tried to watch the broadcast on a monitor in the corner of the room, but the parade of athletes chatting with, playing games with, or in one case cooking with the hosts of *Wake Up, America!* wasn't actually that interesting. They did pull Topher in to help out with the cooking segment—which made sense, given his celebrity cooking show bona fides—so Jake watched that, but once Topher was off-screen, he lost interest again.

He was about to excuse himself to sneak out of the greenroom and "go to the restroom" on the pretense of tracking down Topher when one of the athletes in the room—Jake thought she was a swimmer—said, "Holy shit. Did you all hear this story about the reporter with the gay dating app?"

Jake balked. "What?"

The swimmer was looking at her phone. "Apparently some tabloid reporter installed a bunch of gay dating apps on his phone to find out how many LGBT athletes are hooking up with each other. He wrote a story without naming names, but he gave enough physical description that it's pretty easy to guess who he's talking about. Which means he just outed a whole bunch of gay athletes."

Jake's heart rate sped up. He glanced at Valentin, who raised an eyebrow. Jake's hand went to his pocket, where his phone rested. He had a gay hookup app on his phone but hadn't used it…. Well, he hadn't hooked up with anyone since he'd been cleared to go back to the gym after last year's concussion. It had been all Olympic training all the time since then. He'd gotten only a brief respite eight months ago; Valentin gave his gymnasts a couple of weeks off around the winter holidays, but the relatives from Odessa had flown in for that whole time. It had been easier to spend time with his cheek-pinching aunt than to explain his absences. He wasn't even sure he had any dating apps on his phone anymore.

So logically he knew that the reporter wouldn't have seen Jake's profile in his search—and Jake's phone had been such madness since he'd won the all-around that he'd hardly looked at it because the sheer number of texts and social media tags had been too much to deal with—and yet he still worried he was logged in and active. He wanted to disable the app right then, but not with everyone in the room staring at him.

He cleared his throat. "That's awful."

"I'm not sure what this article is supposed to prove," the swimmer said. "Some athletes are gay."

Valentin coughed.

Jake sank into the sofa he'd been sitting on. He fingered his medal. He'd been pretty cavalier with Topher, hadn't he? That little video Topher had made was up on the various TBC social media accounts now. Topher had called it plausible deniability—they'd been together at the America House the previous night because they'd been recording the video, not discussing how to sneak out to hook up—but what if someone had spotted them together and made an assumption? What if someone saw him at the hotel last night? As far as Jake knew, no one in the media knew he was gay, and although he had no problem with people knowing, being in a foreign country with a huge international group of people, some of whom were from countries that didn't exactly smile on homosexuality....

Also, if Jake came out, he wanted it to be on his own terms. He didn't want to get outed by some dickhead journalist who thought he had the right to announce it. Jake's sexuality had no relevance to his gymnastics.

Suddenly he felt itchy and unsafe, uncomfortable in the greenroom, where the temperature felt like it had just spiked.

A PA stuck his head in the door and said, "Mirakovitch, you're up in ten. Come with me."

Valentin trailed Jake as he followed the PA out to the set. They were deposited in a little area right off set that had a coffee urn and some cups, so Jake poured himself a cup while he waited for the signal to go on set. He felt so jittery now that it was a real challenge to hold the cup still and not pour coffee everywhere.

"Do we have little time?" Valentin asked quietly. "I want to have word with my son before he goes in front of camera."

The PA shrugged. "Sure. You can talk in the hallway. You have about five minutes. No longer or we have to change the show schedule."

"Da. Come, Jakob."

So Jake followed his father into the hallway.

Valentin looked around, probably noting that no one was there. "Your mother said you have someone you like," he said.

Jake balked. Of course his mother had said something. Lana was a loving mother but a terrible gossip, and there were no secrets between her and her husband. "I… yes, but—"

"Do not be foolish. You heard what woman said in greenroom. Anything can wait until home."

"But Dad—"

Valentin held up his hand. "You stay safe. You win event medals. Do not do anything rash or irresponsible."

"Right. Of course."

"Don't take tone like that with me either."

In Russian, Jake said, "You have to let me have a personal life."

In rapid Russian, Valentin replied, "That's not what this is about. You can date whoever you like. Do I care if you're gay? No, I do not. But if there is a reporter lurking around the Olympic Village trying to make trouble, you cannot let him make it for you. Not now."

Jake sighed. In English, he said, "I won't."

Valentin frowned. "I want you be safe."

And Jake softened a little, because although this irritated him, he understood that this was Valentin's attempt to be a caring father. "Yes. I know."

"Da. Go to your interview."

TOPHER WALKED out of his meeting with Joanna and down the hall to the studio. They'd spent part of the morning recutting the phone footage Topher had gotten the day before to do a package to air on TV that was basically meant to show how much fun he'd been having in Madrid. His assignment for the day was to go with a couple of athletes who had finished their Olympic run to the Market of San Miguel for a goofy segment about shopping. Topher wasn't that excited about it, but he could be a team player.

He heard voices around the corner, so he paused to listen. It was Jake talking to someone with a thick Russian accent, probably his father.

"Do not be foolish," said the Russian man. "You heard what woman said in greenroom. Anything can wait until home."

"But Dad—"

"You stay safe. You win event medals. Do not do anything rash or irresponsible."

"Right. Of course."

"Don't take tone like that with me either."

Then they spoke in Russian. Jake speaking in Russian was incredibly sexy… although that wasn't the point right now. Topher had picked up enough Russian over his years in figure skating that he understood words here and there, but they were speaking so fast, Topher couldn't quite decipher it.

Topher didn't have a chance to intervene, because a PA ran past him and grabbed Jake before taking off down the hallway toward the interview set.

Topher glanced at his watch. He didn't have to be anywhere for another hour. He could stick around to watch Jake do the interview.

He snuck onto the side of the set, still out of Jake's vision, and watched as one of the hosts asked Jake a series of softball questions about how it felt to win. Jake had clearly undergone some media training and answered each question with aplomb, or with a canned answer about how he didn't care about the medal as much as putting in his best possible performance.

The interview was brief, just a segment between commercial breaks on the morning show, and when the director indicated they were breaking for commercial, Jake let out a sigh and got up off the prop sofa.

Topher snagged him on his way back to the greenroom.

"Oh!" Jake looked startled. "I kind of expected I'd see you here, but I wasn't sure."

"Listen, can we talk for a minute?"

"My father is probably waiting for me in the greenroom."

"I know, just… okay, so, I was here earlier and over-heard you and your father talking, and I wanted to… apologize, I guess? I don't want to get you in trouble."

"You didn't."

"But your father said—"

"I know." Jake lowered his voice. "He doesn't know about us. Did you hear this story about the report-er who put a bunch of gay dating apps on his phone and started outing athletes in the Olympic Village? Well, not outing them, since he didn't name names, but any-one with a brain can tell who he's talking about from the context and…."

"I read the story this morning."

"Oh."

And Topher had been just as worked up about it as Jake seemed to be. He was frustrated by the fact that it had been so easy for some reporter to learn so much about the athletes in the Village, and Topher was kind of glad he'd disabled all his apps after playing show-and-tell with Natalie the other night. Sometimes it was easier to just remove everything from his phone because he tended to get harassed. Some gay guys could be in-credible assholes when confronted with a photo of a man wearing lipstick and a feather boa. But Topher didn't figure in this story; as a member of the press, he wasn't allowed in the Athlete Village, and he wasn't in danger from this asshole reporter since he was already out pub-licly. But he'd been that terrified athlete not wanting any-thing to distract from his Olympic dream.

Which was why he said, "I read the story. I'll stay away from you if you need me to."

Jake glanced back down the hall toward the green-room. "No, I…. That is, my father is only looking out for me. He doesn't want anything bad to happen. I just need to get in there and win medals and all that. He… means well. I don't… I don't want you to stay away."

Topher smiled at that. "Right." But Topher had been to two Olympics while he was still in the closet, and the second time he'd been dating an ice dancer from Canada who was never going to win a medal but was sweet as pie all the same. And they'd worked so hard to keep that relationship quiet that it had been rather stressful. That hadn't been the reason Topher had choked at the Games—stress, pressure, his legs turning to jelly at the wrong moment, those had all been factors—but he still knew what it was like to be worried about the wrong thing getting out to the press.

Topher lowered his voice. "I was thinking with my dick, not my brain. I think you are so fucking sexy, and I want to spend all of my time feeling you up. And I kept thinking, if I could just get you alone…." He took a deep breath. "Last night was amazing, but you definitely should spend most of your time focusing on your sport. You need to give everything, one hundred percent, to your next competition. I believe you are the best gymnast in the world, and I need you to prove it, for yourself, if nothing else."

Jake let out a breath. "I just… I mean, first of all I find you insanely attractive too, and I want to be with you, and if you think that most of what's been going on in my mind since last night is not a complicated mathematical equation that will get us alone together again, well, you'd be mistaken." Jake rubbed his forehead. "But on the other hand, now I'm terrified we're going to get caught together, and I can imagine the media circus. Chelsea posted one dumb photo of herself and some swimmer she met the other day, and now there are whole stories on the internet about how they're dating, and I don't think Chelsea can even remember his name."

"I get it, Jake. I was you once, you know."

"I *do* know. It's one of the things I like about you."

The event finals were tomorrow. Topher could wait that long. "Tell you what. I don't want anything to jeopardize your chances at the event finals. So let's not make any plans to see each other until the competition is over. But after that, all bets are off. Sound good?"

Jake appeared to think that over. "I... sure. That's probably a good idea."

Topher smiled. "I know it's—"

Mr. Mirakovitch stuck his head out of the greenroom. "Jakob!" he whisper-shouted.

Jake said something in Russian, then turned back to Topher. "Sorry. That's my cue."

And Topher had to be okay with not seeing Jake for the next forty-eight hours. It was for the best. He knew that. "Good luck with the event finals. Win all the gold medals."

Jake grinned. "I will certainly try."

Once Jake was gone, Topher turned his attention back to the real task at hand, which was doing everything in his power to get his commentary gig. He was about to take a second look at his itinerary for the day when Joanna appeared as if from nowhere.

She pulled out a tablet and showed him the playback from a segment he'd recorded the day before. His hair looked a little flat, but some things were beyond his control. He didn't love how nasal he sounded in the recordings, but he couldn't do much about that either.

"This looks good," Joanna concluded when the video finished. "It'll air during the primetime broadcast tonight."

"Thanks again for that opportunity."

"It adds good color to the broadcast. Viewers love the whole package. They want to see the sports, but a lot of viewers aren't regular fans or only tune in to watch every four years. This will keep them hooked. Your segments have actually been getting a lot of positive feedback."

"Yeah?" Topher was glad to hear that. Natalie had mentioned that she'd seen a lot of social media posts praising TBC for hiring him because he was a fresh voice in the broadcast. In an effort to impress Joanna, he said, "I've gotten a ton of social media response. Not all of it positive, of course, but I think some of it is resonating in a good way."

"Oh, definitely. Most of it."

Something about Joanna's tone made Topher's heart sank. "What is it?"

"I don't want to show you."

"You'd better anyway."

"Come with me to my office."

Joanna's "office" was not much bigger than a closet, but it did have a door that closed, which Joanna did. Topher wedged himself in a corner and looked over Joanna's shoulder at her laptop on the desk that took up most of the usable floor space.

And then there it was: she cascaded her windows to show a dozen headlines referring to Topher as "mincing," "flamboyant," "over-the-top." Joanna sighed. "An organization called Concerned Mothers for the Media wants TBC to pull you."

Topher's heart sank, and he stumbled backward and hit the wall. "Are you serious?"

"You won't be taken off the air. TBC has wrestled with Concerned Mothers before. They wanted us to pull

Nikki Kenmore from *Wake Up, America!* too." Nikki Kenmore read the news on *Wake Up* and happened to be an out lesbian who was an outspoken activist and frequent grand marshal of gay pride parades around the country. She currently wore her hair in a funky semi-mohawk and had a legion of fans. Joanna said, "Please don't change what you're doing, because our ratings are up and the feedback on some of the changes we've made to the broadcast this year—including having you do stories—has been overwhelmingly positive. All my bosses really care about are the numbers. Most of the stories are like that one you saw. But these stories exist. I just thought you should know." Joanna gestured to the laptop.

"Let me see."

It took some maneuvering, but Topher and Joanna switched places so that Topher sat in front of the laptop. He knew what he was about to see would hurt. He took a deep breath to steel himself. Most of the stories were not from mainstream sources but rather conservative media outlets, some of which Topher was familiar with and some he wasn't. The stories were all the same. There was a general theme; Topher played around with gender when he presented himself on-air each day, and even though he identified as a man, some writers found his nail polish and lip gloss threatening. Or that was what Topher read between the lines.

He clicked on another tab and found a forum in which sports fans were making fun of Topher for being so flamboyant. "We're supposed to take this... thing seriously as a sports reporter?" one charming fellow wrote.

It was like every fear Topher ever had manifested right in front of him. His stomach flopped and he broke out in a cold sweat. He pressed a hand to his forehead and made himself look at another tab. This was a figure skating message board in which a young, up-and-coming figure skater Topher knew vaguely actually posted that he hated Topher for being such an obvious stereotype.

"Excuse me," Topher said before sliding past Joanna and running down the hall to the men's room, where he lost his breakfast.

When he came back out, still feeling nauseous and generally terrible, Joanna waited for him with a sympathetic expression. "I'm sorry. I probably should have summed up the stories instead of showing you."

"No, it's not your fault. I wanted to see them. And you're not the one saying these things."

"TBC is no stranger to its commentators getting bad press. Our regular baseball guy, Jack Flynn? There are whole websites dedicated to how much baseball fans hate that guy. But he's got a good voice for commentary and he knows baseball better than anyone in the industry, so he's got a job for life if he wants it. Same for any woman who reports on football. I've seen letters sent to the network about Helen Rogers that say the most vile things I've ever seen. But she's a great reporter, so she keeps her job."

Topher leaned against the wall, trying to get his equilibrium back.

Joanna put her hands on her hips. "I'll vouch for you. I know I can be a hardass, but I like the segments you've done, and I think you're a great fit for the types of viewers we get for sports like gymnastics and figure skating. I was thinking it might be fun to have you do some work on diving next week. Or synchronized swimming, even. That doesn't air in primetime, but I thought it would be interesting to do a segment on just how strong you have to be to hold those poses. On how sports like synchronized swimming look silly to audiences but actually require a lot of athleticism. I thought you might know something about that."

Topher nodded, although it felt a lot like he was being pushed into a box.

"The internet always has shitty things to say about the on-air talent. Feel what you feel about this, but then push it aside, because people will say terrible things about you no matter what you do. But if you can let it roll off your back, and you keep being yourself on-air and doing segments like you've been doing? You've got a job, Topher."

"Primetime at the next Winter Olympics?"

Joanna's expression turned wry. "Well, I don't know about all that yet. But you like this work, don't you?"

"I'd like to talk about my actual area of expertise instead of doing puff pieces. But as far as summer sports go, this has been a pretty fun week."

"Am I an asshole for showing you those stories?"

Topher took a deep breath. "No. I'm glad I saw them. And it's not like I haven't heard this kind of stuff my whole life."

"Is it true that you talked Marc Jacobs into designing one of your skating costumes?"

"Oh, honey. That is a *story*. Let me tell you it." Topher hooked an arm around Joanna's shoulders and steered her toward craft services so he could pilfer a pastry. He didn't feel a lot better, although it was reassuring to know he'd have a job. But he told Joanna his Marc Jacobs story—Marc himself hadn't had time to design a costume, but one of his assistants had in the end, and Topher had hooked up with said assistant,

although he left that out of the story he told Joanna—
and he drank coffee and he tried to remind himself
that he was here to do a job, he was good at it, and he
couldn't let some angry conservatives with websites try
to dim his inner flame.

CHAPTER SEVENTEEN

Day 7

TOPHER'S ASSIGNMENT was to do a segment on each apparatus as a way to explain what each event entailed to the audiences who were, for some reason, only just now tuning into the gymnastics coverage. Apparently Jake's gold medal had suddenly caused interest in men's gymnastics to spike, and the network had liked Topher's work on gymnastics earlier, so here he was. Topher was thrilled to be talking about sports instead of paella, and he wasn't about to complain. Natalie was acting as his expert. They were in the gym a few hours before the men's event finals were supposed to begin, so Topher hoped that Jake was off training or sleeping or… not here.

It was stupid that Topher felt so put out about not seeing a guy for a day. If he'd been home and dating someone, probably a week or more would have gone by without them seeing each other. That seemed pretty normal. Topher was always busy.

But in Madrid, where there wasn't a lot else to do except think about Jake, it felt like a major imposition not to see him.

"You okay?" asked Natalie as the cameraman got into place near the parallel bars.

"Yeah, I'm fine. So, my job is basically just to read off the cue cards, right? I read the script TBC provided, but I didn't memorize it."

"Pretty much, yeah. I think it should be pretty straightforward. The way this will go is that you and I will take turns explaining each apparatus. You're the blue letters on the cue card and I'm the red ones. Then we'll say something that will lead to a clip. TBC will splice it all together after we're done and it will air right before the event finals coverage. Got it?"

"Yup. Let's do this."

A PA held up a cue card. Topher waited for the director to signal *action*; then he read off the card. "We'll start with the parallel bars. Unlike the uneven bars in women's gymnastics, male gymnasts use both bars at the same time and do tricks between them. Each routine we'll see today requires six tricks to demonstrate six different skills. These include gymnasts propelling themselves above the bars and then catching themselves on their upper arms." Topher held up his elbow and slapped his tricep to demonstrate where each man would land. "You'll see many of the gymnasts on this apparatus will wear armbands to keep their arms from scraping or bruising."

Then Natalie broke in and said her spiel.

And so it went, across each apparatus. They'd gotten to the still rings when a few of the American gymnasts tumbled out from the locker room in warm-up clothes.

"You know," Topher said, now that the camera was off, "I always heard 'steel rings,' not 'still rings.' Why are they called that?"

Natalie shrugged. "They're supposed to stay still while the gymnasts are on them? I don't know, actually. That's just what they're called."

Jake and Corey O'Bannon walked out onto the floor. Topher and Jake briefly made eye contact.

So much for not seeing each other.

"Hi!" Jake said brightly.

Jake's enthusiasm was disarming. Topher didn't know what to do with his face. Had Topher not been there for their last conversation, he would have greeted Jake just as happily, but this confused him. Weren't they supposed to be cooling it until after the competition? Was Jake not feeling this awful churn in his gut at seeing the object of his affection but having to pretend like they were strangers? How could Jake be grinning so hard?

Probably because there was a camera over Topher's shoulder.

"Er, how are you, Jake?"

A little wrinkle appeared between Jake's eyebrows for the briefest of moments. Then he smiled again and said, "Need any help?"

"Do you have anything to say about the still rings?"

The camera guy was clearly eating this up. Jake grinned and launched into a spiel about the rings that was laden with gymnastics-related slang. Topher couldn't really follow it, but he didn't need to. The fans would probably enjoy something like this, especially since Jake was in such a good mood. When the director called cut, someone said they were moving over to the high bar. The equipment left, and Natalie followed, but Topher lingered for a moment.

"Did they spike your green juice with cocaine or something?" Topher asked. "You're in an awfully good mood."

"Part of that was for the camera, but I actually do feel pretty good. I had an excellent warm-up this morning. I feel strong. I'm ready to get this done."

Across the mats, a British gymnast in his official British uniform did a tumbling pass on the floor, and when he landed it, he let out a triumphant, masculine yell.

"Lot of testosterone in this room," Topher observed.

"You have all this pent-up energy and adrenaline after you nail a routine. For some of these guys, the adrenaline takes over and they need an outlet for it. I've tried to tamp it down. Earlier in my career, I used to shout a lot when I stuck my landings, but my coach has been working to train that out of me. Dad thinks it's undignified." Jake rolled his eyes.

Topher nodded and made a mental note to track down videos of Jake sticking his landings on YouTube when he got back to his hotel later.

Jake's good mood was infectious, so Topher said, "There aren't a lot of he-men in figure skating. I mean, you get an Elvis Stojko every now and then who is all swagger and quad jumps, and there's been this movement to make skating more technical and athletic and less artistic, but if you're over a certain weight, it's pretty tough to get yourself high enough off the ice to complete the rotations. We haven't figured out how to defy gravity just yet."

Jake nodded. "Well, we're pretty brutish over here in Gymnastics Land." He affected a he-man pose and stuck his lower jaw out so that his teeth overlapped his top lip. He grunted and flexed his muscles—good Lord he had strong arms—and stomped around. He looked so ridiculous that Topher laughed.

"Christopher!" Natalie called from the high bar, in her best mom voice.

"That's my cue. I'll see you later, Jake. Good luck today."

"Will you be watching?"

"I think so, yeah. I mean, I still have to film some stuff for the network, but I will watch if I can."

"Cool. I'll see you later."

Topher watched Jake walk back toward his teammates. He wasn't entirely sure what had just happened, but he shrugged and walked over to Natalie.

ALEXEI DID not look pleased.

Jake tried to think back on whether he'd done anything wrong. He didn't think he'd touched Topher or otherwise given any indication that they wanted to get into each other's pants. He glanced back over his shoulder at where Topher was filming a segment for the network. Topher was wearing an iridescent purple T-shirt and a pair of very tight black jeans, but really, he wasn't dressed quite as extravagantly as usual. His hair was done up in the usual pompadour, though, and he'd been wearing mascara and electric blue eyeshadow.

Jake cleared his throat and looked back at Alexei. Corey stood behind him and raised an eyebrow.

Fantastic. He was totally busted.

"You befriend the…" Alexei held his hand in the air as if he were trying to pluck a word out of it. "…crazy reporter."

"We're a little friendly, yes. He interviewed me for TBC the other day. He's a nice guy."

"Your father says… well. We focus on gymnastics now."

"Of course."

Behind Alexei, Corey made a duck-quacking motion with his hand and rolled his eyes. Jake pressed his lips together so he wouldn't laugh.

Alexei had the schedule and rattled off the order Jake would do each apparatus. Jake tried to mentally inventory his gym bag, which he just realized was still in the locker room and not on one of the benches. And he thought the shorts that went with the official leotard he had to wear today were in his locker. He still had to change for the competition and do a bunch of premeet stuff too.

"Focus." Alexei snapped his fingers in front of Jake's face. "No thinking about flowery men."

Jake took this to mean that he shouldn't be thinking about flamboyant men like Topher. "I'm not. I'm trying to remember what I did with my red shorts."

"Good. Because Valentin and I had discussion this morning about what trouble you could get into before finals today. Something about a reporter who is trying to find gay athletes."

"He didn't find me," Jake growled, slipping into Russian. "And I told Dad and will tell you now that I'm fine. I'm focused on the events today. I'm not trying to get involved with anyone here while I'm still competing. How would I even date anyone? All I ever do is train."

"No sarcasm." Alexei held up a finger to Jake. "You do nothing that will take away from your training. You still have medals to win." Then he turned on his heel and walked back to the locker room.

Jake took off after him. "I won't forever, you know!" he shouted in English.

Alexei stopped and turn around. "No. You won't. Your career… it is not forever. But while you are training, while you are under my watch, no funny business. You hear me?" He added in Russian, "No men."

Jake realized that the red on Alexei's face indicated that perhaps Alexei didn't want Jake to be with men… ever. Jake had never had a conversation with any of his coaches about his sexuality because it didn't seem relevant, but everyone at the Mirakovitch gym knew. Jake had always assumed Alexei was okay with it, but maybe that was only true as long as Jake was doing gymnastics.

"Of course," Jake said, trying to sound chastened. Although, in truth, he was more determined than ever to hook up with Topher again before he left Madrid. They'd promised not to see each other until he was done competing, but when Jake had seen Topher standing next to the still rings, he'd gotten excited and hadn't been able to hold in his happiness.

Well, whatever. Jake shook it off and followed Alexei back into the locker room. "I didn't mean anything by talking to Topher. I was just being friendly. Got myself a little bit of publicity with the network. That's good, right?"

"Yes. Be careful."

"I will. I'm always careful."

Alexei grunted. He went ahead and opened Jake's locker, because of course he had the combination. He rifled through the clothes Jake had left there and came up with his red shorts. "You need these, yes?" Then he stalked off.

"Who pissed in his cornflakes this morning?" Corey asked, walking up to his own locker, three down from Jake's.

"Precompetition nerves?"

Corey shrugged and opened his locker. Quietly he said, "Is he mad about you and the figure skater?"

Jake sighed. "Maybe. It doesn't matter. Alexei is mad about… I don't even know. I guess he just doesn't want me to get distracted."

Corey, who was halfway through changing into his competition uniform, stopped what he was doing and tilted his head. "You know what? I think a little distraction is good."

Jake pulled off his T-shirt and tossed it in the locker. "What do you mean?"

"Three days ago, you not only performed well, you won a fucking gold medal. Hell, I finished the best I've ever finished in a World Cup. I've been thinking a lot about what might have happened. And I think a big thing is that you really led the team this year. You finally got your shit together. We all watched you kill it and thought maybe we could kill it too. For once we didn't fuck everything up. So how did you do it?"

Jake shrugged. "I got a good pep talk, I guess."

Corey shook his head. "No. I don't think that's it. I think you met *him*." Corey pointed toward the locker room door, in the direction of the main arena. "And I think he *was* a distraction, but in the best possible way. He helped you get out of your own way. Your head has been in the clouds all week, and I think it's because you're thinking about him instead of saltos and tumbling passes. Which means that your muscle memory can take over and you're able to do what you've practiced instead of trying to force it. I honestly think *that's* why you won that gold medal."

"Really?"

"Jake, I…." Corey paused to wriggle into his uniform. Then he turned toward Jake and put a hand on his shoulder. "You're my best friend. I love you like a brother. And I know how hard you work. I'd be willing to bet there is no single gymnast on Planet Earth, not even your sister, who trains as hard as you do, who puts in as many hours as you do. That's why you're the best in the world. But it's also why you've been really lonely. You never talk about it, but I know it. I see it. If this guy brings you happiness, even if it's only for a few days, I think you should grab on to it. Live your life. Have a crazy week after the rest of us go home. Enjoy the spoils of victory!"

Jake laughed because he couldn't think too hard about what Corey was saying, didn't want to face his own loneliness. "Spoils of victory?"

Corey rolled his eyes and stepped back toward his own locker. "You know what I mean. Don't make fun of me. I'm trying to have a heart-to-heart moment with you here."

"I'm sorry. Thank you. And maybe you're right. I thought about him during the last rotation of the all-around instead of my P-bars routine. It was a strange moment."

"Maybe Brad has the right of it. He puts himself through all this for other people in his life."

"Yeah?"

"I mean, I could go forever without seeing another picture of that baby, but ever since he got married, he's seemed a lot more zen. Remember what he was like when we were kids? He's calmed down so much."

Jake did remember. Brad had been one of those guys Jake had mentioned to Topher who had been all pent-up testosterone. But Corey was right; ever since Brad had met his wife, he'd mellowed out.

"I guess I never thought of it that way," Jake said. "Dad and Alexei are always telling me not to get distracted, that I have to focus, so that's what I do."

"Coaches don't know everything."

Jake mulled that over as he finished changing. Corey was probably right; having something else to focus on had kept Jake out of his own head, which, in turn, had kept him from getting too insanely nervous. He was still nervous—he felt tightness creeping into his muscles now and his heart was starting to flutter in anticipation of the competition, as it always did—but he'd also already won two medals this week. He was the best gymnast in the world. Even if he fell off an apparatus now, it didn't matter; he'd already proven himself. And Topher would be waiting for him when it was all over.

Some of the happiness he'd felt after his warm-up filled up the spaces where his competition-related anxiety usually resided.

He could do this. Hell, he *had* done this.

He smiled to himself. Then he closed his locker and said, "Thanks, Corey."

"Anytime. Win some medals today, okay?"

"You too."

"I'm gonna try."

Jake laughed, unable to help himself now. "Do, or do not. There is no try."

"If we're quoting Yoda before heading to the floor, I think we're going to be okay."

Corey finished changing and hoisted his bag over his shoulder, so Jake did the same. They high-fived. Then they walked out to meet their destiny.

Chapter Eighteen

TOPHER WRAPPED up his work for the network. Natalie had to go call the live broadcast, and no one had anything else for him to do that day, so Topher wrangled a seat in the stands and settled in to watch Jake rake up more medals.

Jake was on parallel bars first. Topher had to sit through three other gymnasts—one of whom looked fantastic until he completely biffed the landing, nearly falling on his ass before catching himself and standing up straight—before Jake walked up and stuck his hands in the bin with the chalk. As Jake chalked up, one of his coaches came over and said something to him. Topher, of course, couldn't hear a word they said, but it was probably some coach-y advice. Jake nodded absently, listening; then he clapped his hands together and sent a cloud of chalk into the air.

Jake stood between the parallel bars. Because of the camera angle on the Jumbotron and Topher's position

in the stands, he couldn't see Jake's face, but the way
he squared his shoulders made him seem determined.
He walked between the bars, paused for a moment, then
grabbed both bars. He lifted himself right into a tuck,
throwing himself over the bar and then catching himself on his upper arms.

Because this was the event finals, there was only
one apparatus in use at a time, and everyone's attention was trained on the parallel bars. Jake made a series
of what looked, to Topher's untrained eye, like long,
smooth movements, handstands that easily transitioned
into somersaults and flips Jake caught as if doing them
was the easiest thing in the world. On the sidelines, the
other athletes—and not even just the Americans—cried
out "Yeah!" and "Come on, Jake!" whenever Jake did
a trick well. The audience oohed and ahhed, everyone
on the edges of their seats. Jake launched himself into
the air, flipping over the bars, and then he caught himself, shifted his arms, and did it again. The height he
got over the bars was nothing short of astonishing—
and explained all those muscles on Jake's arms—and
it was absolutely beautiful to watch. Then Jake did one
last flip, hurled his body over the side of the bars, and
landed just to the left. His arms did kind of a pinwheel
thing after he landed, but his feet didn't move once they
hit the mat. Jake stood up, posed for the judges, then
clapped once and ran off the mat.

He'd nailed it, as far as Topher could tell.

The score was high, but Topher still had to watch
four more athletes, wondering the whole time if any
of them could top Jake's monster score. A gymnast
from Japan was basically perfect and took first; then a
British gymnast came along and there was a nail-biting

moment before his score was posted and he pushed Jake down to third.

Still, a bronze medal was no joke, and Jake had to have been happy with his performance. He'd earned a huge score, he hadn't made any major mistakes, and he still had a few more opportunities to earn gold.

A dais was immediately rolled out and the top three gymnasts were herded over to it. Topher stood as the Japanese national anthem played and watched as Jake stood with a bronze medal around his neck, staring at the flags as if he didn't know where he was.

Then he was sent over to the vault.

As Topher had just explained to a camera, each finalist had to do two vaults in different styles, which Topher understood to mean that they couldn't do the same tricks. Hayden Croft from the American team was also in the vault final. He and Jake conferred with each other on the sidelines, and the men's team coach, Viktor, walked over to speak with them also.

The vault final was over in a blink. Each vaulter ran down the… runway and flipped over the vault table twice. Hayden, it turned out, was the one to beat; he vaulted second, got huge height off the table, and stuck both of his landings. The other finalists chased his score the entire event. Jake was up seventh, and his first vault was beautiful, but in the second, he hopped big enough for Topher to see it from the stands.

So when, again, the dais was wheeled out, the American anthem played, with Hayden standing on top of the podium and Jake with another bronze medal. This time Topher stood and hummed along with the anthem.

Jake got to sit the rings final out, but Corey O'Bannon was up. Corey posted a very high score early in the competition but got edged out by a gymnast from Ukraine in the end, winning silver.

Topher couldn't help but marvel at how well this team was doing. He'd learned a lot about the usual fate of US men's gymnastics. He knew the athletes had a reputation for choking at the Olympics. Jake's concussion during World Championships hadn't helped it. And Natalie had mentioned, when they talked about the floor exercise for the cameras, that Brad had the most difficult routine but often lost points by tumbling out of bounds. It said something about how much this team had trained and how badly they wanted it that Brad only stepped out of bounds once during the floor final but was otherwise perfect as far as Topher could tell, putting him in silver medal position.

But here came Jake again.

Topher wanted him to rake in medals, to earn everything he'd been working his whole life for but that his body had denied him. And suddenly Topher was mentally at his last Olympics, after having done a perfect short program, feeling strong and confident before the long program. He'd landed that quad jump a hundred times in practice. He'd been landing it all week. He'd landed it in the warm-up.

And then his toe pick had hit the ice on his way into the air and he'd completely lost control of the jump. Before he knew what was happening, he'd landed on his ass on the ice.

And then here was Jake, running across the floor, throwing his body into a tumbling pass, then doing some little dance moves across the apparatus, getting the audience really into it. There wasn't music—not like there was for the women's competition—but clearly some song played in Jake's head.

Topher relaxed. Floor seemed pretty safe. Nothing high to fall off of, no handstands on narrow bars; all Jake had to do was tumble and stay in bounds.

Jake stood at the corner of the apparatus and took a deep breath. He ran across half the floor, then launched into a tumbling pass, throwing his body up in the air. And then the last flip....

He lost his footing.

Seeing Jake make a mistake was such a surprise, Topher didn't realize the full extent of what he'd seen until he realized Jake was sitting with his leg at an odd angle. The camera that fed the image to the JumboTron zoomed in on his face, and it was clear that Jake felt an immense amount of pain.

Topher's heart fell to his stomach. Jake was clearly hurt. But how bad was it?

The American coaching staff ran at him, and after consulting with each other for a few moments, they helped him up and escorted him off the floor. There was clapping as Jake gave a gritted-teeth wave to the audience.

What the hell had happened?

The coaches helped Jake onto a bench, where he winced as he sat and gestured at his foot. A medic ran out and attended to him. All proceedings in the arena had stopped.

It wasn't a life-threatening injury, but it likely hurt in more ways than one. Jake still had one more event final. This must be devastating for him.

The competition got back up and running, but Topher's attention remained on Jake, who was having a heated conversation with his coaches and the medic. Then another person ran over; Topher recognized him as a TBC reporter.

Topher waited for the event to finish and for Jake to be carried toward the locker room before he texted Natalie.

Do u know is Jake ok?

Natalie texted back: *We heard sprained ankle.*

Well, that wasn't so bad.

The medal ceremony for floor carried on, with Brad earning a silver medal, as did the pommel horse final, in which Jordan earned a bronze. But Topher hardly paid attention and fretted about Jake instead. Then Natalie texted again:

Jake has not withdrawn from his last final. Reporter asked if he was going to, and he said no.

Only the high bar remained. Topher responded, *He could wreck his ankle in the landing.*

After a beat Natalie responded, *Would that stop you?*

Topher took half a second to mull that over. No, it wouldn't have. At his last Olympics, when he'd been performing at the same level Jake was? No, Topher would have gone out on the ice even if every bone in his body had been broken. Because that was what competition was like at this level. One pushed one's body as far as it would go.

The high bar final was next. Topher scooted forward to sit on the edge of his seat.

JAKE'S ANKLE screamed. Dr. Ruiz wrapped it as Alexei spoke in rapid-fire Russian at Jake, most of it fretting but all of it boiling down to Jake's Olympic career being over.

"It's a sprain," Jake said.

"On foot with torn Achilles," Alexei argued in halting English.

Ah, yes. One of Jake's more glorious moments. At a World Cup meet five years before, he'd pulled a Kerri Strug and torn his Achilles landing a vault at the end of the team competition. Except unlike Kerri Strug, Jake had gone down on the mat and hadn't had the opportunity to do the vault again. Landing badly enough to tear one's Achilles tendon was a lot of deductions, it turned out, and his injury had cost the team a medal.

Because that was Jake's pattern, wasn't it? He did everything perfectly until fate and his body got in the way and he fucked up. He'd been feeling too good; he should have known it was only a matter of time before his old patterns asserted themselves.

On the other hand, he'd gotten this far, hadn't he? Four Olympic medals. One more event. Was he really going to let a stupid mistake derail the whole meet?

No. No he fucking was not.

"I don't need my ankle for high bar."

"You need it to land," said Alexei.

Jake's father ran into the locker room then. "Is it Achilles?"

Jake sighed. "I sprained my ankle. Landed that last tumbling pass on the side of my foot like an idiot."

"You are not idiot," said Valentin. He peered over the medic's shoulder. "Swelling?"

"Yes," said the random medic helping out Dr. Ruiz. "You are?"

"I'm his father. Jakob, did you withdraw from high bar?"

"No. I'm doing the modified Tkatchev."

Valentin shook his head. "No. You are crazy."

That was about when Jake lost it. Dr. Ruiz seemed to sense what was coming, and he stood up and took a step away, motioning for the other medic to follow.

Jake hopped up and stood on one foot. Addressing everyone hovering over him like mother hens, he said, "Look. Let's face facts here. I'm getting to be old for a gymnast. This is my last Olympics. I won't be able to live with myself if I can't finish the competition. It's an ankle sprain. It hurts, but I've sprained plenty of other things. It doesn't hurt as bad as a torn Achilles or a broken bone or a concussion. It'll be fine. I'm going out there to do the high bar final. This is my last shot. None of you can stop me." He pointed toward the door to the arena to emphasize his point.

Valentin looked horrified. "You'll break bones."

"I won't. Doc, put a splint on it or something, will you?" he asked Dr. Ruiz before turning back to his father. "But I'm going to go out there and win a gold medal in high bar, or else die trying." Jake looked Valentin up and down. "Isn't this what you want?"

"I want you to win, but not to hurt yourself."

"You know as well as anyone that you can do a thing well a hundred times and then totally fuck it up on the hundred and first time."

Valentin growled. "Language, Jakob."

"I landed wrong on a tumbling pass I've done literally hundreds of times without error. That's how the Olympics goes. That's how *my whole career* has gone. But I'm done with that. This is my last chance to win a gold medal, and I'll be damned if I'm going to let it pass me by. I'm going out there. Try and stop me."

As Dr. Ruiz finished wrapping his foot, Jake grabbed the crutches that had been left propped up against a row of lockers. He'd had enough foot and leg injuries over the years that he had some facility with crutches, so he hurled himself back to the arena with Alexei, Viktor, and Valentin on his heels.

The audience cheered when Jake emerged.

Valentin wasn't even supposed to be out here, since he was the women's coach and not officially affiliated with the men's team, but apparently security recognized him, and of course, he was Valentin Mirakovitch. Gold-medal winner. Legend. He could do whatever he wanted.

Jake was sick of the Mirakovitch shadow. He was tired of trying to prove he was as good as Valentin, as good as Chelsea. He *was* as good. And he would prove it, even if he could never do gymnastics again.

One of the officials ran over. In a French accent, he said, "You are withdrawing."

"No. I'm doing my high bar routine."

Apparently Jake's tone was assertive enough to make the official back off.

Jake was the best all-around gymnast in the world, and high bar was his best event. He'd be damned if he sat on the sidelines during the final, sprained ankle or no.

When his turn came, he hopped on one foot over to chalk up. He spared a thought for Topher, likely sitting in the stands somewhere, hopefully watching this. Because he was about to see something spectacular.

Jake was done holding back. He was going to win this gold medal. Then he was going to make out with Topher because he could. And if anyone thought Jake's homosexuality somehow tainted his medals, well, fuck them, because Jake was here, he was queer, and this goddamn medal was his.

He chalked up, clapped his hands together a couple of times, and hopped over to the bar.

He felt like he'd fallen into some kind of fugue state, like he'd floated out of his body. He'd done this routine a hundred times just this week. The only thing he had to think about was swapping out one of his re-lease moves to do his modified Tkatchev instead.

He waited until Alexei ran over. "You're sure?"

"Yes. I'm doing this. Help me up."

Alexei grabbed his waist and lifted him up to the bar, which Jake grabbed like a lifeline. He got right into the routine. He rolled around the bar twice, then pushed up off it, flipped in the air, added the twist, jackknifed his legs, and caught the bar between his knees.

He'd nailed it. He'd done his most difficult release move cleanly. Distantly, he heard the crowd cheer.

He finished the routine on autopilot, then did an extra turn before the dismount, because suddenly he was afraid to land on his bum ankle. But then he caught Valentin watching out of the corner of his eye and was suddenly determined.

He could do this. It would hurt like hell, but he could do it.

He launched himself off the bar, stretched out his body, flipped in the air, spotted his landing, and put his fucking feet down on the fucking mat.

Boom. Stuck. Done.

As he straightened and raised his arms, pain radiated up his leg. He didn't care.

Nothing else mattered. He'd gone out there, put every last bit of strength and willpower he'd had into that routine, and he would leave Madrid with no regrets. If he won gold, if he won nothing, it wouldn't matter, because there was nothing more he could have done.

And now the entire lower half of his right leg felt like it had shattered.

He hopped over to the sidelines on his left foot and let Alexei and Viktor help him down.

Valentin was still there too. And he was crying.

What was even happening right now?

Before Jake could answer that question, he was folded up in Valentin's arms. In Russian, Valentin said, "I am very proud of you, my son. Very proud."

"How is ankle?" asked Alexei.

"Hurts like a mother."

Valentin helped Jake sit back on the bench. Dr. Ruiz appeared again, this time with a stool on which to elevate the bad ankle. He took the wrap off and examined Jake's ankle. "We should really get this X-rayed to make sure you didn't damage it further."

"After I get my medal," said Jake.

Jake let Dr. Ruiz and Valentin fret over him while he waited for the last two gymnasts to go. Jake was in first place by a wide margin; not only had his routine had the highest degree of difficulty, but he'd stuck it, with only a few tiny deductions. And apparently that had been enough to intimidate the last two gymnasts, both of whom were normally at the top of their game, but they both made major errors in their routines.

So there it was: gold medal on high bar.

When the final results were announced, Jake stood up on one foot and waved at the audience.

He had no regrets. He let Valentin bully him into using the crutches to get himself over to the podium, and he let the emotional pod person who had taken over the otherwise stoic body of Valentin Mirakovitch hug him a lot more; then he propelled himself over to the dais to accept his much-deserved gold medal.

CHAPTER NINETEEN

JAKE WANTED to have sex.

The team was celebrating at America House, but Jake was on some pretty heavy painkillers and had to sit at a booth with his ankle elevated, so he couldn't have anything to drink. But he didn't need his ankle for sex, so he texted Topher: *They won't let me have alcohol.*

Tragic! Topher texted back.

I don't want to be at this party if I can't drink. Do you know what I want?

Topher texted back a bunch of question marks.

So Jake texted, *Sex. With you.*

Yes, please!

Jake grinned and tried to come up with a scheme. Maybe he could get a cab to Topher's hotel. Maybe he could sneak Topher into the Athlete Village. Maybe he could—

If you're serious, I'm on my way to my hotel now.

I'm going to try to sneak out of here.

Then, just for fun, he sent Topher an eggplant and peach emoji. That should make his intentions clear.

He had all this energy he couldn't do anything with, adrenaline from winning and frustration with being stuck sitting in one place. Chelsea brought him a ginger ale with an apologetic smile, and Jake sipped it resentfully.

"Why are you scowling?" she asked, sliding into the booth seat across the table from Jake. "You won three medals today."

"Haha."

"Does your ankle hurt?"

Jake eyed her glass. It could have been seltzer, or it could have been a vodka soda, and Jake would never know. He raised an eyebrow at her. "It's not bad now, but I've got enough painkillers in me to kill a rhino."

Chelsea laughed. "You don't need alcohol if they gave you the good drugs."

Jake sighed. "I *am* happy. The gold medal hasn't quite sunk in, but holy shit, I can't believe I did that."

"How much more did you fuck up your ankle on the landing?"

"A lot. Tore a ligament."

Chelsea gave him a sympathetic grimace. "Been there. Could have been worse."

"Oh, I've hurt myself worse. It hurt like a mother to land on it, but not like the time I tore my Achilles. Or the time I broke my wrist." That one had been in competition, of course. He'd done a Tkatchev over the high bar and missed the catch. His wrist had broken his fall when he'd hit the mat, and several bones in it had shattered. That had taken him out of competition for the rest of that season. Over the years he'd also broken a few ribs, pulled a few muscles, and hit his head enough that his doctor had tried to talk him out of coming to the Olympics, worried one more concussion would cause permanent damage.

But if a torn ligament couldn't talk Jake out of his Olympic moment, nothing could.

He thought back to what Isaac Flood had told him. Jake had given the competition everything. He had no regrets.

Well, he regretted the torn ligament insofar as he was currently trapped in this booth and not having sex with Topher.

Valentin walked over, exactly the person Jake wanted to see when he was thinking about sex. He tried not to roll his eyes.

"How is foot?"

"It's fine."

Valentin nodded. "You need rest. You too, Chelsea. Your event finals are tomorrow."

Chelsea rolled her eyes. "As if I'd forget."

"I gave you a run for your money," Jake said, tilting his ginger ale toward her.

"Guess I'll have to win *every* final."

Jake grunted at that. The "anything you can do, I can do better" routine had been cute when they were kids, but as his foot throbbed, Jake was reminded—again—that Chelsea would always be better. She had more success, more talent, more of their parents' love.

Leave it to his family to make him feel awful in his moment of triumph. Jake put a hand over his eyes, which unfortunately did not actually make them disappear.

"What did doctor say about treatment?" Valentin asked. When Jake peeked through his fingers, Valentin pointed to Jake's foot.

Jake shrugged. The question struck Jake as odd; Valentin had torn a few ligaments in his day. He knew how this went. "Not a ton you can do. Ice it and keep off it."

"No ice now."

"The ice pack I got at the hospital melted. It's not like I can get up and ask for more ice."

Valentin stared at Jake's foot for a beat, then walked away.

Jake sighed and looked up at the television. Just like any sports bar in the States, all four televisions were tuned in to either TBC, TBC Sports, or the live feeds of whichever sport was happening at that moment. Competition was done for the day now, though, so most of the TVs were showing footage from earlier in the day. The TV closest to Jake showed the TBC late night coverage, which was basically just a talk show with clips. Maybe it was the drugs clouding his brain, but Jake wasted a few minutes trying to figure out if this was the live footage of what would be aired in the States later because of the time difference, and then he tried to figure out what time it was in Texas, but there was too much math involved.

And, oh, there was Topher on screen. White text appeared in the corner and indicated this *was* previously recorded, but Topher—pompadour hair, eyeliner, glittery nail polish, hot pink feather boa, so unapologetically himself that Jake wanted to reach through the television to touch him—sat there and gave some kind of introduction to a video package of himself touring around Madrid with athletes identified as a rower and a weightlifter.

"He's an interesting guy, huh?" said Chelsea.

Jake didn't say anything.

Whispering, Chelsea said, "You're so butch. I imagined you would be attracted to guys who look more like you than like him."

Jake was briefly offended on Topher's behalf, but he realized Chelsea meant well. "I can't explain it. I really like him." Topher was just so... beautiful. Charismatic. Whenever he was near—or on television—Jake couldn't peel his gaze away. Topher was magnetic.

And he was absolutely fucking sexy too. It was the little things. A close-up of his face on screen revealed a sheen of lip gloss on his perfect, kissable lips. He had impossibly long eyelashes, blue eyes that glittered in the harsh lights of the studio, a little birthmark near his eye that made his face even more interesting. The camera panned back again, and the wide shot highlighted how smooth and graceful each of Topher's movements were—years and years of figure skating being the cause, no doubt—and his body was lithe but strong. Jake wanted to touch him everywhere.

He'd had the opportunity once, but it hadn't been enough.

On-screen, Topher wrapped up his segment, and then the host turned toward the camera and started talking. The official gymnastics symbol popped up on-screen, and Jake braced himself for what he knew was coming. There'd be some fawning piece about Chelsea, no doubt. It was just as well that the sound was muted in favor of the classic rock playing over the speakers, because Jake wasn't in the mood to hear it.

Except, no, there was Jake on screen, launching into the tumbling pass, under-rotating, and then the worst thing that could happen: his feet slid right out from under him—he'd hit the landing on the corner of his heel because he hadn't quite gotten all the way around that last flip—and Jake flailing before he hit the mat. That sprain had really only weakened and aggravated him. He watched himself be escorted off the floor apparatus, hopping across the mat, his pride hurt more than anything.

Because, God, he could do everything right, and then undo it in an instant, landing badly on a tumbling pass he'd done successfully literally hundreds of times.

Spraining his ankle hurt, but it wasn't anything compared to… oh, hey, here was the next clip.

On-screen, Jake did his high bar routine, threw in the modified Tkatchev because what did he have to lose at that point? It looked amazing and he'd gotten incredible height above the bar, enough that he impressed even his own harsh inner critic—and then he stuck the goddamned landing. Pain radiated up his leg now at the memory of how it had felt when his feet hit the mat, at once the greatest moment of his life and one of the most physically painful.

"You did that," Chelsea said, pointing to the screen.

"I did."

Corey walked over and motioned for Chelsea to move over before he dropped into the booth next to her, since Jake couldn't exactly move over to let him sit.

"How's the foot?" Corey asked.

Jake sighed.

"He's sulking," Chelsea said.

"I am not!"

Corey laughed. "Sorry about what happened. I don't know if you noticed, though, but that extra weight around your neck is all the medals you won today."

"I know, just… this is not how I pictured myself celebrating."

"He wants alcohol," Chelsea told Corey. "But he's on pain meds."

"We'll celebrate properly when we're back home," said Corey. "I'll be your wingman at that gay bar in Montrose and talk cute boys into buying you drinks. How does that sound?"

It sounded pretty good, actually, but Jake made a show of being pissy and said, "Oh, all right."

"Can I come?" asked Chelsea.

"Turn twenty-one first," said Jake.

"Hmph." Chelsea glanced at the TV. Some bit of understanding passed over her face, but she shrugged it off.

"Actually, there's a bar downtown that's all ages on Thursdays," said Corey.

"Don't encourage her," said Jake.

"Your brother and I used to sneak out at night to go to this place. It was kind of equal opportunity there—whoever you wanted to make out with. Girls, boys, anyone. Jake lost his virginity to a guy we met there."

"Ew!" said Chelsea at the same time Jake said, "Dude!"

"TMI, Corey," said Chelsea.

"Just saying," said Corey. "Or, forget Jake, I'll happily escort you there myself."

"Over my dead body," said Jake. "You touch her and I will throat-punch you."

Corey held his hands up. "It's not like that. You know I love Chels like a sister."

Chelsea grinned. "I don't know if you knew this, but until Jake pulled that Kerri Strug move today and landed his high bar routine despite a sprained ankle, I was the most famous gymnast in the world. I don't see myself having a problem finding someone to make out with. Jake, though...."

"Oh, here we go," said Jake.

"I saw your ankle, buddy." To Chelsea, Corey added, "It swelled up like a grapefruit." He mimed holding a sphere big enough to be a basketball. "That's not sexy."

"Fuck off."

"I told you he was sulking," said Chelsea.

"Leave me to my suffering."

"No such luck," said Corey. He looked up at the TV. "Are they just going to keep showing you sticking that landing on a loop?"

"It was pretty great, wasn't it?" Chelsea asked.

"It was. I'm proud of you, Jake."

Jake scanned the room for his father, who was standing at the bar chatting with one of the gymnasts from the women's team instead of being over here, helping Jake. Valentin had been proud of Jake, or so he'd said, but that was clearly short-lived.

In his peripheral vision, Jake saw Chelsea and Corey follow his gaze. Corey pressed his lips together, probably because he was familiar with Jake's status as the second-best Mirakovitch child.

"I know what's going on here," Corey said. "You do a thing spectacularly a hundred times, but the one time you fuck it up is the one that sticks with you."

"Look, Jake," said Chelsea, "I don't care how many medals you have. I don't care if you're the most famous gymnast in the world or the most obscure.

You're my brother, and I love you. And what you did today was something really special. You pushed past that injury and got your routine done, even though I'm sure you were in a lot of pain. I'm not sure *I* could have done what you did today."

"You don't generally injure yourself in competition."

"No, but… you remember that World Cup when I missed the high bar and landed on my ass?"

Jake did remember. He nodded. But Corey said, "What happened?"

"I broke my tailbone, of all the dumb things." She turned back to Jake. "I dropped out of the competition rather than try to finish it. And, like, I broke my radius falling off the balance beam in practice once, so I'm no stranger to injuries either. But it never occurred to me to push through the pain and finish the competition. There'd be another after I healed."

"This is probably it, you know," Jake said. "There probably won't be another chance for me. Definitely not another Olympics. So I had to finish this one."

Chelsea nodded. She opened her mouth to say something, but then Valentin appeared at the table again, this time holding a towel and a plastic baggie full of crushed ice. "Ice for foot," he said as he examined Jake's foot. He wrapped the towel around the baggie and placed it on the injured part of Jake's leg.

The gesture struck Jake as so odd that he didn't know what to do with it. "You got ice for me?"

"Of course. Best treatment for torn ligament is ice. I want you to recover quickly."

"So I can get back in the gym?"

"So you don't hurt anymore."

Oh.

"Thanks, Dad."

The clip rolled on TV again and Valentin watched it. He turned back to Jake and said, "I'm sorry you got hurt, but I am proud of what you did today."

"Sit, Mr. Mirakovitch," said Corey, shoving Chelsea over in the booth to make more room.

And Jake's father sat. Jake glanced at his phone, at a *Hey, r u coming?* text from Topher, and he mourned the fact that he would not be coming inside Topher anytime soon. Then he turned his phone over and focused on having a drink with his father, his sister, and his best friend. They meant well, and he loved them. What had he been thinking? It wasn't like he could go anywhere without help anyway. So he smiled and tried to push Topher out of his mind.

TOPHER DEBATED how much of himself to strip off in anticipation of Jake arriving at the hotel. He hung the feather boa in the closet and washed his face; then he combed his hair back into place, although he'd be willing to bet it wouldn't last. He changed out of his on-air costume and slipped into a white T-shirt with a bit of iridescent sheen to it and a pair of black skinny jeans. He cupped himself, already hard picturing what he and Jake would do together.

While he waited, he flipped on the TV. The Spanish network covering the Games showed highlights from the day. Topher's knowledge of Spanish was rudimentary at best, but it didn't matter, because the package consisted of mostly images. The Spanish soccer team remained undefeated, a Spanish fencer had won a gold medal, a Spanish swimmer had won a bronze, the Chinese were currently ahead in the medal count, and the men's gymnastics event finals had finished up.

And there was Jake, the clear highlight of the day, landing his tumbling pass badly, spraining his ankle, but going on to win gold in the high bar.

Jake really was remarkable. He had that boy-next-door quality, albeit with messy brown hair and square jaw and bulging muscles. Those muscles strained as Topher watched slow-motion video of the high bar routine, all round curves and cords and sinew. Topher had tasted it all once, but he wanted Jake again, more than he wanted his next meal, and he salivated now in anticipation of tonight.

Of course, it wasn't like they had a prayer of making this anything more than an Olympic affair. Topher knew full well what the life of an elite athlete was like. Jake would go back to training in Houston soon, and Topher would go back to New York to figure out his next move, and that would be it; this funny courtship would be over.

Topher liked Jake a great deal, saw something of himself in Jake, and yet he knew full well that they didn't have a future together. Which didn't make him want Jake any less, of course. And here they both were in Madrid, inside the magic Olympic bubble, so why shouldn't they have tonight?

On the other hand, inside a deep pit within Topher, he wondered what he even had to offer Jake. Maybe the mechanics of this were too difficult. Topher couldn't get into the athlete dorms, so Jake would have to come to him. But Jake's whole family was here in Madrid, and his gold-medal-winning performance today would put him square in the media spotlight. Topher loved the spotlight, but he didn't love his private life being at the center of it. Being with Jake would be complicated. Was it worth it to get ensnared now?

So, actually, maybe hooking up with Jake had not been one of Topher's better ideas, but that didn't mean he didn't want to do it again.

Topher's phone chimed.

Stuck at America House with my family, Jake texted. *Don't think I'll be able to get away.*

Well, there it was, wasn't it? All of Topher's doubts confirmed.

There would be no tonight.

Probably there would be no anything again, because what could they even be to each other? Their night together had been some miraculous fluke. They were attracted to each other, sure. They understood each other. But life wasn't a movie. Topher didn't see any kind of happy ending here.

He texted Natalie. *I need a drink.*

I'm already at the hotel bar, baby.

Topher didn't bother prettying himself up more. He pulled on a sparkly black cardigan to combat the air-conditioned chill of the hotel and headed down to meet Natalie.

"You glitter even when you dress down," Natalie said when she saw him.

"I got stood up."

"I gathered that when you texted me. I don't think I want to know who."

Topher sat at the bar with a heavy sigh.

"You're not wearing makeup," said Natalie, gesturing at his face.

"I don't always."

"No, but your eyelashes are real. That's not fair."

Topher grinned. "Don't hate me cuz you ain't me."

"I wore falsies in competition once. Then I sweat so much during my floor routine that it made the glue start to melt, and I wound up with one stuck to my cheek. I only wore mascara after that."

Topher chuckled. "What would even possess you?"

"The cameras, I don't know. Why do gymnasts put glitter in their hair? The world of women's gymnastics is becoming more athletic, sure, but it still hasn't quite shaken off its history as a sport in which women are supposed to be tiny and cute."

"Female gymnasts are still tiny. I haven't met a single one taller than five two."

"Figure skaters aren't exactly hulking athletes, either."

"Touché."

Natalie grinned. Topher managed to signal the bartender and ordered a glass of wine in halting Spanish.

"Your accent is terrible," Natalie said.

"I speak three languages, but Spanish isn't one of them, I'm afraid."

They drank in silence for a moment. The TV over the bar was, of course, showing local coverage of the Olympics. The clips of Jake played again. Clearly that story was dominating the Olympics coverage worldwide.

"I have to confess something," Topher said. "Cone of silence."

Natalie clapped her hands gleefully. "I love a scandal! What is it?"

"It's not a—" Topher shook his head. "You had mentioned making some discreet inquiries about what Jake's deal is."

"I haven't really had time. Well, I asked Sam, who said there were some rumors about Jake... but you already know, don't you?"

"I do, yeah."

"Did you hit on Jake? That's ballsy."

Topher sighed. "That's not exactly what happened."

Natalie's eyes went wide. "Holy shit. Did you sleep with him?"

Topher's face felt like it was on fire. Rather than answer, he glanced up at the screen again. In slow motion, Jake stuck his high bar landing. "I won't kiss and tell, but let's just say he was going to try to come here tonight, but now he's famous, as you can see." He gestured at the TV. "And suddenly I'm wondering how I could have been so crazy as to think anything between us would work out."

"Wait. You're not kidding, are you?"

"Why would I kid about something like that?"

"The guy who stood you up is Jake."

"Hush. This whole hotel is crawling with media employees."

The look of utter glee on Natalie's face only made Topher feel worse.

"This is the best thing ever," Natalie said. "A perfect sports romance. You'll be, like, the Madrid Olympics power couple. You'll go back to the States and open a gym together and adopt babies who grow up to be Olympic athletes!"

Topher laughed. He… didn't hate the image, actually, but it seemed radically at odds with his current circumstances. "None of that will happen."

Natalie winked. "I bet it will. He's such a sweet guy, and you're my favorite person in Madrid right now, so clearly you're perfect for each other. Unless he's one of those guys who thinks you're too flamboyant. If he tries to douse your flame, he's a dead man."

Topher hugged her, loving her defense of him. "I don't think he would. He seems to like me for me, which is the crazy part of all of this."

Natalie narrowed her eyes at him. "I take it that has not always been the case with the guys you dated."

"Or anyone. I spent a lot of my life trying to conform to how other people wanted me to be. A gay figure skater is such a stereotype that male skaters go out of their way to make skating seem more masculine and athletic. Do you know how many skaters have beards? One of my teammates, who is gay as a rainbow, dated a female Canadian pairs skater for nearly all of his career. She was banging her partner the whole time, it turned out, but that's just... how it works. Every four years, the media combs through all of our personal lives to see what juicy tidbits they can unearth, when all we want is to live and love and compete and not have to apologize for being who we are. So we create these stories for the press and wait until we retire to fade away and live our lives."

Natalie nodded.

"Sorry, that was heavy."

"No, you're right. I never dated during the training season. I met my boyfriend after I retired, and that's hard enough sometimes. I mean, being his arm candy at the ESPN Awards is not the worst time I've ever had, but I imagine it's pretty bad if you're LGBTQ."

"It's better now than it was in my day. But Jake doesn't exactly advertise his sexuality."

"And male gymnasts don't wear sequins."

"That too." Topher sipped his wine. "Anyway, I spent my whole skating career trying to butch it up, and it's exhausting, and I'm not willing to do it anymore. My agent made that very clear to the network, and luckily the feathers and sparkly nail polish are part of my appeal." Although Topher could also tell that he was being set up as the butt of the joke sometimes. He was supposed to look ridiculous and frail, despite the strength he had after years of elite athletic training. That bothered Topher sometimes, that he still wasn't being taken completely seriously.

Natalie smiled. "I should show you this."

Topher felt a spike of anxiety. Natalie pulled her phone out of her purse and started sliding her fingers over the screen. Then she handed it to him.

She pulled up an article... about Christopher Caldwell.

"Do I want to know?"

"I saw it this morning. The subtitle is 'The Unexpected Star of the Summer Olympics.' CliffsNotes version is that young women—the prime demographic for Olympic sports like gymnastics and figure skating—think you are precious and are totally buying whatever you're selling. You're becoming something of an internet celebrity. There are stories about you on fanfic sites."

Topher recoiled. "Who am I fucking in these stories?"

"Mostly other athletes. A lot of them pair you up with Timmy Swan. He's an out gay diver."

"I've never met him."

"He's very cute, but he's no Jake Mirakovitch."

"And this is why skaters have fake relationships."

"This is good news, Topher. You have a fan base."

"In other words, TBC is probably keeping me because my sassy self makes for good ratings."

"That's exactly what I'm saying."

"Well that's neat." Feeling a bit gratified, Topher looked at the article on Natalie's phone. So maybe he wasn't a *complete* joke. The article was posted on one of those sites that mostly posted buzzy news and listicles. The story contained a ton of photos of Topher in some of his more fashionable outfits—he was particularly proud of the Prada suit he'd worn to the ESPN Awards a few years ago, and there it was—and it included a ton of tweets praising Topher for being so zany and unapologetic. "Wow. I guess we have come a long way. Text this story to me?" He handed the phone back.

"Sure thing." She fiddled with her phone, and a text with the link showed up on the screen of Topher's.

He opened the article and scanned it again. So maybe he wasn't a joke, at least not in the eyes of everyone. Maybe he could use this as leverage to appeal to whoever at TBC made decisions about who would do the commentary for the next Winter Olympics.

Buoyed, he smiled, closed the article, and sipped his wine.

Natalie leaned close. "Now, back to the fanfic *I'm* writing about you and a certain gymnast…."

CHAPTER TWENTY

Day 8

TOPHER HAD the day off, which seemed like a reasonable excuse to spend the day moping around the hotel.

This Jake thing upset him more than it should have. Jake hadn't made any promises the night before. He didn't owe Topher anything. He'd said he'd try to sneak out... of the party thrown in his honor; of course he couldn't get away. Nor would he probably be able to see Topher much before he flew back to the States. Then he and Topher would likely never see each other again.

That didn't change the reality that Topher really liked Jake. Leaving things unresolved felt a little like leaving something important behind on the ice after finishing the long program. So Topher got dressed, ate breakfast with Natalie, and then kind of wandered around aimlessly for a bit, mourning what might have been. He took a walk up and down the street and took some photos of the architecture, which he threw up on social media to appease the TBC powers that be, but mostly he just mulled over his own thoughts.

When evening rolled around, he ate tapas at the bar while nursing a glass of rioja blanco—when in Madrid, he'd decided—and he watched the local coverage, which, perhaps fortunately, was not focused on gymnastics. A Spanish men's beach volleyball team occupied the screen instead, and they were beating the pants off a team from Australia. One of the Spanish players was a beardy guy who was quite foxy, so Topher was entertained at least.

He was into his second glass of wine when a shadow appeared over the seat next to him and someone said, "This seat taken?"

Jake.

"It is now," Topher said. "What are you doing here?"

Jake smiled. He propped a set of crutches against the bar, sat on the stool beside Topher, and ordered a mineral water. "I want a beer, but it's probably a bad idea to mix painkillers and alcohol," he said when the bartender slid a glass in front of him.

"You didn't answer my question."

"So, fun story." Jake took a big gulp of his water. "I spent the day watching women's gymnastics. Chelsea, of course, won gold in everything except the balance beam—she got bronze—because that's her worst event. Chelsea's weakness still earned her a bronze— think about that. And there was, of course, a raucous party to celebrate, because the American women will be bringing home a wheelbarrow full of medals, and I went to part of it because she's my sister. Then my father started doing his 'You need rest, Jakob' routine, which I think might be his way of telling me that he's concerned about me. I saw Natalie at the party, and I know you guys are friendly, so I asked if she knew where you were, and she directed me here. She said you had a day off. So I told my dad I was going to sleep and then caught a cab over here with Natalie." Jake eyed Topher and sipped his water. "You were here all day?"

"I was. It sucked."

"Oh no. Really? Why?"

Topher considered lying, but Jake was here, so he said, "I was bummed about you not coming here last night."

He felt self-conscious for having admitted that, but Jake nodded. "I thought about you all day."

Aw. "Really?"

"Yeah. I didn't get good crutches until this morning, though, so my mobility was severely limited. And it's probably just as well, because I had to get up at the crack of dawn to do the morning show on TBC."

Topher smiled. Having Jake sit beside him thrilled him beyond reason. "Now I'm picturing you being carried around on a chaise, a litter of hot young men hoisting you up on their shoulders, you lounging casually atop it, eating grapes."

Jake laughed. "If only. It wasn't nearly that glamorous. Mostly my teammates let me lean on them while I hopped around on one foot."

Topher watched Jake for a moment. Jake shifted his weight and managed to get his injured foot propped up on the empty adjacent stool. He winced as he moved, belying how much pain he was probably in.

"That was an incredible thing you did yesterday," Topher said. "And clearly everyone is in agreement, because I've seen the clip on TV today about three hundred times."

Jake pressed his lips together. "Well. There is that, I suppose."

Topher suddenly became conscious of the fact that he was talking to a man who was now one of the most famous faces at the Olympics, and that several pairs of eyes were trained on them. He reached for his wallet and extracted enough euros to cover his meal. "Do you think it's wise for us to be seen together?"

Jake looked startled. He looked around, then looked back at Topher. "Oh. Probably not."

Topher stood. He leaned close to Jake, slipped a key card into his hand, and whispered, "Come up in five minutes."

THIS TIME Jake didn't hesitate to meet Topher in his room. Sure, his parents were in this hotel, so he had some plausible deniability. But did he really care if he got caught? Not much.

At Topher's door, he pressed the key card against the lock until the green light flashed. When Jake walked into the room, Topher stood with a grin on his face. He'd dressed down that day—something Jake had noticed as soon as he'd walked into the hotel bar—but "dressed down" for Topher meant looking impeccable in a white button-down and dark jeans, with a bright red cravat tied at his throat, a belt with a glittery buckle, and his hair done in its customary pompadour.

Jake was wearing an old warm-up suit and felt like he'd come from a different planet.

"This is almost familiar now," Jake said.

Topher undid his cravat and raised an eyebrow at Jake.

Jake sighed and stepped forward. He pressed his face against Topher's shoulder for a moment, and Topher cooed something and rubbed his back.

"How much does your leg hurt?" Topher asked softly.

"Hardly at all. That's mostly due to the painkillers, though."

Topher smelled amazing, and Jake enjoyed being pressed against him, but he wanted to elevate things. He leaned up to kiss Topher but nearly fell over when he forgot he was on crutches.

Topher laughed softly. "Okay, I got you. Hand me your crutches."

Jake took the crutches out from under his arms and handed them to Topher, who propped them up on a wall between two of his suitcases. Jake stood on one foot and leaned against a dresser. Topher walked over to Jake and cupped his cheek; then their lips met in a searing kiss.

"How much time do you have now?" Topher asked.

"I mean, I should probably get back to my dorm before anyone misses me, but I can give you a few hours, I think."

"Good. Lie down."

That seemed like an excellent idea, since putting weight on his injured foot just made it throb. Jake hopped over to the bed and lay down, happy to be off his feet. He pulled off the sneaker on his good foot, tugged off his hoodie, and shucked his pants carefully, leaving him in just the wrap around his ankle and a pair of plain red briefs. There was no need to beat around the bush this time. He wanted to get right to it.

Then Topher, with his eyes on Jake at all times, pulled the cravat from his throat, took off his shirt, and pushed his jeans to his ankles. He'd been wearing fussy slip-on shoes, which disappeared in the pile of his clothing. Topher glanced at the discarded garments on the floor, then shrugged and climbed onto the bed with Jake. Topher wore flimsy white briefs this time, and they hid nothing. Jake smiled and took Topher into his arms.

Topher whispered, "I'm game for anything, but maybe we could switch it up. I'd love to be inside you."

Jake's cock pulsed in response. "I was imagining doing just that last night."

"You and your fruit emojis," Topher laughed softly.

Jake laughed. "Your ass is amazing. How could I resist fucking you? But now I want to try something else."

"I bought a box of condoms from the hotel shop last night in anticipation of this. They're in the drawer on your side of the bed."

"I've got a couple in my pants pocket. I didn't think you'd be expecting me today."

"Look at us, being all prepared."

They made quick work of preparing each other, and then Topher was inside Jake. Jake threw his head back and pulled Topher down to kiss as they writhed against each other.

And *this* was exactly what Jake had wanted the night before as he'd sat trapped in that booth at the bar. He'd wanted pain and pleasure and sweat, two men kissing and touching and finding release in each other. He'd wanted this elemental thing he and Topher had together, the pleasure of Topher's company, the feeling of Topher moving inside him.

Topher wrapped his hand around Jake's cock, and Jake nearly leaped off the bed as excitement zipped through him. This coupling would be hard and fast, and

Jake wanted that. He wanted Topher inside him, in his arms, muttering sexy talk in his ear.

When Jake came, it was the sweetest bliss, and he dug his fingers into Topher's back as his body tightened and expanded and he spilled all over his own belly. Topher kept pumping inside him, then closed his eyes and seemed to lose himself, coming inside Jake and grunting as he did.

LATER, THEY lay panting in each other's arms.

"Amazing," Topher said. "Even better than last time, but with less mystery."

Jake tightened his arm around Topher. "There's plenty of mystery. We're just starting to get to know each other."

Topher shot Jake a crooked smile. "Aw. We've gotten to know each other quite well, I'd say. You're toppy and athletic and are in the middle of what I have to assume is one of the most incredible weeks of your life, bum ankle notwithstanding."

"Sure, but I don't know a lot of things about you. How do you like your coffee? What kinds of books do you like to read? What's your favorite TV show?"

Topher looked up toward the ceiling as if he was thinking about Jake's questions. "Well. Light and sweet. Old romance novels. *RuPaul's Drag Race*. I'm such a superfan of that last one I got to be a guest judge last season."

"Wow, really?"

"Yeah, I had to film a segment in which I taught the queens how to walk more gracefully. Also, I blended right in there, as you can probably imagine. What about you? Coffee? Books? TV?"

"Just milk. Literary thrillers. And I like trashy reality TV."

"Really?"

"I love the Kardashians. Don't tell anyone."

Topher laughed. He put his arms more firmly around Jake's shoulders and kissed his forehead. "I won't. This delights me."

"I don't watch a lot of TV, and when I do, I'm so tired that I just want something fun and unchallenging."

"I met Kim at Fashion Week last year. She knew who I was, and I almost died right there."

Jake felt himself drifting off to sleep. He pressed his ear against Topher's chest and listened to the thump of his heart for a moment.

"We haven't talked about it, but you really did something amazing yesterday," Topher said. "You've got a lot more hardware."

Jake held Topher close. "So people keep telling me. I still don't entirely believe it."

Topher rolled over to look at Jake. "You're leaving the Olympics with a wrecked ankle. How does that feel?"

Jake grinned. "I have no regrets."

Topher laughed. "I left my last Olympics with a huge bruise on my hip from where I hit the ice when I missed that quad jump, thus not winning a medal. I had a lot of regrets." He ran a hand down Jake's torso, taking stock of the muscles there. "So how do you feel about… everything? The competition and whatnot."

"It hasn't sunk in yet," Jake said, "that I actually pulled it off, I mean. I can't wrap my head around it. I spent most of my party last night thinking that I didn't need my foot in order to have sex with you."

Topher leaned over and kissed Jake's nose. "That's the spirit."

"I mean, I should have celebrated more maybe. I don't know. All I know is that I was standing in the locker room before the high bar final and I'd had it. I knew if I didn't do everything in my power to get that medal, I'd regret it, and I wouldn't let anyone stop me. I've probably damaged my foot and ankle permanently, but I don't even care, because I did it. So that's where I am mentally right now."

Topher admired that. He kissed Jake's forehead. "You're pretty awesome, you know that."

Jake smiled. "You're great too. You… you live the way you want to now. You express yourself unapologetically. I really admire that."

"Thanks, but this is your moment." Topher appreciated how Jake saw him, that he didn't expect Topher to be anything but who he was. But he also wanted Jake to feel his victory.

Topher was touched that Jake had decided to sneak over here so they could be together. He lay back down beside Jake, and Jake grabbed his hand, lacing their fingers together. Topher took in the whole picture of them together, their bodies stripped naked save for the wrap on Jake's foot, a reminder that he'd sacrificed something for his medal the day before. Topher admired Jake, admired the strength it took to stumble like he did but still get up and win a medal.

He cared about Jake too. He cared that Jake hurt, that Jake had excelled, that Jake was here and sexually satisfied. He cared about how Jake felt, about what he thought. He cared about Jake, period.

It was an odd thing to realize in the context of their recent sexual encounter. Topher had compartmentalized their encounters in the "hot sex" box, but there was clearly more here than that. He and Jake understood each other, had many similar experiences in their histories, cared about each other.

This would be hard to walk away from.

He rolled over onto Jake, and Jake immediately put his arms around Topher. Jake sighed happily.

"How's the leg?" Topher asked.

"What leg?"

Topher laughed. "No, seriously. How do you feel?"

"I feel great. A good orgasm is just what the doctor ordered. I think if I had a few more, I'd be all healed in no time."

"That's the painkillers talking, big guy."

"Mmm. I could fall asleep here. Should I?"

"I won't kick you out. But you're right, someone will probably notice if you do."

Jake sighed. "The crutches complicate everything. I can't just walk out of here when I want to. I can still say I was here to see my parents if I get out by midnight. I think it'll look fishy if I stay later than that, not that anyone would likely ask."

"Well, you never know. You *are* the most famous gymnast in the world right now."

"What time is it?"

"Uh… twenty-two-something. That's, what, after ten?"

"Yeah. Good. Time to squeeze in another orgasm. Or three."

"Three?"

"I won a gold medal with a sprained ankle yesterday. Anything is possible."

Chapter Twenty-One

Day 9

THE ARTISTIC gymnastics competition had ended; the Palacio Vistalegre was being turned over for
rhythmic gymnastics, Chelsea recorded another interview for TBC, and most of the team and coaching staff
was packing up to fly home within the next twenty-four
hours.

Jake's flight home wasn't for another eight days;
he'd wanted to stick around for the Closing Ceremony
and soak up as much Olympic spirit as he could, given
that this was likely his last one. He had tickets to a few
events, and he hoped to squeeze in some sightseeing.
And he definitely hoped to spend more time in bed with
Topher. In fact, he had big plans to move to Topher's
hotel just as soon as his parents were out of his hair.

But first he had to survive a team meeting in a conference room somewhere in the bowels of the Palacio,

where Viktor and Valentin gave what seemed like a grim postmortem considering the USA Gymnastics team had brought home more medals than they ever had before.

Then again, in all of Jake's twenty-six years of life, he'd rarely seen Valentin smile.

With very little emotion, Viktor wrapped up the meeting by saying, "We are proud of both teams. You did good. Take a few weeks to celebrate. Practice resumes in September."

Some pep talk.

When that nightmare at last ended, Valentin walked over to Jake and said, "Your mother and I will be on plane tonight."

Jake nodded. USA Gymnastics had chartered a flight home that was open to whoever wanted to take it. Jake had chosen to spend his well-earned endorsement money on a flight without everyone else on it. "Is Chelsea going with you, or did she decide to stay?"

"Don't know. Chelsea!"

Chelsea had been flirting with young Paul. She patted his shoulder before trotting over to talk to Valentin. Paul's face turned the brightest crimson, and he sheepishly ducked out of the room.

"You come home with us?" Valentin asked.

"I'm staying for Closing Ceremony," Chelsea said, her tone all, "get with the program, Dad." "I told you that, like, six times. I'm in the running to be the flag bearer."

"Where you stay?"

"Olympic Village." Then she glanced at Jake. She probably knew Jake was planning to move to the hotel, but she also probably sensed that Jake didn't want this to be public knowledge, so she stopped talking.

"Good. Any other girls stay?"

"Jessica, Ashley, and Danielle. I won't be alone, Dad."

"I worry, is all."

"I'm also nineteen. So technically, I'm an adult."

Valentin turned to Jake. "You keep eyes on her, *da*?"

"Of course."

Valentin didn't seem terribly satisfied with that, but instead he said, "Have lunch with me and Mama today before we get on plane." It wasn't a request.

They ironed out plans and Valentin departed. Jake lingered, steeling himself for going outside on his crutches, so he and Chelsea ended up leaving together. It took longer to move out of the building than it would have if he'd had the use of both feet, but Chelsea slowed to his pace and walked beside him.

"You *are* moving to a hotel, aren't you?" Chelsea said as they walked toward the exit.

"That was the plan, yes." He told her which one.

She nodded. "Are you staying with your new boyfriend?"

"He's not—no. I've got my own room. Which you can't share with me."

"Ugh, no. I'd rather fall off the balance beam. The girls and I were talking about calling around to hotels to see if they have any vacancies and then all sharing a room. I don't want to spend the next week in the athlete dorms. It's so loud and crazy there. I've got track athletes on either side of me, and they've been doing sprints in the hallway outside my door. I almost got trampled when I left this morning. No, thank you."

"I guess that will make it easier to follow Dad's orders to keep an eye on you."

Chelsea rolled her eyes. "I'm an adult."

"Barely."

Chelsea pushed open the door on the way out of the athlete entrance and held it open for Jake. They were almost to the designated spot where the shuttlebus would pick them up when all of a sudden, what seemed like a hundred flashes went off in front of him.

"Jake! Chelsea! How does it feel to be gold medalists?"

Fortunately a bus pulled up right then. Jake said nothing, but Chelsea waved before pushing through the crowd to reach the bus.

"This is my life now, isn't it?" Chelsea said.

"This is both our lives. What have we done?"

"Well, I didn't tear any ligaments before triumphantly winning a gold medal at my last event, so my story's not as good as yours, but I did medal in every event final."

Jake decided not to hear the note of bitterness in her voice. They could share the spotlight. Or she could have all of it, because Jake had no desire to talk to the press. He propelled himself over to the bus and Chelsea helped him board.

An hour later Jake and Chelsea were on their way out of the Athlete Village to get a cab to the restaurant Valentin had chosen for lunch when, once again, a slew of cameras showed up to take their picture. They made Jake tremendously uneasy, but he reasoned this was one more reason to move to the hotel. There were so many people that there wasn't room for the cab to pull up to the curb, and a security guard yelled at everyone to get out of the road… in three languages.

The Olympics sure were an experience.

They seemed to have shaken off their tail by the time they got to the restaurant. Lunch mostly involved Lana Mirakovitch gushing over how well her children had performed in the Games and Valentin admonishing them to behave during the rest of their time in Madrid. It felt so routine and normal—although the food was spectacular and Jake ate until he thought he might burst, despite Valentin saying "You want to eat that?" three or four times in a tone that said, "You want to be fat?"—that Jake had almost forgotten he and Chelsea were celebrities.

As soon as they exited the restaurant, the cameras were back. And now there were reporters. Dozens of flashes exploded in Jake's face. He'd posed for plenty of photos in the lead-up to the Olympics, but he didn't like being ambushed like this.

Valentin had clearly been planning some kind of grand goodbye even though they'd all see each other again in a matter of days, but all the reporters and paparazzi outside the restaurant waylaid those plans. "Come to hotel," Lana said as she pushed through the mob to hail a cab.

So they all piled into the cab and took it to the hotel, which was, of course, full of media company staff from various countries.

No one really bothered them as they cut through the lobby to the elevators, at least. Maybe there were rules about talking to athletes or staff inside the hotel.

But this was really bad. If that many reporters were following Jake and Chelsea around, they were bound to catch Jake in a compromising position. It didn't dampen his desire for Topher at all, and he still intended to move into the hotel, but it was giving him second thoughts. What would happen if some paparazzo caught Jake and Topher together? What would happen if Jake got outed publicly?

Jake had no answers to these questions.

But God, last night had been amazing. It would have been a crime not to sleep with Topher again. As much as possible.

He mulled that over as he settled into a chair in the corner of his parents' room and propped his foot up on an ottoman. This room was much bigger than Topher's, so there was room for Chelsea to sit too, as she rattled off the list of events she wanted to see that week. Jake sat while they all made small talk, tuning them out and getting lost in his own thoughts.

"I'm worried about the press," Jake said as he watched his parents pack the rest of their things.

"I said to be careful," said Valentin.

"That's… not even a little helpful, Dad."

"Why you worry?" Lana asked.

Jake switched to Russian because he figured it would make everything easier. Both of his parents understood English perfectly fine but were generally more comfortable conversing in Russian. They'd even encouraged their children to speak English as often as possible when they'd been young. But a perk of being bilingual was that as adults, Jake and Chelsea could switch back and forth with relative ease. Now Jake said, "If the press is following me around, they might find out things we don't want them to know."

Both of Jake's parents stopped what they were doing and stared at him. "Such as?" asked Valentin in Russian.

"What happens if they find out I'm gay?"

"We will manage," said Valentin.

"It's fine, Jakob," said Lana. "We love you no matter what. And your friends do too."

Jake smiled at that. "I know. Thank you. I love you too, Mom."

"The media could still cook up a scandal," Chelsea said, carrying on the conversation in Russian, "or catch Jake with the guy he's been making eyes at in Madrid."

"Thanks, sis," Jake said in English.

"I told you to stay away from him," said Valentin.

"It's not how Chelsea is making it sound," said Jake, returning to Russian.

"There's no reason for your private life to be public," said Valentin.

"I agree with you. I don't want anything private to be public. But you saw those reporters."

"Are you dating someone, Jakob?" Lana asked. "That boy you told me about?"

"Not… really. It doesn't matter. We were just… having a little fun before going back home. He lives in New York. There's no future in it."

"Don't do anything stupid," said Valentin.

"I wouldn't." Jake let out a breath. "I don't want the press to find out about my private life, but that doesn't mean I can't have one, does it? I have a week off in Madrid. I don't want to spend all of it hiding."

Valentin went back to folding up his T-shirts. "Be careful," he repeated.

Jake rolled his eyes. Topher wasn't in the hotel, which Jake was able to ascertain with a few covert text messages. He was busy at the broadcast center. He probably would be most days, so Jake could go see some diving or track events and no one would be any the wiser. But still, the hotel was crawling with press. With American media, more to the point. All it would take was for that gossipy reporter from *Hollywood Tonight* to catch them and everything would be out there.

Jake adjusted his weight in the chair, grunting as he moved his ankle. His pain meds were wearing off, and it throbbed uncomfortably. As he shifted, all three sets of eyes in the room looked his way. Valentin wore a concerned expression as he looked over at Jake's foot.

In Russian, Valentin said, "I know you're thinking about retiring. We talked some at lunch yesterday but didn't decide anything."

"Do I have to decide anything right now?"

"No. But I've been thinking about it."

"What do you think I should do?"

There was a long pause. Then Valentin said, "In 1989, I broke my wrist falling from high bar. The X-rays showed I had a hairline fracture in my radius too, that had probably been there for a long time. And the arthritis in my knees was starting. And I realized that my body was falling apart. I think… I think maybe you know something about that."

Jake looked at his foot. "I do know something about that."

"The ligament will heal, but the next injury may not. I worry about you hurting yourself permanently."

Well. Jake's heart swelled a little; Valentin did care after all. He knew deep down that Valentin cared about him, loved him even, but he was so used to working for that love that these rare moments of affection still felt odd.

"It's not easy being your son," Jake said quietly.

"I know."

"I wanted to be what you wanted me to be."

"I know. But I know what it's like to be a gymnast with the weight of expectation on my shoulders, and I know I don't make things easy. But you *are* the greatest gymnast in the world, and you are also my son, and I want you to be safe more than I want you to win another medal. We can talk about another season when you get home, but if you want to announce your retirement, I will accept it."

"Thanks, Dad," said Jake.

He was still mulling that over when he and Chelsea left the hotel a short while later.

"This sucks," Jake said as he and Chelsea waited for their cab back to the Olympic Village, after being accosted by a British reporter who wanted an interview. Jake had begged off, saying he needed to get off his feet.

"The ankle?"

"The ankle. The media attention. All of it."

"Give it another day. Someone else will dominate the news. Some marathon runner who overcame cancer or a cyclist who recovered from a grave injury will win a medal and that will take over. I mean, hey, the soccer finals are coming up and Spain is still in it. This city loves soccer. All of those players are far more famous here than you are."

"Thanks?" There was some truth to that, though. Once track got rolling in earnest or once some bigger Olympic story took over the headlines, no one would remember who Jake was anymore. Hopefully.

Chelsea shrugged. "I love you, Jake, even if you're a big idiot."

"Love you too, Chels. Am I really going to have to keep an eye on you this week?"

"I promise to be a perfect angel." She shot him a sweet smile.

"That's not reassuring."

CHAPTER TWENTY-TWO

REPORTERS HAD taken to hanging out around the gate between the athlete-only part of the Olympic Village and the public area, which went a long way toward convincing Jake that being in the hotel would help him keep a lower profile. He and Chelsea had managed to get a cab without too much trouble this time around, but Jake still found himself having an awkward conversation with a hotel manager about security. Also, it was hard to keep the media out when the TBC staff, as well as staff from the networks of three other countries, were staying in this hotel.

The saving grace was that the elevators needed a key card to work, so only hotel guests could access the upper floors.

Chelsea's three teammates rolled into the lobby as Jake was wrapping up a conversation with a security guard. A flurry of glitter and girlish laughter collided with Chelsea, who giggled and hugged each girl, even though they'd all seen each other earlier that day. "This is going to be so much fun," Jessica said.

"Good clean fun, right?" said Jake.

Chelsea rolled her eyes. "Ignore my big brother. He thinks he's my chaperone."

"Hi, Jake," said Ashley, batting her eyelashes. "I didn't get to tell you, but that high bar final was amazing. How much longer do you need the crutches for?"

"A few days. I know the drinking age is sixteen here, so you're all legal, but don't get too crazy, okay?"

"Sure, *Dad*," said Chelsea. "Come on, girls, we have a room upstairs. See you later, Jakey."

Jake tried not to think too hard about what kind of trouble a group of teenage girls could get themselves into at a hotel in a foreign city.

A bellhop loaded all of Jake's bags onto a cart, even though Jake was perfectly capable of carrying a couple of bags up to his room. Jake was about to protest when Topher and Natalie came in through the front door.

Topher looked upset.

Unable to stop himself, Jake walked over to him. "Is everything okay?"

Topher looked startled. "Jake! What are you doing here?"

"I'm checking in to this hotel."

Natalie touched her nose. "Good thinking."

"Why?" asked Topher. "Not that I'm sad I'll be able to see more of you, but…."

"This is brilliant," said Natalie.

Topher turned to her, looking appalled. "Are you serious? What if we—?"

Under her breath, Natalie said, "The TBC powers that be want their Olympics broadcast to be wholesome and scandal-free. Athletes are just here to triumph in their sports, smile for the cameras, and go home. They do not have sex with each other. My thought? If someone from the TBC staff catches you two together in a compromising position, they'll try to squash the story for the sake of keeping the Olympics a precious, perfect thing."

Topher let out a breath. Jake nodded. That made sense.

Natalie leaned away and shoved her hands into her designer jeans pockets. "Think about all the things they *don't* broadcast."

And that was a valid point. The previous Olympics had been in a South American city plagued by political violence and pollution, but the entire broadcast—Valentin had made him watch it when they got home as a way to demystify international competitions so that Jake would stop biffing them—had been about the beauty of the country and how happy its people were to be hosting the Olympics. Never mind that a couple of fencers had gotten mugged and protesters had delayed a bunch of the track events, among other things that happened throughout the Games that TBC hadn't broadcasted.

"Fair," said Jake.

"I think you're safer here than you would be anywhere else. Also, is it my imagination, or are there way more security guards in the lobby than usual?"

"The paparazzi followed me and Chelsea around Madrid all day. The fact that they're crawling all over the public areas of the Village is part of the reason I moved over here. There's only so much the hotel can do. But if anyone gets out a camera and starts taking photos without permission, they will be escorted out."

"That's something."

"How does it feel to be famous?" Topher asked.

"It's not the best," said Jake.

"Señor Mirakovitch?" asked the bellhop.

In Spanish, Jake said, "Take my bags up, please. I will be there in a few minutes." He passed the bellhop a few euros.

"How many languages do you speak?" Topher asked, a little bit of awe in his voice.

"My Spanish isn't the best, but I live in Texas. I think I picked it up by osmosis."

"You're bilingual, though, aren't you? Russian and English?" asked Natalie.

"I also speak Spanish and a little Chinese."

Topher shook his head. "You missed your calling as, like, a UN ambassador or something."

"Looks like I'll be retired from my current gig at the ripe old age of twenty-seven. I'll need a hobby or something."

Topher laughed. "You're funny, kid."

"Let's get out of the lobby," said Natalie, pushing Jake and Topher toward the hotel bar. They found some big, comfortable chairs and sat down together.

Jake wanted to get up to his room, but he also wanted to get to the bottom of why Topher's expression had been so grim earlier. "Why were you upset when you came in?"

"Well, fun story. Teenage girls love me. Old white guys in flyover states don't."

Jake looked at Natalie, needing a translation.

Which she gave him. "I found an article the other day about how young women think Topher is completely fabulous. They're tweeting about him and creating memes and writing fanfic."

"Fanfic?"

Topher rolled his eyes. "The erotic stories about me and various out gay athletes at the Games are my favorites."

"Is it wrong that I feel a little jealous?" asked Jake. He glanced at Natalie, who didn't react, so Jake assumed Topher had told her about what was happening between them.

Topher smiled. "That's the good news. The bad news is that for every three posts about how adorable and sparkly I am, there is one calling me a fag or a sissy. A conservative group has started a letter campaign to get me pulled from the air, although my TBC handler insists they won't."

"They won't," said Natalie. "Didn't you hear that ratings are up? The viewership wants younger, more diverse talent calling the events, instead of the same old white guys who have been on-air since 1984."

"It makes me nervous. I *really* want the figure skating commentary gig. Even if they don't pull me off the air, this Concerned Moms group could keep me out of primetime. So I'll either get stuck doing fluff pieces or they'll only let me cover, like, the European Championships, which airs on one of those channels only people with the good cable sports packages get." Topher sighed. "I'm not going to tone myself down to keep from offending some bigoted ladies' sensibilities, but the damage is done either way. So, I don't know. Have I completely fucked this up?"

"No," said Natalie. "I think you're doing exactly what you should be doing. TBC wants fresh voices, and that's exactly what you are. And look at how fast you adapted to talking about gymnastics. You're great on the air, Toph. If anyone says otherwise, they're an asshole."

"Yeah, but some of those assholes are in charge of making hiring decisions."

Jake was reminded again of the conversation he'd had with his parents that morning. Sure, they would love him no matter what, but if he were outed in a big way? How would that affect his future employment? He still wasn't completely sure what he wanted to do after his retirement. His rough plan had been to take some classes at a school in Houston and coach the young kids at the Mirakovitch gym, but he wasn't married to that plan. Would conservative parents pull their kids out of his classes if they knew he was gay? He didn't think so, but weirder things had happened in Texas.

"I need to let it roll off my back," said Topher. "There's nothing I can do about it right now."

Jake let out a breath. "Are you guys done for the day?"

"Yeah," said Natalie. "You want to have dinner with us? We were just going to eat at the restaurant on the other side of the lobby."

That seemed easy enough. "Sure, let's do it. Let me just finish checking into my room."

TOPHER SETTLED against Jake's side in the bed, and Jake folded his arms around Topher's chest. Topher had been right; being wrapped up in Jake was magnificent.

Topher closed his eyes and savored the postorgasmic glow. After dinner Jake had followed Topher back to his room—conveniently, their rooms were a few doors down the hall from each other—and after an athletic bout of sex, they'd hopped in the shower and somehow summoned enough magic to do it again under the spray of water. There'd been a brief moment when Topher had worried he'd drown, but it almost didn't matter. Things got tricky with Jake's injured foot, but Jake didn't seem to mind much.

Topher had committed those moments to memory. Being with Jake was amazing. He hadn't clicked with a man in bed in this way in a very long time.

"How do you like living in New York?" Jake asked.

It was an odd question, but Topher had learned enough about Jake to guess this was going somewhere. "I love it. I mean, part of why I moved there was that I'd retired and decided I'd do all the things I hadn't been able to do when I was training. I took a few classes, I went dancing in a bunch of clubs, I met some guys, I walked in Fashion Week, and now I'm trying to get a more long-term position at TBC. I guess I don't have to be in New York for that, but I don't know, I like the city. It has some magic to it."

Jake squeezed Topher gently and sighed. "Athletes joke that they live in the gym, but it's literally true for me. And now my body is so banged up that the next time I injure myself, it could very well end my career. My plan right now is... to keep training gymnasts. To stay in the gym."

"I can't imagine the kind of pressure you must have dealt with. My mom is not an athlete."

"What about your dad?"

"He died before I was old enough to remember him."

"I'm sorry."

"Don't be." Topher rubbed Jake's arm. "My mom was the only parent I ever needed. She's just... she's incredible. She always supported me and worked extra jobs to pay for my lessons and rink time. She sewed some of my early costumes." Topher let out a breath. His mother really had been his rock during his career.

"She couldn't come to all my competitions when I was a junior because she had to work so much to pay for everything, but as soon as I brought in enough money, I told her to quit one of her jobs. When I started getting endorsement deals, I bought her a house. And I still feel like I'll never be able to pay her back for everything she gave me."

"Did you always feel that way?"

"I questioned my choices a lot, especially at some practices when I was on my twentieth figure eight and my coach was yelling at me about how I was an inch off the line. But yeah, I think I always kind of knew my mom was something special."

"And not a Soviet gymnast."

Topher laughed. "No."

"Some former gymnasts keep their kids as far from the sport as possible, but my parents tossed us right in. It's… it's so much to live up to."

"Do you want to leave the gym when you retire?"

"Not sure." Jake shifted a little on the bed but tugged at Topher so he'd settle back against Jake's body. "I've thought about teaching—I really love working with young kids. But part of me also thinks it might be a good idea to get as far from Houston as possible. Figure out how to be something other than an elite gymnast. Do something completely different."

Topher wove his fingers with Jake's. He really couldn't imagine what it must have been like to come from a whole family of elite gymnasts and to spend so much time in their shadows. But Jake had proven himself this week, and Topher felt weirdly proud of him. "So you're thinking hard about retiring, then."

"I hurt myself doing a tumbling pass I've done hundreds of times. And I was having the meet of my life. I think that's a sign that my body can't take much more. Maybe one more season, but then that's probably it." Jake sighed again. "I feel like I put my whole life on hold for this. I'll miss gymnastics, of course, and part of me isn't really looking forward to retiring, but on the other hand, I can't wait to finally start living my life."

"Yeah. I know a little about that."

Jake pulled away slightly and propped himself up on one elbow. Topher rolled over to look at him. "So, when you got to New York, did you just fuck your way through it, or…," Jake asked.

Topher laughed. "No, darling, not quite. I did party quite a bit. Dated a man for almost a year, but it didn't work out. Dated a few others. I learned how to cook, though. Turns out that when you spend your whole life pushing your limits to be the best at something, you can apply that drive to other pursuits."

"Is it crazy that I want you to cook for me sometime?"

God. Jake looked so earnest and sweet, his face showing all his emotions. His disheveled hair and those amazing, strong arms were so perfect. Topher suddenly had a vision of waking up beside this face for many mornings in the future. "Not crazy at all."

Jake smiled. "I will admit, I feel pretty safe in this hotel, but sneaking around with you for a whole week could get dangerous."

"Are you worried about getting caught together?"

"I can't decide. Should I be?"

Topher considered. He hadn't expected them to be in much of a position to be caught together, but Jake had a lot of idle time over the next week. That could mean they'd spend a lot of time together, if the network didn't keep Topher busy. And spare time was a real possibility, because despite Joanna's reassurances, some of his scheduled appearances had been cancelled. That could have only been because he'd been bumped in favor of a splashy interview with an athlete who had unexpectedly excelled, or that the network didn't want to put him on-air so much. Topher couldn't say, and it was taking a lot for it not to bother him.

He took a deep breath and tried to focus on Jake's question. "I don't know. It's not like people don't know I'm gay. And I like you a lot and am certainly not ashamed to be seen with you. But you're already in the media spotlight, and this is bound to increase its brightness. Are you ready for that?"

Jake flopped onto his back. "No. I don't want to be in the media spotlight. I wanted to win a gold medal... or a few... and then I wanted the press to leave me alone. Chelsea thinks some other story will emerge and the press will follow that one."

"That's true. There's a Dutch rower who got some press today because he's a cancer survivor and had to miss the previous Olympics because he was doing chemo, but now he's cancer-free and he won a gold medal by a crazy margin today. Everyone at TBC was talking about that this afternoon."

"Huh. Well, there you go."

"And one of the female Chinese divers got engaged to her coach-slash-boyfriend."

Jake raised an eyebrow. "That doesn't seem shady at all."

Topher laughed. "The Olympics are basically built for these kinds of stories. Your performance at the event finals could very well be on highlight reels for years to come, but it won't be as immediate tomorrow as it was yesterday. The press will back off."

"I asked my parents what would happen if I got outed."

Topher leaned closer and pushed some of Jake's hair off his face. Now that it didn't have gel in it, it kind of just flopped around everywhere. Topher wasn't upset about that, because Jake had really soft hair, and Topher liked running his fingers through it. "What did they say?"

"Mom said she loved me no matter what and Dad just told me to 'be careful,' but I don't really know what that means. Bottom line, though, is that everyone who matters already knows I'm gay, so if the general public finds out… I don't know. Does it change anything? Probably not. But you're right, it could put the spotlight back on me. And I'm also kind of worried some parents might pull their kids from the classes I teach at the gym."

"Is that a rational fear?"

"I don't know. And then I keep wondering if you and I even have any kind of future. Is this one of those relationships that burns fast and is over when we fly home?"

A knot formed in Topher's throat. Here it was, wasn't it? They were about to have The Talk. Topher had been hoping to avoid this, to just keep floating along and enjoying themselves. Alas. "Is that what you want?"

"I don't know! I mean, no, not really. I want to get to know you because I feel like there's some real potential between us. Do you know how hard it is to explain my life to nonathletes? How many relationships have fallen apart because the guy I was dating couldn't understand why I had to put in the hours at the gym that I do?" He gestured at himself. "But you understand it perfectly, don't you? You know what it takes to put your whole body into something in order to achieve a goal. And you know how crushing it feels when you defeat your own damn self because you make a dumb mistake on the world stage. No one I've ever been with has come close to understanding that."

"So what are you saying?"

"I hate that the Olympics is cutting that potential short, because I'll wake up in the morning a week from now and get on a plane and very likely never see you again."

Topher supposed he should have expected that answer, but for a hot minute he'd thought maybe Jake was proposing that they keep seeing each other after the Olympics were over. And Topher admitted to himself that he kind of wanted that, because he really liked Jake. And Jake was right—they both knew something that only elite athletes knew. They understood each other. It seemed a shame to throw that away over a small issue like geography.

"You're probably right," Topher said.

"Or, I don't know." Jake met Topher's gaze, a bit of daring in his expression. "I could take some time off and spend it in New York. See if the potential between us is real."

Topher's pulse kicked up. "Yeah?"

"I mean, it's just a crazy idea. Would you even want that?"

"I would, actually." There was no sense in playing games or mincing words. Topher leaned over and kissed Jake slowly, giving them both time to savor it, and perhaps offer a reminder of what they'd be giving up if they said goodbye after the Closing Ceremony.

When Topher pulled away, Jake was smiling. "This is insane."

"I know. And who knows, maybe once the bubble bursts, we'll hate each other."

"I don't think that's true."

"No?"

Jake kissed Topher, mimicking Topher's move of slowly sliding their lips against each other. "No. I think that I will spend the rest of my life reliving these two weeks. In a good way."

"Well, we have this week. Maybe we shouldn't make any decisions yet."

Jake nodded. "You know, I have a room here by myself. I don't think anyone would miss me if I didn't go back to it tonight."

"You want to spend the night with me? Is that what you're saying?"

"If that's okay."

"It's more than okay." Then Topher dove for Jake and vowed to make it worth Jake's while.

CHAPTER
TWENTY-THREE

Day 12

AFTER A few idyllic days and nights in Jake's bed, Topher was in a wonderful mood as he walked into the network staff meeting. Only it didn't last. To Topher's surprise, Joanna had pitched a story to her athlete commentators about the triumph and tragedy of the Olympics that involved the clip of one Christopher Caldwell falling on his ass. Topher had been reluctant to balk too hard at the idea lest he anger the people in control of deciding how much airtime he got, but he'd had a word with Joanna about it after the meeting, asking her to leave it out. Natalie had backed him up, patiently explaining that most athletes didn't enjoy having their failures broadcast on national television again and again.

It was still too raw. That gut punch of fucking up when the moment was his, when that gold medal was so close that he could touch it. He couldn't blame it on being outskated, because he wasn't; if he'd landed that jump that gold medal would have been his. It hadn't been the ice conditions, it hasn't been his skates, it hadn't been audience distractions. It had been one hundred percent his own failure to perform when it counted.

It still hurt. It would probably never stop hurting. That knowledge of what could have been still hung in front of him.

"She wanted to put my worst moment ever on-air," Topher said later. He and Jake were walking hand-in-hand through the Casa de Campo, a huge public park in the center of Madrid. Jake had given up on the crutches, but he didn't have the full range of motion of his ankle yet, so they were moving very slowly.

"I have, like, eight of those, so I sympathize."

Topher looked around. Jake had wanted to get out and walk after a being cooped up in the hotel for a couple of days. They'd decided on wandering around outside in the relative anonymity of the park. Neither wore anything that indicated their country of origin or that they were in town for the Olympics, and Jake had put on mirrored aviator sunglasses that obscured his face pretty well. Topher still stood out a bit, but he hadn't noticed any kind of tail. So he'd felt pretty comfortable taking Jake's hand. The way Jake kept squeezing it indicated he liked holding hands.

They got a few hairy eyeballs from passersby, but so far they'd been left alone.

Not that holding hands in a public park meant they were a couple or anything. They were just exceedingly fond of each other.

"Can you imagine?" Topher asked, still a little offended by Joanna's story pitch.

"I don't want to. They keep showing me falling on the floor exercise. On the floor! Nobody fucks up on the floor! You hop out of bounds, sure, or you sit at the end of a tumbling pass because you under-rotated. But tumbling passes are Gymnastics 101. It was such a dumb mistake. And I feel humiliated all over again every time I see it on a TV out of the corner of my eye."

"It feels like it matters more than the gold medal does."

"Yeah. I mean, I fought for that gold medal. It's mine, and no one will ever take it from me. But I keep reliving the worst parts of my career. All the times I've fallen off an apparatus or, I don't know, banged my leg on the pommel horse, or torn a muscle doing practice on the rings, or that time I got a concussion at the World Championships because I missed the landing on a vault." Jake sighed and hopped a few steps. "Sorry. I don't mean to rant, but I don't love that the networks keep showing that clip."

"No, believe me, I get it."

"You said Natalie talked Joanna out of it?"

"Well, she talked Joanna into making participation voluntary instead of mandatory. I opted out. I don't need to relive *not* winning a gold medal."

"Yeah. I could do without seeing myself tripping over my own feet every time I look at a television." Jake sighed. "Are you okay with all this? I mean, I can't help but think… you don't resent me, do you?"

"What? No. Not at all."

"I guess I worried."

"No, Jake, I'm so proud of you. You did something I couldn't have. I still have nightmares about quad jumps, and that Olympic experience is seared in my brain. But that's my issue, not yours. You grabbed that opportunity and went for it, and watching it was exciting! I'm thrilled you won, I really am. I could never resent you."

"Okay. Sorry I asked. I must seem selfish."

Topher took a deep breath. He completely understood where Jake's fear came from, but he was glad Jake had taken the opportunity Topher hadn't been able to. "You're not selfish. You care about me and want to make sure I'm okay, right?"

"Yes, I care about you a lot." Jake hopped again.

Topher wanted to talk about that more, to find out how much Jake cared, but Jake seemed distracted by his leg. "Your foot okay?"

"Eh. It's starting to throb."

"I think I see the street over there."

"Where are we?" Jake pulled out his phone and touched the icon for the maps app.

"I don't know, but where there's a street, there's a taxi."

Jake laughed. "Fair enough."

Topher squeezed Jake's hand. "This is nice, you know. Us just hanging out. Chatting. Holding hands."

"It is nice. Maybe we should think about finding ways to do it more often."

"I mean, I guess I'm not opposed to visiting Houston. I hear there's a nice…. Actually, I know absolutely nothing about Houston."

Jake laughed. "We've got some good restaurants. If you come in March, we can go see the rodeo. That's kind of a big deal. There's… I don't know. The NASA Space Center. And it's right on the Gulf Coast, you know. I like the beach in Galveston."

"All right. New York has all the New York things you probably already know about."

"I've been a few times. I was just there a few weeks ago. *Wake Up, America!* had me on to do an interview as part of their series on 'Olympic hopefuls.'" Jake made quote fingers. "I was in and out pretty quickly because it was the middle of training camp, but there's a gym in New Jersey I use when I'm in that part of the country. It's owned by a former Mirakovitch student, so Valentin trusts that she won't corrupt his teachings."

"Do you often call your father by his first name?"

Jake shrugged. "He's kind of a special case. Valentin Mirakovitch is a force of nature. If you ever get to meet him, you'll see. He has the authority of an Eastern European dictator and does not like jokes or disagreements. He's the most serious person I have ever known. My mother is a good influence on him because she gets him to lighten up, but when he's training gymnasts, there is no levity. It's intense."

"I can imagine." Topher liked the idea of getting to meet Jake's father someday, in the context of them being in a relationship. He took a moment to imagine some future dinner in which they all sat down and Topher tried to impress Valentin with his rudimentary Russian, the same way he had Lana Mirakovitch that night they'd met.

Was it dangerous to think that way? Topher thought it might be. Then again, here they were, holding hands and talking about how they'd go see each other after the Olympics. So maybe there was some hope.

"Can we sit for a sec?" Jake asked, leading Topher over to a bench at the side of the path.

Topher sat beside him. "I guess it feels pretty silly to complain about my old pain when you are literally still healing from an injury."

Jake frowned. "Nah, not really. I totally understand why you wouldn't want to have to talk about your Olympic experience. I don't really want to talk about mine either, even the good stuff." He leaned back on the bench. "Doc says it's a grade two sprain, which means I don't really need the crutches anymore, but I'm out of the gym for six weeks. Which means I'll get a late start on training for next season."

"Really? When does training start?"

"Time off is not really a thing I ever get. Except when forced on me by injury."

"In other words, if we're going to go to the beach or steal a space shuttle from NASA, we should do it in the next six weeks."

Jake laughed. "I suppose so."

"Good to know. I'm mentally penciling you in on my calendar."

"I'd love to see you. I mean that. You don't have to come to Houston. You can take me to eat good pizza in New York instead."

Topher tilted his head back, letting the sun beat down on him, the warm air envelop him. Sitting beside Jake and talking as though they had a future made him warm inside too. He took Jake's hand again, feeling content. "If I come to Houston, be prepared for *a lot* of 'Houston, we have a problem' jokes."

"So noted."

Topher leaned over and kissed Jake's cheek. "We're really doing this, aren't we?"

Jake smiled. "Yeah, I think we are. The more I think about us spending time apart, the more it upsets me."

"Me too. Turns out I like you."

"I like you too."

And even though they were in public, because Jake was so damned irresistible, Topher leaned over and placed a soft kiss on Jake's lips. Jake lifted his hand and cupped Topher's jaw.

Yeah. They were doing this. Topher could see himself falling in love with this man. Would it be easy? No, definitely not. Jake still had a lot of decisions to make and Topher still traveled a lot and there was still so much to negotiate, but Topher decided to savor the promise of a happy ending with Jake.

Jake pulled away slightly and said, "So, about that taxi."

"Yes, sir." Topher hopped up and then helped Jake to his feet. "Your chariot awaits."

Jake's foot was obviously really hurting him now, because he hooked his arm around Topher's and mostly hopped to the street, but Topher didn't mind holding Jake up. He hoped to keep doing it for a long time.

JAKE HEARD the text message alert on his phone as if it was underwater.

It wasn't worth pulling out of the tangle with Topher's limbs to check on it. In fact, Topher was currently trailing kisses along Jake's jaw, and it felt too good to stop.

Jake put his arms around Topher and pulled him close. "I want you inside me this time."

Topher moaned. "Yes. Perfect."

The text message alert went off again. It occurred to Jake to wonder if something had happened, but he pushed it aside. Instead, he grabbed a condom from the drawer and rolled it on Topher. Topher had the bottle of lube in his hand and got to work preparing Jake. Jake shifted his hips up, spread his legs wide, and tried to keep his injured foot out of the equation.

And then Topher hovered over him. They'd swapped back and forth quite a bit over the past couple of days, and they'd had so much sex that they had some understanding of each other's bodies now. Topher had a tattoo of the Olympic rings on his right buttcheek, which Jake loved. Jake's own Olympic tattoo was on the underside of his right arm. But Topher also had a tattoo on his hip.

"Infinity sign?" Jake asked, rubbing his finger over it.

"Figure eight."

"Oh." Jake laughed. "Of course."

Topher grinned and shoved two fingers inside Jake. Jake threw his head back and moaned. God, that was just what he needed. No, he needed more.

"I want your cock," Jake grunted.

"Then stop making small talk."

Topher tossed the lube aside, then positioned himself between Jake's legs. Jake felt the blunt head of Topher's cock against his entrance and tried to push himself forward on it. He really wanted the burn of it, the pleasure only Topher could give him. Topher hooked Jake's knees around his arms and shifted his hips forward, finally sliding inside Jake.

God, Topher felt amazing. Jake's body stretched to accommodate him, and it stung, but in the best possible way, the fiery promise of future pleasure. Jake's body relaxed to let Topher in and the pain became pleasure.

"More," Jake moaned.

"You are insatiable, darling," Topher said, a little breathless.

Topher picked up the pace, pushing in and out of Jake. Topher's skin had a sweaty sheen to it, and his hair had become messy. And then he looked up and met Jake's gaze.

Jake could get lost there. He could see every nuance of color in Topher's bluish-gray eyes. There was an icy quality to them, or Jake was imagining it. It didn't matter, because that connection between them made Jake's heart flutter.

He put his arms around Topher and pulled him close. It occurred to Jake to whisper that he loved Topher, but it was far too soon. He wasn't ready to make that kind of declaration, didn't trust his feelings yet, didn't want to say such things during sex. He felt a lot of things for Topher, but he wasn't sure they were love yet.

But some of this was heat and magic, because it was there, where their bodies met. Topher wrapped his hand around Jake's cock and started stroking, and Jake began to feel like he was all nerves everywhere. His skin tingled, his insides melted, and an orgasm building somewhere near the base of his balls.

Topher closed his eyes as if he was about to surrender to everything. "I'm gonna come," he mumbled. "But it's too soon."

"I'm close too."

Topher increased the pressure on Jake's cock, squeezing it an exquisite way, coaxing the orgasm out of him. Jake groaned and distantly heard his phone chime again, but it didn't even matter because suddenly he was coming, shooting between himself and Topher.

Then Topher said, "Oh God," and crushed his lips against Jake's, taking a searing kiss as he came inside Jake.

A few moments later Topher said, "You are too fucking sexy. It's hard to draw things out between us."

"Well, if we're going to visit each other in the future, we'll have some time to practice."

Topher laughed softly. "An excellent point." Then Jake's phone chimed again. "Someone is really trying to get in touch with you."

Topher hoisted himself out of bed and went into the bathroom. Jake wasn't eager to put his foot back down on the ground, but with a groan, he forced himself out of bed and limped into the bathroom, since Topher had left the door open.

Apparently they'd already reached the level of intimacy where they could pee in front of each other. Okay.

With a laugh, Jake went to the sink and washed his hands, then washed the drying cum off his abdomen.

"Don't know if you knew this," Topher said, nudging Jake out of the way so he could wash his own hands. "But you and I are spectacular in bed together."

"I may have noticed that."

"I had a lot of fun with you today. I just wanted to tell you that before we re-engage with the real world. I lost track of how many texts you got while you were scrambling my brains, but it sounded like kind of a lot."

"It's probably just Chelsea."

"Or your other boyfriend."

"Ha ha." Jake kissed Topher and let it linger for a moment. "I had fun with you too," he said.

Jake hopped back to bed and grabbed his phone. Eight text messages, most of them from Chelsea. He opened the text app.

"Oh," Jake said as he read. "Apparently I'm in the running to be the flag bearer at the Closing Ceremony. I got a text from a swimmer named Melissa, who I guess is kind of the de facto Team USA leader. She says there have been a half-dozen names suggested, then all the athletes will vote. They want me to be the flag bearer?"

"Of course they do!" Topher sat next to him. "Do you know how many athletes would have quit after getting injured? You did something really brave, and probably a little stupid, but you won a gold medal anyway. Of course they want you to be the flag bearer."

"Chelsea is, of course, also in the running, so she's taunting me over text."

"Gives new meaning to sibling rivalry."

"I'm not even sure I can walk far enough to do it. The ankle feels better, but it still hurts a lot. On the other hand, I'll never have this opportunity again. I just… wow."

"If you feel well enough when the day arrives, I think you should do it."

"It's not mine yet. The other athletes still have to vote."

"Still, if you do get it? Go for it. Show all the doubters that they were wrong. Show how good and how strong you really are."

Jake ducked his head, suddenly embarrassed. "It's just the flag."

"I know, but it's still a big deal. Just think about it, all right?"

"I will."

CHAPTER
TWENTY-FOUR

Day 13

THE BUZZ around the International Broadcast Center was mostly focused on track and field. An American sprinter with a doping charge in his past was suddenly among the favorites to win the 200-meter final. Topher knew even less about track than he did about gymnastics prior to the Games, but this sprinter, Jason Jones Jr., was a handsome guy who liked to bling up his uniforms on the track, and Topher was intrigued enough to ask about the possibility of interviewing him. Joanna seemed delighted by the idea.

Others had already focused their attention on the Closing Ceremony. Apparently the contest for the flag bearer position had gotten quite contentious. There were a half-dozen finalists. In the past Topher hadn't cared much about the Closing Ceremony. Mostly he'd wanted to hide his face. But he was excited for Jake.

In the meantime, the competition was still on. Topher's schedule for the day put him at the Olympic Stadium to talk about some track events. As he headed for the elevators, Joanna stopped him. "I know you're kind of in your head about how the media has been talking about you, but honestly, please just be yourself. Go do social media from the track like you've been doing. Make it fun and positive. Draw a little attention to yourself. Yeah?"

"I'm on it," Topher said with more confidence than he felt.

He got a cab at the broadcast center and then promptly got stuck in traffic. So he let his mind wander.

He would take Joanna's advice and act like he didn't know a conservative group was gunning for him. He knew he couldn't change anything. He drew attention to himself, both deliberately and accidentally sometimes, so he supposed he should have expected some pushback. He was loud, brash, flamboyant—he put himself out there. Figure skating fans wrote blog posts about his post-Olympic life full of speculation about who he was dating, and it had never occurred to him to mind until Jake walked into his life. Because Jake was special, because they had something real, and Jake didn't want this spotlight.

Jake, who just that morning had kissed Topher sweetly before heading off with his sister and her friends for some sightseeing in Madrid. Topher probably had hearts in his eyes whenever they looked at each other.

Topher had once been a champion figure skater, and he supposed his inner flame shone bright enough that no one was really surprised when he came out publicly. He'd often demurred in interviews before that, afraid that the figure skating establishment would condemn him for upholding those old stereotypes. Not to mention, he'd had enough male skaters over the years tell him to tone it down, to wear fewer sequins and ostrich feathers, to not be so fey. Once in a locker room before the World Championships, a Russian skater had cornered Topher in a locker room and called him a fag before putting him in a headlock tight enough to leave a bruise on Topher's chin. He'd had to get out the heavy makeup to cover it up, which hadn't helped his cause much.

But skating was such a beautiful sport, and Topher had always wanted to honor its artistic origins. He'd wanted to express himself with music choice and costumes. It wasn't just about landing quad jumps or completing all the required skills in a program. It was about artistry and beauty and grace. And that was something men's figure skating had been losing lately as it became a contest to see who could land the most quad jumps. Topher and Jake had talked a lot about gymnastics moving away from the artistic and more toward the athletic, and that was all well and good, but Topher missed the artistic. Skating was less for it, in his opinion.

Topher sighed. He'd been so tired of getting harassed in locker rooms and on figure skating social media that when he'd retired, he'd vowed to live his best life, to express himself however he saw fit, to be himself and nothing else. And he'd lived up to that all week, which of course now meant that people on the internet were making fun of him and calling him ridiculous. But Jake hadn't seemed to mind any of that. Jake seemed to like everything about him, in fact. He wasn't judgmental and wouldn't ask Topher to change; he liked Topher for who he was, and was attracted to the parts of Topher that others found outrageous.

Just the night before, Jake had spent a few minutes looking at all the clothes hanging in the closet. Why had Topher packed a little faux fur jacket for summer in Madrid? Why not? It was cold in the broadcast center. And Jake had held up some garments to Topher and asked to see them modeled, and that had led to some sexy fun. Jake wasn't afraid of any of this. Hell, he'd even draped the hot pink feather boa around his shoulders as he'd examined things, which had spurred Topher into imagining how Jake would look with some eyeliner and some more gender ambiguous clothing. The image didn't quite work—Jake's body was remarkably different from Topher's and he wore Topher's accessories differently—but that was okay.

Because Jake had strong arms and was easygoing and he liked Topher. Jake understood what the weight of expectations and the pressure to succeed felt like. He knew what it felt like to fuck up on the world's stage. And he'd figured out how to conquer his past failures, and Topher remained incredibly proud of him. They understood each other.

Topher's last boyfriend had been like, "You went to the Olympics. So few people will ever do that. You're still special."

But that wasn't the point. And Jake got that.

The traffic finally broke, and Topher soon found himself in front of the Olympic Stadium. He felt newly determined to show everyone exactly what he could do and exactly why he should have this job.

JAKE AND Chelsea had broken off from the rest of the girls to take a closer look at an exhibit at the Prado while everyone else went to find a restaurant. When Chelsea asked how things were going with Topher,

Jake had tried to put her off, but she was persistent. Well, she let it drop at the museum, but once they'd gotten the text with directions to their lunch spot, she started again.

"How have you handled this with guys you've dated in the past?"

"I don't date. Who has time?"

Chelsea's face softened. "I bet you've figured out how to make time, but you don't want to tell me about it, and that's fine. I don't want to know. Although, and don't tell a soul about this, but I'm kind of seeing a guy who plays for the Rockets."

Jake balked. "You are not."

"It's not serious. But we go out if we both have a night off. Also, I'm nineteen."

"Nope. You're my little sister." God, when had Chelsea grown up? This was unreal. "For the Rockets? Which player?"

"Would you know him if I told you?"

"Nope. I know next to nothing about basketball. But is he, like, three feet taller than you?"

"Yes. Well, a foot and a half. He's six five."

"Wow. I'm really strong, though. I bet I could take him if I had to."

Chelsea rolled her eyes. "We're not talking about me. We're talking about you."

Jake sighed. He did not want to talk about himself. He wanted to be able to spend time with Topher in Madrid without anyone caring. He wanted the anonymity of being a failure back. He let out a wheezy breath.

"All right, let's back up," said Chelsea. "Topher. You like him, right?"

"Yes. A lot."

"In an 'I'd like to get to know him better after the Olympics way' or in—and trust me, as your sister, it pains me to say this—a 'the sex is super smoking hot' kind of way?"

"Honestly? Both."

Chelsea laughed. "All right. Well, that's something. And you're nervous about going public."

"I just… I don't want to invite the whole world into my private life, and I'm worried people will give me a hard time."

"That's fair. I can't even say that won't happen, because it probably will."

"It's not even getting outed. I can take care of myself. I can face whatever happens with that. It's more about me and Topher. Will we last or not? Who knows? I'd like to be able to figure that out before I say anything to anyone outside of the circle of people I trust."

"I hear you."

"I just… I need more time."

"I don't know him, obviously," Chelsea said, "but he is very cute, and he seems like a good guy."

"He is."

"You don't have to take this from me, because I totally get that I'm younger than you and you're more worldly or whatever, but I've figured out that you and I—we do not have normal lives."

Jake scoffed. As if that wasn't obvious.

"And because we don't have normal lives, we don't get to have normal love lives. How many times in your life has a guy you like as much as Topher even shown interest in you?"

Jake closed his eyes. He'd made eyes at guys in gay bars, he'd had one-night stands without getting to know the man beyond the surface, and he'd met plenty of guys he'd liked over the years who were straight or not into short guys or who really just did not understand Jake's life. Had he ever met someone who he clicked with, the way he did with Topher?

"Never. This is pretty much the only time it's happened."

Chelsea nodded. "After the Olympics, all of this will blow over and most of the American public will go back to not knowing who you are. They'll show that clip of you sticking the landing in your high bar routine in Olympics clip shows for a few decades to come, probably, but that still means people will only remember you for two weeks every four years. That means that once we get back to the States, none of this will matter." Chelsea gestured to her phone. "You know what does matter? Finding someone to spend the rest of your life with. Because I heard what Dad said—you're planning to retire soon, and you have to build a life for yourself outside of gymnastics. And I'm guessing that could get pretty lonely... although Mom will probably still make you come over for dinner."

Jake laughed. She was right. The only time the media even showed up at the Mirakovitch compound just outside Houston was if there was some gymnastics-related story in the news. The doctor who'd been arrested for molesting his patients while employed by USA Gymnastics had been a huge story. Valentin had never trusted that doctor or let him near his own gymnasts, and the doctor had been let go when Valentin took over as head coach of the national team, but a bunch of reporters had shown up at the gym to ask questions anyway. But that was a rare situation. Chelsea was right; most Americans probably couldn't pick Jake out of a lineup.

"So what you're saying is," Jake said, "that I should be with Topher and not worry about what the fallout might be."

"Basically, yeah."

Jake looked at his sister. Hadn't she just been a little girl five minutes ago? He shook his head. "How did you get so wise?"

Chelsea grinned. "The magic of gymnastics." She patted Jake's shoulder. "You'll be okay, you know. The whole family, all of your teammates, we support you."

"I know. Thanks, Chels."

"I mean, Dad will totally have a coronary the first time he meets Topher, but he'll recover. He loves you and wants you to be happy."

After seeing the way Valentin had worried over him the last week, Jake believed that more strongly than he ever had before. "I know."

"And it's totally going to be me bearing the flag."

"Sure. We'll see."

CHAPTER TWENTY-FIVE

Day 15

TOPHER LOST the lottery to get a Closing Ceremony ticket, which was a bummer considering Jake
and Chelsea both planned to go regardless of who was
chosen to be flag bearer. Topher and Jake had spent every available moment together over the past week—a
lot of them in Topher's room, which felt safe. The good
news was that they hadn't tired of each other or run out
of things to talk about. It had been a fantastic week.
And now Topher's flight home was two days away, and
he wasn't looking forward to it.

He browsed the craft services area of the TBC
floor of the broadcast center, snagging a slice of cheese
and a handful of crackers.

Joanna appeared at his side. "Can I talk to you for
a sec?"

"Sure." Topher kept his tone light, although Joanna's serious expression was worrisome. She was probably about to tell him that this had been fun and all, but TBC would not be needing his services anymore. There'd be no commentary gig at the Winter Olympics or even at the US regional figure skating championship on an upper-dial cable network. Topher had pushed it too far, he was too flamboyant, too gay, too—

"I'm passing along that this Olympics broadcast has been a great success, and the powers that be have decided it's because they hired personalities that appeal more to younger viewers. Our ratings with eighteen-to-thirty-five-year-olds have gone way up over the last Olympics, and we think it's because of people like you."

Topher's heart pounded. That sounded like… good news. "Well, that's good to know. Glad I could help."

"Here's the deal. The network wants to hire you to do commentary at the next US Figure Skating Championships, in January."

Topher's heart rate sped up. "Are you serious?"

Joanna nodded. "Yes. And if that goes well, then other figure skating competitions that we air are yours too. TBC Sports usually covers the European Championships and World Championships in between Olympics. And if you do well on all *those*, well, Tim Preston plans to retire. So that job's yours."

Topher felt faint suddenly. Tim Preston was a retired figure skater whose heyday had been in the eighties. He'd been calling figure skating for TBC since the early nineties. Topher found Tim highly irritating—his approximate level of enthusiasm was that of college football cheerleader—but recently there had been some rumors about Tim trying to assert his heterosexuality by feeling up women without their consent. Topher wondered if Tim wasn't retiring so much as being pushed out by the network because of the rumors. Either way, Topher was happy to take his job.

"You're serious. That is so amazing. I can't even…." Then Topher took a deep breath and tried to calm down. He cleared his throat. "I mean, I'm thrilled for the opportunity."

"The network liked the work you did here. You made gymnastics accessible for the regular person who only tunes in every four years. Bring that energy to calling figure skating, and you'll do just fine."

"I swear, you and TBC will not regret it." It started to sink in that Topher was getting exactly what he'd wanted. He'd passed the test. That job was his. "Thank you, thank you."

His various retirement projects had been fun. Participating on that cooking show had been a blast. And having so many designers now wanting to give him red-carpet outfits or have him wear their clothes at Fashion Week felt like a coup, and some of the modeling work he'd done had been fun. But he missed figure skating. Not even the skating itself; he still had access to a rink in New Jersey any time he wanted to get back on the ice. He still got asked to do easy routines at exhibition shows once in a blue moon, although he usually turned those down. But more than that, he missed talking about skating, he missed the community, he missed the energy in an arena during competition.

This was his ticket back in. And he wouldn't risk bruises or broken bones if he did this.

He couldn't keep the grin off his face. "Thank you so much, Joanna. This will be amazing. I'll totally be going to the next Olympics."

"You'll have to call pairs and ice dancing and everything. Not just men's and women's."

"Not a problem."

Joanna winked. "I mean, we have Tana Barber for ice dancing. Do you know her?"

Tana Barber was half of a silver-medal ice dancing pair. "Of course, darling. Tana and I vacation together. She's one of my skating besties."

"And we're thinking about having you call with Marilyn Chen."

Topher knew Marilyn well from their years traveling to competitions together. "She's a goddess."

Joanna smiled. "This will all work out just fine, then." She glanced at a plate of pastries on the craft services table as if it were calling to her. "Seriously, congratulations, Topher. I know I am not always the easiest person to work with, but you made these last two weeks a lot more fun than I imagined it would be."

Topher couldn't keep the grin off his face. "I will admit, I kept wondering for the last two weeks if my getting sacked was imminent. I know I can be a lot."

"We like you because you're a lot." Joanna winked. "If I still have this job in two years, it will be a lot of fun to work together again." She patted his shoulder. "Seriously, good luck with everything. Someone from TBC will be in touch with your agent when we're all back in New York, and we'll set up meetings to deal with the details. But in the meantime, welcome to the TBC family, Toph."

Topher couldn't help it—he hugged Joanna. She stiffened and seemed taken aback, but then she laughed and patted his back. "Congratulations."

"It's gonna be great. I can't wait to get started."

THERE WAS a knock on the door of Jake's hotel room. He paid for the room mostly for show, since he hadn't spent a single night here. It was basically just a place to store his stuff. But he'd been changing clothes here, and now his backpack had to be repacked, which was an unfortunate sign that the end of the two most amazing weeks of his life were at an end.

Jake answered the door and found Topher there with a wide grin, a bottle of wine, and two glasses that looked like they'd been stolen from the hotel bar.

"We're celebrating," Topher said.

"All right. What are we celebrating?"

"Two things. First, you are looking at the new figure skating commentator for TBC, at least for next year's US Championships. And if I kill it, which I totally will, I'll be the commentator at the next Olympics."

Jake felt a warm swell of pride in his chest. He threw his arms around Topher. "Oh my God. Congratulations!"

"And—one of the reporters decided not to go to the Closing Ceremony, so I scored a ticket for that too. I won't be on-air or on the field with the athletes, but I'll be in the stands. So I'll be watching you."

"That sounds ominous." Jake took everything from Topher and pulled the cork out of the bottle.

"At least I won't be stuck here watching it on TV."

Jake poured two glasses and handed one to Topher. "Congrats on the commentary gig."

Topher clinked his glass against Jake's. "Thanks. I'm really excited. Which leads me to the another thing, which you apparently don't even know about yet. I got it from the horse's mouth, though. You and Chelsea were elected as co–flag bearers."

"What? Really?"

"Yeah. It was a tie, apparently. I just talked to Melissa Lowe before I left the broadcast center. She said they planned to ask both of you. I've totally ruined the surprise, haven't I?"

"No, that's… that's perfect. I gotta call Chelsea. But, like, in a few minutes." Jake grinned at Topher and took a healthy sip of wine. "So, I had a crazy idea."

"Uh-huh." Topher leaned forward, his expression eager.

Jake leaned over and put a hand on Topher's thigh. "Well, if I have to be out of the gym for five more weeks, I might as well make the most of my time. So I started looking at apartments I could sublet for a month. In New York City."

Topher's eyes went wide. "Are you serious?"

"I am. I thought maybe I'd see New York and some other places on the East Coast and also spend time with you and see if what we have has staying power outside of the Olympic bubble. What do you think?"

The utter glee on Topher's face was all Jake really needed to see to know his answer. Topher leaned forward and kissed Jake. "I think… I think I might be falling in love with you. So, yeah, I think this does have staying power. And I'd love to have you visit me in New York. You can save your money on the sublet."

"I didn't want to presume."

"I've got a two-bedroom apartment if you really need your own space. I use the second bedroom as an office-slash-closet."

Jake opened his mouth to ask about that, but he thought better of it. Given how much luggage Topher had brought to Madrid, Jake could only imagine how much real estate his clothes took up in his apartment.

Then something Topher had said caught up with Jake. His pulse picked up. "Did you say you might be falling in love with me?"

Topher took Jake's hand. "I think I might be. Is that crazy?"

Jake grinned. He wove his fingers together with Topher's. "Nope. I think I might be falling in love with you too."

Topher leaned back and grabbed his wineglass. "Let's drink to that."

EPILOGUE

A year and a half later....

TOPHER WALKED into the booth with Jake on his heels. There was still an hour before Topher actually had to be here, but he wanted to get the lay of the land. He'd be commenting on the primetime broadcast of Olympic figure skating. The first event, the new team event, would happen first. Topher picked up his headset and put it on experimentally.

"Did you... bedazzle your headset?" asked Jake.

"At least I know which one is mine."

Jake rolled his eyes.

"We've still got some time before things really get underway. I could track down Joanna and talk her into letting you do some segment for TBC."

"Nah, that's okay. I'm happy to just relax and watch events. I'm meeting up with Natalie in an hour.

We're going to go eat our weight in sushi, and then we've got tickets a few rows up from the ice."

Topher laughed. Since he and Natalie were basically besties now, he was glad Natalie and Jake got along. Natalie was in town in a capacity similar to what Topher had been doing in Madrid, but she'd also done more general sportscasting for TBC in the year since, working full-time for the TBC Sports cable channel. TBC had her assisting in calling some of the events that had been imported from the X-Games, like snowboarding and freestyle skiing.

"Well," said Topher, snaking his arms around Jake's shoulders, "if you have some time to kill." Then he leaned in for a kiss.

"Ugh, get a room," said Marilyn Chen, another retired skater who had been paired up with Topher to do most of the commentating, as she walked into the booth. They'd be joined by a guy who normally called hockey for TBC but who was there to ask leading questions about triple toe loops and how the scoring system worked.

When Topher looked at her, she was smiling.

"You're early," said Topher.

"So are you. Did you really sneak your husband in here to make out?"

"That wasn't my *original* plan. More of a spur-of-the-moment decision." Topher slowly lowered his hands and reluctantly stepped away from Jake.

"Far be it for me to interrupt the Olympic It Couple," said Marilyn.

Jake rolled his eyes. "I hate when people call us that."

"Stop being so adorable, then," said Marilyn. "Did you know that at least once a broadcast, whenever you're in the audience, Topher tries to find you so he can say something cheeseball like, 'There's my handsome husband.'"

Jake grimaced. "Ew, really?"

"I thought we agreed we would not be telling Jake that," said Topher.

Marilyn crossed her arms. "I agreed to no such thing. How are you, Jake? Having a fun week?"

"Yeah. Toph and I caught some short track speed skating this morning. That shit is intense!"

"Oh, yeah. I hope to catch some of that this week," said Marilyn. "I'll watch any sport done on skates."

"Anyone I should watch out for tonight?" Jake asked.

Marilyn looked at Topher but said, "The American pairs team is the first competitive one we've fielded in years. They're called E-squared. Elliot and Eliza. They are painfully adorable."

"Allegedly, they're a couple," said Topher, "and we've been instructed to comment on how romantic they are, but secretly, I think Elliot is skating for our team, if you know what I mean."

Jake snorted.

"And Blake Ferrer is the male skater for the team event, at least for the short program," said Marilyn. "He is *smoking* hot."

Topher couldn't argue with that. "He has the most perfect ass you've ever seen."

Jake made a show of looking behind Topher. "Better than yours?"

"I mean, I've never seen my ass up close, but I'm assuming yes."

"Have you seen Blake Ferrer's up close?" asked Jake.

"Are you jealous, baby?" Topher threw an arm around Jake.

"No," said Jake. "I'll have to render a verdict on who has a better ass, though. For science."

"For science. Of course."

Marilyn grinned. "How's retirement treating you, Jake?"

"Oh, it's actually pretty great. I haven't been retired long enough to miss gymnastics yet, though. Talk to me in six more months."

After his foot had healed, Jake went back to the gym, decided he felt pretty good, and finished one more season after all. Since Topher traveled so much for his TBC job anyway, he sublet his apartment and rented a place in Houston while Jake was training. Jake called his last season his victory lap, and he won medals all over the world before deciding he wanted to go out on a high. That, and after he banged up his knee at World Championships—he'd badly whiffed a move on the pommel horse—his doctor basically told him he had to retire.

Living in Houston had been a strange experience for Topher. It wasn't even that he stood out, although he did sometimes. It was more that the Mirakovitches were… overwhelming. Once Jake and Topher announced they were officially in a relationship, Lana insisted on having Topher over for dinner a few times per week, which put Topher under the discerning gaze of Valentin. Topher got the impression that Valentin thought he was pretty ridiculous. The one thing that saved Topher was that he was an athlete. When Valentin started asking what his training regimen had been like and Topher successfully demonstrated that he led a life with a great deal of discipline, Topher seemed to win

Valentin over. And if Topher was not mistaken, Valentin's eyes had gotten a little watery at the wedding.

Jake had retired finally just the previous September. And after much crying from both Lana and Chelsea, Jake packed up and moved into Topher's apartment in New York for good.

Then he'd slept for what seemed like a month.

So, yeah, he'd barely been retired long enough to miss it. TBC was trying in earnest to get him to join their Olympics coverage, but currently Jake was eyeing an elite gym in New Jersey that he hoped to buy and possibly run. Topher knew it wouldn't be possible for Jake to quit gymnastics cold turkey.

"You know what I did when I retired?" said Marilyn. "I went on *The Dance Off*."

"Is that the celebrity ballroom dance show?" asked Topher.

"It sure is. Athletes tend to do well on the show too, because we know all about practice and discipline and can make our bodies do amazing things."

"There you go, Jake. There's your retirement hobby. Ballroom dance."

Jake grimaced. "I've never had much rhythm. I don't know about that. *You*, however, would be great on that show. I've seen a few episodes." He turned to Marilyn. "I have a lot of free time on my hands now."

Topher laughed. "I'm clearly not keeping you busy enough."

Marilyn put up her hands. "There's a dirty joke brewing and I don't want to be here to witness it. I'll leave you guys alone for a minute. But I'll be right back, so don't desecrate the announcer booth."

"Like we'd be the first ones to have sex in it," said Topher.

"Keep your pants on. I'm serious. I'm just going to get some water and maybe see if anyone has some loose rhinestones so I can make my headset as sparkly as yours."

Topher laughed as Marilyn left. Then he kissed Jake.

"I wanted to finish the thought from when Marilyn interrupted," Topher murmured. "She probably will return in, like, two minutes, which isn't enough time to do anything."

"It's okay." Jake put his arms around Topher's middle. "I'm just happy to be here with you."

"I'm glad you agreed to come with me."

"Am I going to get in trouble for sneaking into booths with you and stealing donuts from craft services?"

"Nah. Joanna knows you're here. Also, you heard what Marilyn said—we're the Olympic It Couple. It's our job to follow each other around and look adorable."

Jake laughed. "All right. I should probably leave you and Marilyn to do your thing and go meet Natalie so we can get our sushi on."

"All right. I'll look for you in the stands. I might say something schmoopy about you on camera."

"I guess I can live with that."

Topher smiled and kissed Jake's forehead. "I love you."

"Love you too." Jake pulled away gently. "Just, like, don't embarrass me or say anything too suggestive. My parents will be watching."

"Valentin's going to show up on our door one evening and kill me, isn't he?"

"He will if you make a joke about sexing up his son on national television."

"So noted."

"Have a good broadcast, Topher. I know you'll kill it."

KATE McMURRAY

RACE *for* REDEMPTION

BOOK THREE · ELITE ATHLETES

Coming in Fall 2020

Race for Redemption

An Elite Athletes Novel

Sprinter Jason Jones Jr., known around the world as JJ, is America's hope to take the title of Fastest Man in the World, the champion of the Olympic 100-meter sprint. Two years before, a doping scandal brought his winning streak to a crashing end, and even though he's been cleared of wrongdoing, he's finding it hard to escape the damage to his reputation. At the Games in Madrid, no one believes he's innocent, and officials from the doping agency follow him everywhere.

It just fuels JJ's determination to show them he's clean and still the fastest man on earth.

If only he wasn't tempted by foxy hurdler Brandon Stanton, an engineering student and math prodigy who views each race like a complicated equation. His analytical approach helps him win races, and he wants to help JJ do the same. But JJ's been burned too many times before and doesn't trust anyone who has all the answers. No matter how sexy and charming JJ finds Brandon, the Olympics is no place for romance. Or is it?

www.dreamspinnerpress.com

Chapter One

Two years before the Olympics....

JJ COULDN'T breathe.

He woke up the morning of the 100-meter sprint world championship feeling like someone had shoved wads of wet cotton balls up his nose.

That was really bad news.

Anything that might inhibit his breathing could be the difference between winning gold and being left out of the medals, but this wasn't a mere case of the sniffles. JJ sat up and felt it all hit him: feverish body aches, drippy nose, his throat feeling as if he'd swallowed a knife.

This was really, really bad news.

JJ had won six international races. He was in great condition and had been training his ass off all year. The thing he coveted most in the world was the title of "World's Fastest Man," which was bestowed on the winner of the 100-meter sprint each year. Yesterday he'd been gunning for the world record. Today he had had a cold.

After a long, hot shower, JJ assessed that yes, some virus had taken up residence in his body. He texted

Marcus, his coach, then headed for the stadium. This fucking virus would probably keep him from the podium, but he'd hate himself if he didn't still try.

When JJ walked into the locker room at London Stadium, Franco Greer, a friend and one of the other Americans who had qualified for the gold medal final the day before, stood waiting near JJ's locker. "Marcus said you had a cold."

"Yeah, feels that way." And boy did it. His head felt so foggy, it was as if he were floating out of his body. All he really wanted to do was lie on the bench in front of his locker and sleep there for three days.

"I have some cold medicine. You want some?" Franco held out his hand; two white pills lay on his palm.

JJ reached for them and then withdrew his hand, thinking better of it. "This gonna get me in trouble with the drug testers?"

"Nah. These have that other decongestant in it— not the stimulant one. They don't work as well, but they're better than nothing, right?"

"Yeah." JJ hesitated before taking the pills from Franco, knowing it wasn't smart to take something if he didn't know what was in it. But Franco was his teammate and his friend. He'd never given JJ any reason not to trust him. And if JJ could put his cold on hold until after the race, he wanted to.

So he took the pills. He walked over to a refrigerator at the end of his row of lockers and grabbed a Gatorade. He swallowed both pills. Then he found a massage table and lay on it while he waited for the medicine to kick in.

He could breathe again, mostly, by the time his race started an hour later. The gold medal final had three Americans, two Jamaicans—including the reigning world champion and world record holder—a teenager from Kenya, a white guy from the UK, and a Canadian sprinter who came in second in this race a lot. The Jamaican champion was thirty-two years old now and past his prime, and there were unsubstantiated doping rumors swirling around the team, so JJ felt like this race was his... if he was healthy.

All he could do was run his heart out.

He tied the laces on his neon green sneakers, then undid the laces and tied them again. He'd painted his nails the same color as the sneakers, but now he was regretting that choice. Neon green wasn't really a color associated with luck, was it? Suddenly it looked just like snot, or was that the cold medicine talking? JJ suppressed a groan, and he felt tired and gross instead of flashy and ready to race.

"On your marks."

JJ got himself into the blocks, kissed the little gold pendant his mother gave him, and carefully placed his fingers behind the starting line.

"Get set."

At the gun, JJ leapt off the blocks and pumped his legs as hard as he could, running with everything he had. The other runners stayed very close, and really, any of these guys could run a hundred meters in less than ten seconds and therefore had a shot at this medal. JJ could see the yellow jerseys of the Jamaicans on either side of him and felt new determination to beat them. His lungs burned, his throat scratched, but he pushed through all that. Adrenaline coursed through him, powering him further, and the roar of the crowd motivated him too, and he felt a burst of energy.

He could do this... he could do this... he could do this.

His whole body screamed, his legs and his lungs straining from this burst of energy, less than ten seconds of pushing his body as far as it would go.

He ducked at the finish line, hoping to get his nose ahead before anyone else, but he realized suddenly that he had crossed the finish line alone, followed a beat later by the rest of the field.

He'd... won.

He'd won!

He looked up at the scoreboard and saw his name, Jason Jones Jr., and the time 9.84 seconds. Not a world record, but fast enough to win the world championship, despite his cold. Marcus ran out onto the field and handed him an American flag, so JJ raised it, still feeling dazed. He'd done it. Holy shit, *he'd done it*! So much joy coursed through his veins that it needed an outlet, so he yelled at the sky. Marcus yelled too, and slapped him on the back.

JJ was the fastest man alive.

And then he dropped onto the tracks, utterly spent.

Jones Caught Doping, Medal Rescinded

LONDON, ENGLAND—American sprinter Jason Jones Jr. has tested positive for a banned substance at the recent world championships, according to the International Association of Athletic Federations (IAAF), the governing body that oversees all track and field competitions worldwide.

Jones was found to have taken a banned stimulant, according to officials from IAAF and the World Anti-Doping Agency, who administered tests at the recent world championships in London.

As a result of the positive test and IAAF's no-tolerance policy for doping, Mr. Jones has been suspended from IAAF events for six months and was asked to return the gold medal he won in the 100-meter sprint final. Jones has filed an appeal, and a hearing is scheduled on September 9....

JJ SAT in a blandly decorated reception area outside of a conference room, slowly losing his mind.

He'd tested positive for pseudoephedrine, which the World Anti-Doping Agency banned because it was a stimulant. The only place it could have come from was the cold pills Franco had given him. Had Franco known the cold medicine had pseudoephedrine? Was it sabotage or an accident? Either way, JJ was furious.

He'd won that race on the power of his own body, even with a pretty bad cold. Said cold had kept him in bed for a week after he got home from Worlds. He didn't take performance-enhancing drugs. He knew "I love the sport too much" was a cliché, but it was true for him. Running was among the purest of sports, just the human body powering itself down a racetrack. It didn't require much in the way of special equipment, and athletes didn't need to have been training since the womb to be good at it. Running was raw, close to nature, one of the oldest sports on earth. JJ respected that. Took pride in it.

He would never try to enhance his performance with anything illegal, and he was deeply offended anyone would think he did. And yet here he was, his heart pounding as he paced up and down the length of the small reception area, waiting to march into a room and try to explain all that to a panel of strangers.

Marcus stood on the other side of the room. "You have to calm down."

"Calm down? Are you fucking kidding me? My future in this sport is on the line. They took my medal away. But I'm supposed to be calm?"

"Yes. You can't go off half-cocked in front of this panel. You have to be calm and reasonable."

JJ swallowed. Unfortunately Marcus was right. Yelling would not accomplish what he needed to do here.

The silence rang in JJ's ears as he tried to get his breathing under control. There were several long, uncomfortable moments when JJ tried to keep a lid on his rage at the situation he found himself in.

And then Marcus muttered, "Of all the things to get caught taking."

JJ grunted. "I didn't know. I had a cold."

Marcus stood and crossed the room. He stood close to JJ and whisper-hissed, "You want to play around with this stuff, you have to come to me."

"I don't—"

"I could get you on a regimen, you know. None of this namby-pamby over-the-counter shit. I've got a doctor on staff who understands what these things do to the human body. If you want to try it, we should do it right."

JJ balked. He couldn't believe what he'd just heard. "Are you kidding me right now?"

"You want to win?"

"Not like that."

Marcus rolled his eyes. "Your competitors are all doping, you know. Everyone does. You won't be able to compete if you don't."

JJ shook his head. "Uh, hello? Do you not hear what I'm saying? I had a cold so I took a couple of cold pills. Only I didn't know they contained pseudoephedrine. I wasn't trying anything."

"Sure. That's a great line, kid. Say it just like that to the committee."

JJ growled in frustration. "I won a gold medal running on my own power. The IAAF wants to take it back. That's the whole fucking reason I'm here right now. Remember? I don't need your fucking regimen to win races."

Marcus backed up and looked JJ up and down. "How many races do you think your principled stance will win you?"

Before JJ could answer, Tom McCoy, JJ's lawyer, buzzed into the room. "Sorry I'm late. They start yet?"

JJ shot Marcus what he hoped was a disdainful look before stepping away.

A few moments later a woman with mousy brown hair and wearing a sensible pantsuit stuck her head into the waiting room. "Mr. Jones? We're ready for you now."

They convened in the conference room. The officials from the IAAF sat in a row on the opposite side of the table from JJ, who was flanked by Marcus and McCoy. They sat primly and listened as JJ explained about the virus and the cold pills of unknown origin. JJ broke out in a cold sweat as he spoke and his voice shook a little. "I just wanted to breathe during my race. I took what my teammate offered. I didn't know the pills had pseudoephedrine in them."

McCoy took over then, putting verbal pressure on the IAAF panel to exonerate JJ. They went back and forth for what felt like an hour, mostly hurling legalese at each other. JJ struggled to follow it, but he tried to keep his mind from wandering, because whenever it did, he managed to convince himself this one stupid incident spelled the end of his career. The panel asked Marcus questions, and he denied any knowledge of the incident.

JJ turned over what Marcus had said in the waiting room. He knew plenty of other runners were doping. He liked to think the American team was clean, but one of his teammates had been suspended the previous season after testing positive for anabolic steroids. JJ knew also, because he talked to other athletes, that there was a whole black market of drugs out there, stuff the World Anti-Doping Agency didn't know existed yet. Athletes were using it during practice but quitting long enough before competition for everything to work its way out of their systems. JJ also knew that shit ended careers early and made men impotent and had a lot of weird side effects. But some guys didn't care as long as the drugs made them stronger or faster. The goal was to win. The cost was immaterial.

And yet JJ had gotten busted for taking a couple of cold pills.

"So, you're saying it was inadvertent use," one of the IAAF officials asked JJ.

JJ knew *inadvertent use* was the official term for using a banned substance without meaning to do it, and it was something that often got athletes off the hook. Not that JJ was trying to…. He sighed. "Yes. That's exactly what I'm saying."

But athletes had been suspended for lesser offenses. JJ fretted and checked back out of the conversation as McCoy gave what was probably an eloquent speech about how JJ believed in the beauty of running and only wanted to win the right way and that he never would have taken anything to put his medal in jeopardy.

When JJ checked back in again, one of the officials was arguing about the medal, saying that he didn't like the precedent it set to excuse JJ with no penalty if he wasn't denying taking a stimulant to begin with. JJ tried to keep his anger in check, but the more this guy talked, the angrier JJ felt.

"You really expect us to believe that you were stupid enough to take some unlabeled pills without knowing what they were?" said the official.

That was when JJ lost it.

He shot to his feet. "Fine. You want the medal? Yes, I'm that stupid. I trusted my teammate, and that was my mistake." It took everything in his body not to drop an f-bomb. He took a deep breath and tried to get a handle on his emotions. As calmly as he could, he said, "I'm sorry. I genuinely am. If I have to surrender the medal to end my suspension, then I'll do it. The medal is not important so long as I can run again and have an opportunity to win another."

"JJ...," said McCoy.

The members of the panel looked at each other. "We need to consult," said the woman in the mousy suit. "Please wait outside."

JJ resumed pacing in the reception area, mulling over whether Franco had intentionally torpedoed his whole career. He wouldn't look at Marcus, not now that he knew Marcus was willing to hook his athletes up with a drug regimen. How many of JJ's training partners were doping? And how was it only JJ got caught?

Now he knew he was losing it. He was a corkboard and a ball of red yarn away from going full conspiracy theorist crazy.

The mousy lady appeared again. "You can come back."

Everyone filed back into the room. JJ sat and closed his eyes for a long moment, wondering if this was how criminals felt before a jury delivered a verdict.

The mousy woman said, "The commission has ruled that the evidence indicates the consumption of the pseudoephedrine was accidental. The ruling stands on the championship medal, but we agree to lift your suspension, Mr. Jones, if you agree to regular drug testing."

JJ let out a breath. It felt like the best outcome he could have hoped for. He mourned the loss of his medal—he'd fucking earned that medal—but getting back on track, literally, was what he wanted most.

Marcus and McCoy both started to speak, but JJ held up his hands. "I'm fine with that."

"It was an accident," McCoy said. "Surely you can consider restoring the medal."

"We take doping very seriously," said another official. "We want to send a clear message that we run a clean operation here. Track and field must remain untainted by allegations of doping. Do we understand each other?"

JJ just wanted to get out of there. He understood the theater of all this. An aggressive approach to doping violations gave the appearance that track was clean, even though the World Anti-Doping Agency had a dozen countries on its watch list. Track was hardly free of cheaters.

"It's fine, really," JJ said. He felt resigned. Underneath everything, he was still angry as hell that he'd been put in this position to begin with, but as long as he could run, well, he'd just have to win other medals.

McCoy pursed his lips for a second but said, "If you're okay with the ruling, then I guess we're done here."

On the way out of the building, McCoy rattled on about how they should do a press conference in which JJ defended himself, and JJ responded with, "Yeah, fine, whatever." But his suspicions of Franco were plaguing him now. *Had* Franco lied about the pills having pseudoephedrine? Had he known? Had he done it on purpose? How would JJ ever trust anyone again?

When they got outside, McCoy shook JJ's hand and said he'd be in touch before he walked off.

"You want a ride back to the hotel or…," said Marcus, pulling his keys out of his pocket.

JJ stared at his coach for a long moment.

"Nah, I'll get a cab. And Marcus? You're fired."

KATE MCMURRAY writes smart romantic fiction. She likes creating stories that are brainy, funny, and, of course, sexy with regular-guy characters and urban sensibilities. She advocates for romance stories by and for everyone. When she's not writing, she edits textbooks, watches baseball, plays violin, crafts things out of yarn, and wears a lot of cute dresses. She's active in Romance Writers of America, serving for two years on the board of Rainbow Romance Writers, the LGBT romance chapter, and three—including two as president—on the board of the New York City chapter. She lives in Brooklyn, NY, with two cats and too many books.

Website: www.katemcmurray.com

Twitter: @katemcmwriter

Facebook:www.facebook.com/katemcmurraywriter